SINCE last Summer

SINCE last Summer

a novel by

JOANNA PHILBIN

poppy

LITTLE, BROWN AND COMPANY
New York   Boston

Copyright © 2014 by Joanna Philbin

Poppy

Hachette Book Group
237 Park Avenue, New York, NY 10017
lb-teens.com

Poppy is an imprint of Little, Brown and Company.
The Poppy name and logo are trademarks of Hachette Book Group, Inc.

The publisher is not responsible for websites (or their content) that are not owned by the publisher.

First Edition: June 2014

Library of Congress Cataloging-in-Publication Data
Philbin, Joanna.
    Since last summer / Joanna Philbin.—First edition.
        pages cm
    "Poppy."
    Sequel to: Rules of summer.
    Summary: Eighteen-year-olds Rory McShane and Isabel Rule are back for another summer in East Hampton, but their friendship is put to the test as each girl deals with boyfriends, summer jobs, and family issues.
    ISBN 978-0-316-21209-0 (hardcover)—ISBN 978-0-316-21210-6 (electronic book)
    [1. Friendship—Fiction.   2. Dating (Social customs)—Fiction.   3. Social classes—Fiction.
4. Wealth—Fiction.   5. Summer—Fiction.   6. Hamptons (N.Y.)—Fiction.]   I. Title.
    PZ7.P515Si 2014
    [Fic]—dc23

                                                                          2013022286

10 9 8 7 6 5 4 3 2 1

RRD-C

Printed in the United States of America

Book design by Tracy Shaw

Also by JOANNA PHILBIN:

The Daughters

The Daughters Break the Rules

The Daughters Take the Stage

The Daughters Join the Party

Rules of Summer

To Annabelle,
who was with me every minute

CHAPTER ONE

She almost missed the sign, but Rory McShane made the turn at the very last second, guiding her uncle's sputtering Honda onto the smooth blacktop of Lily Pond Lane. The street was just as quiet and still as she remembered it. The midday sun filtered in through the canopy of tree branches overhead. A jogger ran gracefully on the other side of the street. She turned down the radio and lifted her hands from the steering wheel. Her palms were slick with sweat.

Relax, she thought. *Everything is going to be great.*

But there was no getting around it: Eleven weeks was a very long time. A record for them, in fact. They'd talked on the phone almost every day, and Skyped and texted and IM'd countless times, but she and Connor Rule hadn't been face-to-face since her last trip to LA in March, and from the moment she'd crossed out of New Jersey, doubts had begun to overwhelm her. What if they didn't know what to say to each other? What if things were awkward? What if she got to the house and realized that she was actually still the errand girl?

That's not *going to happen*, she reminded herself. For ten months, she and Connor Rule had managed to be in a happy, healthy, drama-free relationship, all while living on opposite sides of the country. Eleven weeks apart wasn't going to change anything. All those years of being single had screwed up her hold on reality, she thought. They'd been looking forward to this all year. East Hampton was where they'd met and fallen in love, after all. Everything was going to be just fine.

She turned into the break in the hedges and pulled up in front of the iron gates. After she typed the code Connor had given her into the silver intercom box, the gates swung open. She pressed the gas, rounded the turn, and began driving down the gravel path, past the Rules' immense front lawn.

The house, perched on a slight hill above the lawn, was still intimidating from a distance. But as she got closer and the faded silvery-gray shingles and bright white paint of the windows came into view, she remembered how familiar the Rules' mansion had become to her last summer. She pulled up to the bank of garages. She left her purse on the passenger seat and got out of the car. The sea air was bracing. In the distance, she could hear the roll of waves and the squawk of seagulls. The breeze whipped up her dark curls, unsticking them from the nape of her neck. She was finally here.

You're still coming out for the summer, right?? Isabel had texted Rory a few months ago. Yes? I hope? My bro hasn't done anything to piss you off?

Wouldn't matter if he had, Rory had texted back. You're the one who invited me, remember?

She walked around to the trunk of the car and unlocked it. She heard the back door of the house open with a creak.

2

"Finally," a voice said. "I almost sent a helicopter to come get you."

Connor stepped out of the house and walked through the rose garden, sunlight glinting off his blond hair.

"I didn't want to speed," she said, her heart pounding rapidly.

"I would have paid the ticket," he said, coming toward her.

She walked into his arms and tilted up her head to kiss him. As their lips touched, a jolt of electricity bounced around her rib cage, shot through her stomach, and made the backs of her knees loose and light. Instant bliss.

"So that was a long time," he said, looking down at her when they were done.

"Eleven weeks," she said. "And three days."

"And every one of them sucked," he said with a smile.

"Tell me about it." She leaned in to kiss him one more time.

Despite her nerves, it felt good to be back on familiar ground. The first time she'd visited Connor at USC had been a little bit of a shock. Up until then, she'd only known him as Connor Rule, Isabel's sweet, self-effacing, gorgeous brother. But at USC, he was CONNOR RULE. They couldn't walk around for five minutes before some guy passed and gave him a silent bro-shake, or some girl smiled shyly and said "Hey, Connor" under her breath. His years on the swim team had made him a bit of a celebrity. And his friendliness and golden-boy looks didn't hurt, either. Even his professors seemed to adore him. "Mr. Rule, would you like to comment on this?" was a common question whenever Rory sat in on one of his classes.

Around his friends, Connor was even more in demand. And his friends were, well, interesting. The girls were all skinny and tan and wore blousy silk tops with extrawide armholes so that people could see their lacy bras underneath. The guys drove sleek black BMWs with tinted windows and flashed gold credit cards at the campus snack bar. Sitting with them at a meal could send her self-esteem into a tailspin, as they discussed their White House internships or their summer jobs at Goldman Sachs or their plans to teach English in Uganda. *What is he doing with* me? she'd asked herself, more than a few times. *Me, a high school senior who doesn't even have her own car?*

Fortunately, Connor didn't seem to be thinking that. He always introduced her as his "ultra-high-achieving girlfriend" who made him "feel like a slacker." When she'd gotten in to Stanford early, he bragged about it to everyone they came across. But it was never enough to put her at ease. Going home to New Jersey was always a relief. Back in Stillwater, she could still be Connor's girlfriend without having to fit into his college world. It was kind of the ideal situation, when she thought about it.

"It's good to see you," she said, pressing her face against his neck and breathing in his smell of soap, laundry detergent, and shaving foam.

"How'd the speech go?" he asked. "Did you do that line at the end about the promise of a new generation?"

"No. It was corny."

"Come on! That was the best part!" he said.

"*You* thought it was the best part," she said. "Everyone else told me to cut it."

"Okay, fine, I'll take your word for it. I wish you'd let me come."

"To sit in my school gym with my mom and her tattooed boyfriend?" She took his hand. "I don't think so. It was just a graduation."

"And you were *just* the valedictorian," he said with a smile. He kissed her again.

"So," she asked when they'd finished kissing, "how does it feel to be home?"

"Oh, you know," he said, looking at the house over his shoulder. "This place never changes." He stepped in front of her and grabbed her suitcase out of the trunk. "Come on," he said. "Let's go inside."

After hoisting her duffel over her shoulder, she followed Connor over the paving stones and through the rose garden, with its abundant red, pink, and fuchsia blooms. She lifted her wrist to look at the gold charm bracelet, the one Isabel had given her at the end of last summer. The *I* and *R* charms shone in the sun. "Isabel isn't here yet, is she?" Rory asked.

"Nah, she's coming tomorrow with Fee," Connor said over his shoulder. "She's flying back from California today."

Inside the house, a ball of barking white fluff charged toward her down the hall.

"Trixie!" Rory said.

Trixie circled Rory's legs, trying to stand on her tiny back feet.

"Hi, sweetie pie! I've missed you!" Rory put down her bag and crouched to pet Trixie on the head.

The dog responded with a few sharp, happy barks. When Rory stood back up, Trixie trotted behind them down the hall.

"I think she wants you to take her to the beach," he said.

"Only if Bianca isn't here."

"I told you," he said over his shoulder. "My mom fired her."

"I know. But you didn't tell me why." Bianca, Mrs. Rule's house manager, had been horrible to Rory last summer, but Rory had assumed Mrs. Rule was happy with how she ran things.

"No clue," Connor said. "I try not to get involved with any of that domestic stuff." He stopped in front of the door to her old room. "Okay. The sleeping arrangements. You can have your old room again. *Or*"—he gave her a sly look—"you can be in my room."

"Are you kidding? What about your mom?"

Connor shrugged. "She likes you now."

"I'll just be in here again, if that's okay," she said, opening the door.

She walked into the cream-and-blue-colored guest room and looked around with a smile. She'd longed for the quiet luxury of this room so many times over the past year. The king-sized bed with its downy soft mattress, the comfy club chairs, the elegant writing desk, the nautical map of Long Island hanging over the headboard—it all looked exactly the same. The only changes were the more current hardcover novels stacked on the nightstands and a vase of white-and-pink peonies on the desk.

"It's so pretty in here," Rory said. "And I love peonies." She dropped her bag on the rug and walked over to the flowers. Trixie was circling her feet, eager to be petted. "They're beautiful," she said, bending down. "But not as beautiful as this little dog right here."

"*You're* beautiful," Connor said, crouching behind her and kissing her on the neck.

She turned toward him and kissed him on the lips. He pressed her close to him and slowly pulled her down to the floor.

"Wait," she murmured. "Are we alone?"

"Pretty much," he replied, still kissing her.

The sound of approaching footsteps down the hall made them both shoot to their feet.

"Rory, is that you?" said a familiar voice. "May I come in?"

"Uh, sure, Mom," Connor muttered, and Mrs. Rule strode into the room.

Once again Rory was struck by how such a tiny, slim woman could exert the presence of a person twice her size. Especially because Mrs. Rule seemed to have gotten even tinier and slimmer since last summer. Her roomy boatneck sweater hinted at a significantly narrower chest, and her skinny jeans showed off legs that looked like toothpicks. Rory wondered if she'd been sick. But Mrs. Rule's hair was fuller and lusher than ever. It fell in loose, beachy waves past her shoulders.

"Rory," she said, coming straight toward her. "You're here." She grasped Rory's hand and leaned in to give her an air-kiss on the cheek. "You didn't need to bring your own car. We could have found one for you here. I think the Mercedes is probably free—"

"Oh, that's okay," Rory said. "I didn't mind driving. And thanks for having me again. It's really good to be back."

Mrs. Rule smiled. "Well, we're all very happy you chose to come back. Especially Connor." She looked approvingly at her son. "Steve didn't come back. He's decided to teach tennis down

7

in Palm Beach. As if anyone would want to be *there* for the summer." Mrs. Rule gave a dismissive shrug. "And if there's anything you need—more hangers, a shoe tree—just let me know." Mrs. Rule's gaze lingered on Rory's duffel bag on the floor. "When do you start your job?"

"You mean my internship? I start Monday."

"What is it called?" Mrs. Rule asked. "The East End Festival?"

"That's right," Rory said. "It's sort of a film festival slash music festival. Like South by Southwest."

"South by South...what?" Mrs. Rule asked.

"Hey, Mom," Connor broke in. "Rory also got into Princeton. But she decided on Stanford."

"Really?" Mrs. Rule took a slight step backward. "That's wonderful."

"Thank you," said Rory.

"Stanford is an excellent school," said Mrs. Rule. "But I know the tuition is pretty steep."

"They gave me a really nice package," Rory said.

"Rory was class valedictorian," Connor added.

"Oh," said Mrs. Rule. Her steel-blue eyes seemed to peer right into Rory's soul. "How nice."

She knows, Rory thought. *She knows that I know.*

The secret about Mrs. Rule and Isabel's real father had gnawed at Rory all year. It felt a little unethical—and icky—to know something so shocking about Connor's family that even he didn't know. How did you tell your boyfriend that his mom had been in love with another man eighteen years ago and that his younger sister was actually his half sister? Was that even some-

8

thing you *did* tell your boyfriend? The easy solution had been to push it to the back of her mind and spend the school year making sure it stayed there. After all, she reasoned, it wasn't her place to say anything. Especially since Isabel had sworn her to secrecy. But now, being back under the Rules' roof, it seemed inevitable that Connor would find out. And when he did, Rory was going to have to pretend she didn't know. Just thinking about that gave her a stomachache.

Mrs. Rule continued to give Rory a penetrating stare for a few more seconds, and then she turned to Connor.

"So, we're having some people over for dinner tonight," she said. "I hope you two can join us? Sloane and Gregory will be there, too."

Phew, Rory thought. She was in the clear.

"Sure," Connor said.

"Do you need any help?" Rory asked before she could stop herself. "I mean, not with serving or anything but—"

Mrs. Rule smiled and gave Rory's arm a little pat. "Don't be silly. You're our guest now. You relax and have fun." She turned back to Connor. "How about some Ping-Pong before dinner? Six thirty?"

"Great," Connor said.

"Wonderful." She turned to Rory. "Once you're all unpacked, you should go down to the pool. It's a lovely day. Best not to let it go to waste." Mrs. Rule eyed Rory's bag one more time. "Come on, Trixie. Let's go."

Trixie gave Rory one last hungry glance and then followed Mrs. Rule out of the room.

"That was the longest conversation I've had with your mom since last summer," Rory said.

"What about Christmas?" Connor asked.

"Asking me to pass the sweet potatoes doesn't count," she said. She reached into her suitcase and pulled out a small wrapped box. "So I know I'm a little bit late with this, but I wanted to give it to you in person."

"Ror," Connor said gently. "I told you no birthday gifts."

"But you got *me* something in March," she said.

"That's different. You're my girlfriend." He kissed her again on the cheek.

"Oh, just take it," she said, handing him the present.

She held her breath as he ripped open the paper and then opened the small box. "Wow." He removed the silver Swiss Army knife and held it up to the light. "This is cool."

"Here, look," she said with relief, turning it so he could see the inscription on the underside. RM+CR.

"Very old school," he teased. "I like it."

"Do you really?"

"No. I *love* it." He kissed her. "I'm coming up north every single weekend next year."

"Oh, really," she said. "Is that a threat?"

"It's a fact," he said, wrapping his arms around her. "I may even have to get a little place up there. Palo Alto, here I come."

His lips met hers again, and this time Rory felt a surge of need for him. Normally she had to be around Connor for at least a couple of days before she could be this unselfconscious. Now she didn't care. She ran her hands over his shoulders and down his back. He pulled away from her and turned to close the open door.

"But what if your mom comes back?" Rory asked.

"You're a guest here," he said, shutting the door with a grin. "You're going to have to get used to having a little privacy."

The door shut with a click.

Isabel drummed her nails on the arm rest and stared out the plastic window at the empty blue sky. Somewhere below the cloud cover was the Sierra Nevada mountain range. Isabel grabbed hold of her white wine and took another long sip. The only good thing right now about going home was flying first class, even if the seats on this plane weren't as big and roomy as she would have liked.

"Do you mind?" asked the man next to her. He was a businessman in his forties. Up until this moment he had been hard at work, pounding the keys of a tiny laptop. The screen was filled with numbers.

"Sorry," she said.

He eyed her wine.

"I'm a nervous flier," she explained. "I'm twenty-one," she added.

The man shrugged and went back to pounding his keyboard.

Isabel turned back to the window and constructed another sentence in the e-mail she planned to write to Mr. Knox. *Flight was uneventful. Got kind of buzzed on plane. Thought a lot about what you said at dinner. Determined to be positive.*

Maybe it was a lame idea to write so soon, and about such

trivial stuff. But Mr. Knox—Peter, he always kept telling her to call him Peter—had insisted.

"I know you're going to be far away from now on, but I still want to be in touch," he had said to her the night before in the crowded Beverly Hills restaurant. "Send me an e-mail when you get home. Let me know how it's going."

"I can tell you right now how it's going," Isabel said, poking at her penne pomodoro. "Terribly. You sure there's no way I can just stay with you for the summer?"

Peter gave her a pained smile. "I would love that, but Michelle wouldn't be comfortable, and Holly and Krista, well..."

"That's okay," Isabel broke in. "I get it. Your family doesn't know—my family doesn't know."

"I'm just waiting for your parents to take the lead with this, Isabel," he said, giving her a gentle smile. "Out of respect for your mom."

A waiter came by to clear their plates.

"So, what do you have planned for the summer?" he asked, changing the subject. "Anything fun?"

"Rory will be there," Isabel answered. "But she's dating Connor, so..."

"So what?" Mr. Knox asked, sipping from his glass of red wine.

"So I don't know. It's different. I mean, we're still friends totally separate from that. And I'm happy for them. I really am. But when your friend is dating your brother..." She let her voice trail off. She was pretty sure Mr. Knox wouldn't know what she was talking about if she'd finished the sentence. "Anyway, I have no interest in hanging out at the Georgica. So I'm not sure. I think I'll try to go into the city as much as possible. Get ready for NYU in the fall."

"That's exactly right. It's your last summer before college. Have fun. Do something you'll never forget. If I could tell you how many times I wish I'd had more fun when I was your age—"

"Dessert?" the waiter asked. His face was Hollywood actor–handsome, with the requisite chiseled features and light blue eyes, but there was a streak of edge to him. A definite bad boy. Last year he would have been exactly Isabel's type: hot, older, dangerous.

"Sure," said Mr. Knox. "What do you recommend?"

"Well, the tiramisu is very good."

"I'll have some," Isabel said, smiling at him.

"Wonderful," the waiter said, grinning at her. He took their menus away and gave her a pointed, but discreet, smile.

"If I can ask you one favor," Mr. Knox said, folding his hands on the table, the candlelight flickering across his face. "Go easy on your mom this summer."

Isabel snorted.

"I know how much she loves you."

"Please," Isabel muttered. "If she loved me, she would have told me the truth herself. And she'd let my brother and sister in on this. Instead of making me the lucky one."

"We all come to things in our own time," Mr. Knox said as he leaned back in his chair and patted his stomach. "Be patient with her. And if you have to, vent to me. I won't say a word."

"Thanks for being so cool this year," Isabel said. "Coming

up to school to visit me, taking me out to dinner down here, the e-mails … It's all been really nice of you."

"I'm your father," he said. "Better late than never, right?" He stood up. "I'll be right back." He left to go to the men's room, and a moment later the waiter returned with the tiramisu.

"Here you go," he said. "Will there be anything else?"

"I think just the check," she said.

The waiter cocked his head and smiled at her. "I get off in an hour if you want to hang out," he said. "We could go get a drink."

It was tempting. The past nine months had been extremely quiet. All by choice, of course. Nobody at school had seemed that appealing. And her last relationship had been a disaster.

But as she looked at this guy now, something told her to stay away from him. *Too dangerous. And too good-looking.* If she'd learned anything last summer, it was to stay away from both of those things. "Maybe some other time," she said.

The waiter had seemed surprised. "Enjoy," he'd said, giving her a smile that promised a rain check on his invitation, if she wanted it.

"Excuse me?" she said to the flight attendant walking by with bottles of wine. "I'll have another, please," she said, holding up her cup.

The attendant tipped more white wine into it.

Beside her, the businessman subtly shook his head with disapproval.

"If you were going home to my house for the summer," Isabel said, "you'd get hammered, too."

"Sparkling or flat?" asked the young man in a polo shirt and khakis, displaying the two different European water bottles he held in his fists.

"Um, flat," Rory said. "Please."

He poured her glass to the brim and moved on. Rory wished she could follow him. Attending one of these dinners had turned out to be much more stressful than serving at one of them. She'd learned that during Christmas with the Rules, when she'd eaten her salad with the wrong fork and then used the wrong bread plate. Luckily nobody had said anything—she'd felt like more of a ghost than a guest that day—but the sheer possibility of someone noticing had made her a nervous wreck. She took a sip of water and turned to smile at Connor next to her. He reached for her hand under the table. Feeling him squeeze her palm reminded her of their hookup in her room, and she almost blushed.

"So what happened to that plot of land you were trying to buy last year?" asked the silver-haired magazine mogul sitting next to Mr. Rule. Mrs. Rule had introduced him as Jay Davenport. "Not that I think you two should move, but it sounded like a helluva property."

"That fell through," Mr. Rule said quietly. "One of those crotchety old farmers; you know what sticklers they can be. Covenants, and all the rest."

"That's a shame," Mr. Davenport said. "Though it's hard to believe it was more spectacular than this place."

"I, for one, am very happy about it," said Mrs. Rule from the head of the table. "I love this house. I grew up in it."

"So, Rory," said Mr. Rule.

Rory let go of Connor's hand and sat up.

"I heard you're going to Stanford," he said. "Congratulations. That's an excellent school."

"Thank you," she said, trying to make eye contact with him.

"What are you going to study?" Mr. Rule went on, sipping his glass of bourbon on the rocks.

Rory debated what to say. She still felt odd talking about her hopes for a film career around the Rules. She got the feeling that she wasn't interesting or mysterious enough to qualify as an artist in their eyes. "Probably a double major in poli-sci and film," she said.

"Ah," he said, and took another sip. "Poli-sci. I was almost poli-sci."

"You were?" Mrs. Rule asked. "I thought you were always a business major."

"I was, but I thought about doing poli-sci," Mr. Rule answered, a ribbon of tension threading his voice. "It was just a thought." Maybe it was a trick of the candlelight, but Mr. Rule also seemed thinner and younger-looking than he had last summer. Gone was the pinched, somewhat painful expression he'd worn most of the time. Now he looked content and rested, as if he'd spent the past few months at a spa.

"Rory is Connor's girlfriend, everybody," announced Mrs. Rule at the opposite end of the dining table. "She's from New Jersey."

"Oh," said Mr. Davenport. "What part? Morristown? Basking Ridge?"

"Stillwater," she answered. "It's near the Pennsylvania border."

"Never heard of it," said Mr. Davenport, picking up the tiny artichoke soufflé in the center of his plate and putting it in his mouth. "Stillwater. Hmmm."

Rory glanced at Sloane and Gregory Rule on the far side of the table. They watched her eagerly, waiting for her to speak. Connor's older brother and sister had finally warmed up to her this past year, but they could still go quiet and ultrapolite when she was in their presence, as if she were a foreign exchange student they might offend. At Ping-Pong they'd played her and Connor quietly, refraining from any of the whoops and hollers that she'd noticed when the family played one another.

"There are some *beautiful* parts of New Jersey," said Sloane.

"There certainly are," exclaimed the Rules' other dinner guest, Beatrice Lank. She was a famous interior decorator whom Sloane was assisting this summer during the week. "Just *beautiful*. I don't know why it gets such a bad rap."

Connor cleared his throat.

"How did the two of you meet?" asked Mr. Davenport.

"I worked here last summer," said Rory.

"You did?" Beatrice asked. "As what?"

"I was the errand girl."

Mrs. Lank looked at Mrs. Rule. Mr. Davenport coughed.

"But now she's part of the family," Mrs. Rule said with an iron smile. "Does anyone know if the McAndrews are having a Fourth of July party?"

And…done, Rory thought. She could now relax. She felt Connor take her hand under the table again and gave him a quick smile that she hoped said *Everything's cool; I'm not embarrassed.*

After dessert, which was a panna cotta with berries and cara-mel sauce, Rory felt her eyelids start to droop. The air in the dining room had turned close and warm, and she felt herself dangerously close to a yawn.

"Sloane is *such* a quick study," the decorator was saying. "All my clients love her. And she has *such* a good eye."

Sloane took another tiny bite of panna cotta and put down her fork. "I still have a lot to learn."

"She could be another Bunny Williams one day, if she keeps at it," said the woman.

"That would be nice," said Mrs. Rule. "It's always handy to have a decorator in the family. But what I could really use is a dress designer. We have so many events coming up in the fall it's hard to keep track."

"You both are chairing the Alzheimer's benefit at the Wal-dorf this year?" asked the mogul.

"No, I don't think so, not this year," Mrs. Rule said. There was an awkward pause as Mr. and Mrs. Rule regarded each other with alarm, as if they'd messed up their lines.

"Then let's hope whoever does keeps the price of the tables down," the mogul said. "Ten grand is as much as I go for food at the Waldorf." He laughed.

Mrs. Rule laughed, too, and brought her wineglass to her lips. The moment had passed. Rory glanced at Connor to see if he'd noticed the awkwardness, but he only smiled at her, oblivious.

Mrs. Lank glanced at her watch and placed her napkin on the table. "Well, that was divine. *Divine*, Lucy dear. It's always so good to see the both of you."

"Thank you for coming," Lucy said.

As everyone got up, Rory stood and then almost sat back down again. Her foot had fallen asleep. "Thanks, the meal was fantastic," she said to Mrs. Rule.

Mrs. Rule nodded slightly, and Rory realized that this had been another faux pas. "You're welcome," Mrs. Rule said in a low voice.

Rory followed Connor out of the dining room, trying not to limp. Out in the hall, Rory held on to a chair, trying to shake out her sleeping leg.

"You want to go to your room?" Connor asked. He peered at her. "What are you doing?"

"My leg fell asleep," she said. She sat down on the chair and shook it some more. Her new navy-and-white Jack Rogers sandals, bought especially for this summer, had already given her a blister.

Back in her room, Connor lay down on the bed and clicked on the TV. "What do you feel like watching?"

"Is the French Open on?" she asked, going into the bathroom. Her head pounded. She wasn't sure if it was from the stress of sitting at the Rules' dinner table or from the glass of white wine she'd drunk at dinner. She rifled through her toiletry bag, looking for Tylenol, and then remembered that it was in her purse, which she'd left on the front seat of the Honda.

"I have to get something out of the car," she said, walking back into the bedroom.

"You want me to go?" Connor asked, still flipping through channels.

"That's okay. I'll be right back."

The night was cool and smelled of roses as she stepped out the back door. The roll of the waves in the distance seemed louder than it had been this afternoon. She walked slowly over the paving stones, allowing the pins and needles in her leg to fade, and was almost at her car when she heard the jingle of keys. In the moonlight, she saw that she was not alone. Mr. Rule stood next to his Porsche and then a moment later folded himself inside it. The engine started, the brake lights glowed red, and before Rory could take another step, the car backed up and peeled off down the gravel drive.

Rory checked her watch. She wondered where Mr. Rule could be going at ten o'clock. There was something about how quickly he left, too, that seemed strange, as if he couldn't wait to get away from the house. She pulled open the door of her car and felt around on the passenger seat for her purse. At least she didn't have to worry about anyone stealing it here.

When she got back to her room, Connor was watching highlights from the French Open on TV. "I just saw your dad take off," she said.

"Yeah?" he asked.

"Yeah," Rory said, putting her purse on the dresser and then sitting down next to him. "Was he going back to the city for something?"

"No. I don't think so." Connor sat up and cleared his throat. He kept his eyes on the screen. "He was probably going home."

"Home? What do you mean, home?"

Connor muted the TV with the remote. "My dad's renting his own place in Sagaponack," he said quietly.

"Why?"

"Because my parents are taking some time apart."

"They *are*?" she asked, before thinking.

Connor looked down. Rory regretted sounding so shocked. "Yeah," he said. "It's no big deal."

No big deal? Rory thought. "Why didn't you tell me?" she asked.

"I wanted to, but then I thought you might not want to come out." He glanced back at the TV.

"Are they gonna get a divorce?" she asked.

"I don't know."

"So why was he here tonight? It seemed like they were still totally together."

Connor coughed into his fist. "Well, they are. For dinner parties and public stuff like that." He blinked a few times and looked at her questioningly, as if he wasn't sure she'd accept this as an answer. "I guess they're keeping it to themselves for now."

"Do you know why they're separated? Is there a reason?"

"Not that they've told us," he said, shrugging. "I don't think there's ever one reason for something like this, you know?"

She looked over at the glass clock on the nightstand. She realized that she knew the reason: Mr. Knox. She felt sick to her stomach. "I'm so sorry," she said. "How long has it been going on?"

"They told us a few weeks ago," Connor said. "But my mom said it's been in the works for a while. He has his own place in the city, too."

"So, they're not telling anyone?" she asked.

Connor shifted a few inches away from her. "That's the way

21

they want to do it," he said. "It's seriously not a big deal. I'm not freaked about it or anything."

"Well, that's good," she said, not sure she believed him.

"All my friends, their parents are divorced. And it's not like it's going to ruin the summer. Too many other good things going on," Connor said, smiling at her in a sly way. "You're here."

"Yeah. And no more groupies stalking your every move."

"Huh?"

"No more girls doing this." She batted her eyes and said in a breathy voice, *"Hi, Connor. What's up?"*

"Oh? So someone's jealous?" Connor asked, wrapping his arm around her. "Is that it? Someone's a little jealous?"

"You wish."

"Yeah, I think you are," Connor said. "I think you're jealous."

He kissed her again, and she let herself forget all about the Rules, and polite dinner conversation, and unsettling secrets. At least for a little while.

CHAPTER TWO

The next morning Rory woke early. She showered, then sat on the edge of her bed for a good twenty minutes, listening to the stillness of the house and wondering just what to do with herself. Last summer she would have been on her way to town by now, getting newspapers and doughnuts for the Rules' breakfast, and whatever last-minute items Erica, the former chef, needed from Citarella. But now she was a guest here, which meant that there was nowhere she needed to be and nothing she needed to do. She tapped her foot on the carpet. Her blister still ached. She thought about sneaking upstairs to see if Connor was awake, but she didn't want to run into Mrs. Rule. At last she decided to take Trixie for a walk on the beach. The poor dog probably still hadn't touched sand since she got here.

She opened her bedroom door and watched as Trixie trotted toward her from her bed down the hall. "Let's go for a walk, okay?" she half whispered.

At the word *walk* Trixie ran straight to the back door.

"That's what I thought," Rory murmured.

She let Trixie lead the way out the back door. The sky was overcast, and the wind blowing in from the ocean made the tips of her ears tingle. Steam rose off the glassy surface of the pool. The American flag snapped and curled in the breeze. Beyond the dunes, she could see a thin line of grayish-blue ocean. Everything looked exactly the same as it had last summer. But everything was different. She'd been wrong about Lily Pond Lane, Rory thought. Things did change here. More than she'd expected they could.

She walked down the beach, throwing a smooth piece of driftwood at regular intervals for Trixie to race toward, grab with her tiny teeth, and retrieve. Up ahead she could see the brown-shingled snack bar of Main Beach. On her left, tacked to a crooked fence sunk into the sand, was a sign that read DO NOT ENTER—PIPING PLOVERS NESTING AREA. She still hadn't actually seen a piping plover, but apparently this was their turf.

It wasn't entirely surprising that the Rules were headed for a divorce, she thought. She knew too much about them to believe in their facade of perfection anymore. But even headed for divorce, the Rules still made her feel inadequate. Last night, as she and Connor had kissed and fooled around, she couldn't relax. *Am I pretty enough for him?* she'd wondered. *Does he like what I'm doing right now?* She'd hoped Connor couldn't tell.

By the time she returned to the path of wooden planks that led up the sand dunes to the house, the clouds had burned off. A dull, hazy sun beat down on the top of her head and shoulders, and she could tell that today would be hot.

"Come here, Trix. Let's rinse you off," she said, crouching

down by the hose near the dressing cabana. As she rinsed Trixie's sandy curls, she heard a car crunch over the gravel and come to a stop, then a car door slam. It had to be Isabel.

Rory dropped the hose and turned it off. Trixie paused a moment and then shook her coat, sending drops of water all over Rory's face. "Thank you," Rory muttered, and then stood up, wiping her eyes. "Isabel?" she called out, rushing past the pool. "Hey!" She was almost at the back door when Isabel walked into view.

"Hey, McShane!" Isabel called, sauntering past the roses. She was still stunning. Her denim cutoffs and sleeveless crocheted tank showed off her long, golden limbs. Her hair was pin-straight and streaked with buttery highlights, courtesy of the California sun. Looking at her now, Rory found it hard to believe that some modeling agent hadn't snatched her up for the next J. Crew catalog. "God, it's been forever." She wrapped her arms around Rory. "Ugh! Why are you wet?"

"Trixie just soaked me," Rory said, hugging her back.

"Gross," Isabel said, rubbing her arms. "But how are you? How was graduation?"

"Okay. I survived the speech."

"Did the breathing exercises help?"

"Not really. I told you I wasn't a yoga person."

"You don't have to be a yoga person to breathe, Ror."

"I know. How'd the play go?"

"Oh, it was awesome," Isabel said, closing her eyes and savoring the memory. "Rosalind is an amazing part. And I finally got Shakespeare. All this time I thought he was boring. Turns out he was a genius."

"Yeah, well…" Rory wasn't sure how to respond to that.

"When did you get here?" Isabel asked.

"Yesterday."

"Connor must have been happy to see you," Isabel said with a sly smile. "Not that I want to hear details."

"Don't worry," Rory said. "You won't. What are you guys doing here so early?"

"Fee wanted to beat the traffic."

Just then, Rory caught a glimpse of her aunt Fee walking over from the driveway. Now that she'd replaced Bianca as house manager, Fee's uniform had gone from a unisex green polo and khaki pants to a more elegant outfit of a belted shirtdress and round-toed flats. It was as if Aunt Fee had finally earned the privilege, in the Rules' eyes, of dressing like a woman.

"Fee!" she yelled.

"Hello, my dear!" Fee said, rushing over to hug her. "Welcome back!" In two seconds, Rory was engulfed in one of her aunt's iron embraces.

"Nice duds," Rory said when she pulled away.

"You think so?" Fee said, glancing down at her dress. "I'm a little on the fence about it, to tell you the truth. I feel like a nurse. How was last night? Everything go okay?"

"There was a dinner party." *At which I totally embarrassed myself,* she wanted to add.

"I'm so glad I missed that," Isabel said, rolling her eyes.

"Well, you girls get caught up. I need to run off to the market with Mickey and do some shopping."

Rory had met the new chef before dinner, and he seemed

even more intense than Eduardo, the first chef she'd met last summer. Mickey had worked at some restaurant in San Francisco and talked ceaselessly as he moved around the kitchen, as if he were directing staff. *All right, let's get this one cooking—more fire under that one! How about a teaspoon of cilantro there—no, the saffron!* It had been a little unnerving, and she'd made a quick and silent exit.

"You need me to come? I can help," Rory offered.

"Not at all," Fee said. "You're a guest this summer. Mickey and I can take care of most of it." She gave Rory's arm a squeeze. "Come visit me later," she said before walking into the house.

"Where is everyone?" Isabel asked. "Still sleeping?"

"I think so," Rory said. "No one was up when I left."

"Good," Isabel said, grabbing her arm. "'Cause we need to catch up. Come on," she said, picking up her carry-on and leading the way inside the house.

Up in Isabel's room, Rory settled herself on a chair and eyed the pile of enormous FedEx boxes that lay in the middle of the ivory shag rug. "Are you starting a business or something?" Rory asked.

"Oh, this is my stuff from school," Isabel said, kicking one of the boxes. "It's so much easier than shipping it regular mail."

"Right," Rory said, pretending to agree.

Isabel dropped her carry-on on the floor and then went to the window to pull open the curtains. "God, this is weird," she said, looking out at the front lawn.

"What's weird?"

"Being back here." Isabel stared out the window. "Don't be offended or anything, but I tried to stay in California."

"You did?"

"Yeah. Mr. Knox was going to try to get me a job as a PA for one of the movie studios. But my mom wouldn't let me do it. What a surprise."

Rory sat down on the bed and scratched at a mosquito bite on her knee. "Is it because of what's going on with your parents?" she asked.

Isabel turned from the window.

"I heard," Rory said. "Connor told me. I'm really sorry."

"Yeah, well, we both saw that one coming, didn't we?" She sat down on the floor and reached for one of the FedEx boxes. "I can't believe it took them this long. The more important thing is that I'm going crazy."

"Crazy?"

"Guy deprivation," Isabel explained. "It's finally kicked in. It's been almost a year since I kissed someone."

"But that was by choice, I'm sure."

"Maybe." Isabel ripped open one of the boxes. "But it's over now. I think I've reached my breaking point."

"Are you going to get in touch with Mike?" Rory asked, as delicately as possible.

Isabel froze. "Uh, no. Why would you even say that?"

"Because I'm sure he's still around this summer."

"So what?" Isabel said, pulling out a cluster of blouses on tied-together hangers. "He never called me once all year. Not once."

"Well, you did break up with him."

"Yeah, but he could have at least tried to call me and get me back. That's the *least* he could have done."

"When you were in California?" Rory countered.

Isabel gave Rory a look and pulled out another cluster of blouses. "Forget it. But I'm totally open to a very cute, very nice stranger. Not that I would have any idea what to say if he started talking to me."

"I'm sure it'll come back to you," Rory said.

"Isabel?" Mrs. Rule called from out in the hall. "Are you here?"

"Oh god," Isabel groaned. She looked up at the ceiling. "I'm not ready for this."

Mrs. Rule breezed into the room and stopped short in front of the barricade of boxes around her daughter. "How are you, honey? How was the trip out?" She seemed more hesitant, less imperious, than she had been waltzing into Rory's room yesterday.

Isabel ripped open another box. "Fine," she said tonelessly.

"I'm surprised you got such an early start."

"I couldn't sleep."

There was a pause. Mrs. Rule glanced at Rory and gave her a tight smile. "We're all just going down to breakfast now."

"I already ate," Isabel said sullenly.

"That's okay." Mrs. Rule pursed her lips. "Tonight is First of Summer."

"That's great," she said icily.

"I'd like it very much if you'd come," Mrs. Rule said. Her voice sounded needy.

"You know I didn't want to come back here," Isabel said.

"Isabel, it's one night of your life. Everyone else is going—"

"So?" Isabel dumped a pile of jeans on the rug. "I have plans."

Mrs. Rule turned around and closed the door behind her.

Rory knew what was coming. "Isabel," Mrs. Rule said, visibly trying to stay calm. "I don't want to start off the summer like this. You've been home five minutes—"

"Why is it so important we all go to the Georgica?" Isabel asked, finally looking at her mother. Her eyes flashed with anger.

"Because it's our club. It's the beginning of summer. It's a family event."

"No. You just want to parade us all around—so nobody'll know that you guys are getting a divorce."

Mrs. Rule's smile disappeared. Rory wished she could melt into the bed. "Fine, stay home, if that's what you want," she said. "But I want you to know that this rebel-without-a-cause routine is getting a little old."

Rory noticed that Mrs. Rule didn't deny the divorce.

"I don't know why you made me come back here," Isabel said. "Mr. Knox said he could get me a job in LA this summer. He was all set to help me—"

"Do not talk about that man in this house, do you understand me?" her mother said sharply. "I have no interest in what he has to say. None."

Rory stared at the rug. She hoped she'd never have to look Mrs. Rule in the eye again.

"Fine," Isabel said. "Be in denial. You can't make me be there, too."

"I'm going downstairs," Mrs. Rule announced. "I hope you can bring yourself to say hello to the rest of the family."

"Except for Dad, right? I'd have to go to his new house to do that."

Mrs. Rule made a sound of disgust. "Good-bye, Isabel," she said. Then she turned on her heels and shut the door.

There was silence for a few moments.

"That was fun," Isabel quipped.

"So your parents are getting a divorce?" Rory asked.

"Yup." Isabel started to fold the pile of jeans.

"Connor said he didn't know. That he wasn't sure. He made it sound like they were just separated."

"He would," Isabel sniffed.

"So he *does* know?" Rory clarified.

"My mom called us all a couple of weeks ago," Isabel said. "She told us that they'd decided to separate and that they were headed for a divorce by the end of the year. And that my dad was getting his own place in Sagaponack and that we were all going to 'proceed normally' for now, i.e., hide it from the rest of the world."

Rory felt a pit form in her stomach. Connor had deliberately downplayed the situation to her, then. That wasn't good. "Is it about the thing with Mr. Knox?" Rory asked.

"What do you think? Of course."

"But Connor doesn't know about it," Rory said.

"Nope. My parents don't want anyone to know. You haven't said anything, right?" Isabel said.

"Nope. Haven't said a word." *Not that it's been easy*, she wanted to add.

Isabel looked at her watch. "I have a riding lesson. You want to come?"

"No, thanks," Rory said, remembering her one experience at Two Trees with Isabel and Connor's ex-girlfriend Julia.

31

"Okay. What about later? We can go to the beach, right?" Isabel asked.

"Sure. And what about tonight at the Georgica? I'm pretty sure I have to go. And it's not like I'll know anyone there."

Isabel scratched her arm, mulling this over. "Okay. I'll go. I mean, if you're gonna get dragged there, then it's the least I can do."

"Thanks," Rory said, getting to her feet. "Have a good ride."

"I'll try."

As Rory left the room, she realized that the pit in her stomach had doubled in size. If she'd thought that being an errand girl for the Rules was hard, being a guest of the Rules was going to be even harder. At least last summer she could pretend not to know about any of the Rules' private drama. Now she was right in the middle of it, whether she wanted to be or not.

Isabel turned onto Montauk Highway, thinking about the question Rory had posed about Mike. Truthfully, he had popped into her brain a few times on the flight home. But how couldn't he have? The last time she was in East Hampton she'd been crazy in love with the guy. Or at least she thought she'd been at the time. But she had no plans to call him. When she thought about him now, she knew that it hadn't been love. It had been sex. Pure physical attraction, and not much else. He didn't know anything about her school, her family, or her friends. Looking back, she wasn't even sure what they'd talked about in between their hookup sessions. Even so, it had taken a while for his spell to finally dissipate. When she got back to school, there would be times walking around campus when he'd suddenly invade her thoughts and she'd have to force herself not to call him. Then there'd be times when she'd be hit with a hookup flashback so intense it would distract her for the rest of the day. And still other times she'd obsess over how carelessly, and cruelly, he'd hurt her. Using their relationship to get info about a stupid real estate deal of her dad's…stringing her along so he could report back to his uncle…it was unforgivable, really. She'd let him off way too easy that day at the stand. For a good two months afterward she'd worked on the speech she should have given him, just in case he called. But he never did.

By Christmas, the pain had lessened. But that didn't stop her from having those flashbacks. Her and Mike in his tiny, stuffy room, shadows on the walls from the votive candle flickering on the bedside table, Bob Marley playing from the iPod dock— *Is this love? Is this love? Is this love?* And her on his bed, kissing him, reaching to pull off his T-shirt and then running her hands down his back, his chest, the hard terrain of his stomach…

Suddenly the white SUV in front of her slowed down. She slammed her foot on the brakes. With a screech, her car came to a stop, but not before her front bumper just touched the back of the SUV.

The SUV turned its hazard lights on.

Great, Isabel thought.

The other car moved slowly out of the traffic jam and into the parking lot of a roadside bagel shop. Isabel followed. Being at boarding school, she'd gotten a little rusty behind the wheel. But at least she'd stopped. And bumpers were made for bumping. Weren't they?

Isabel pulled into the empty spot beside the SUV. The car's engine turned off, and the driver-side door swung open. A small, wiry woman wearing yoga pants and a tank top emblazoned with the Hindi symbol for *om* walked right around to her back bumper without saying a word. Isabel got out of her car.

"So sorry about that," Isabel started, and then the woman whirled around.

"Didn't you see me stop?" The woman pointed to her bumper. "Look at that dent! Look at that!"

Isabel searched for the imaginary dent. It looked perfectly fine. "I don't see anything—"

"There's a scratch right there," the woman said, cutting her off. "Don't you see it?" She pointed, and Isabel leaned in closer to look.

"I honestly don't see anything."

"Uh, you guys need help with something?" a voice asked.

Isabel turned around. A guy about her age was walking toward them from the bagel shop. In his hand was a brown paper sack.

"She rear-ended me," the woman snapped. She folded her toned arms. "Look at that dent."

The guy walked up beside Isabel and took a look. "I don't see anything," he said.

"It's right there," the woman said, pointing.

The guy turned to Isabel. His expression seemed to say, *Is it me, or is this woman totally nuts?* He was actually kind of cute. Messy bed-head hair that hovered between dirty blond and

34

brown. Large olive-green eyes. Friendly eyes. "I gotta be honest," the guy said, turning back to Yoga Woman. "I don't see anything."

"Whatever. This isn't any of your business." The woman turned to Isabel. "Can I get your insurance information?"

"But there's nothing there," Isabel said.

"I've always been a big believer in letting things go, personally," the guy said. "You know, not sweat the small stuff. Live and let live. Be kind to your fellow yogi."

The woman narrowed her eyes.

"Not take-advantage-of-your-fellow-man, extort-helpless-young-girls-for-money stuff," he added with a grin. He held up his hands. "Sorry. Thinking out loud here."

"How deep," she said. Then she glanced at her watch. "I have a class to teach. But you," she said, pointing a finger at Isabel, "you watch where you're going, do you understand?"

"Uh, sure," Isabel said, trying to keep a straight face.

The woman got into the car, and they both watched as the SUV pulled back onto the highway.

"I have this theory," the guy said, turning to Isabel. "The higher up you drive, the farther you reside within your own butt."

Isabel laughed.

"It's a theory, still working it out."

"Well, you might be on to something," she said, smiling at him. "Thanks for your help. She was kind of a nightmare."

"Just another blissed-out yoga person," he said with a slight roll of the eyes.

"You got it," she said. She looked down at the bag in his hand. "Those smell good."

"You want one?" he said, opening the bag of bagels. He pulled out a cinnamon raisin. "It's all yours. I got way too many."

"You're sure you don't mind?" she asked.

"No, no. Take it."

She took the bagel, which was still warm, and tore off a piece. She popped it in her mouth. "Wow, that's good," she said, savoring the sweet taste of the bread.

"Do you not have food where you live?" he asked.

She giggled. "I'm hungry."

"I can see that. I'm Evan."

"Isabel. And I don't do yoga."

"No wonder you're such a happy person." He looked back at the parking lot. "I should probably get going. My roommate'll kill me if I don't bring these back," he said. "But..." He reached into his back pocket and took out what looked like a crumpled receipt and a pen. "If you have any more fender benders, you can always give me a call. Be warned, though. I might have to charge you next time."

Isabel smiled. "That's okay."

He scribbled a number on the receipt. "Here," he said, giving it to her with a flourish. "That's until I have business cards."

She took it. "I'll let you know."

"So...yeah," the guy said, smiling and walking away. "Stay safe out there."

She chuckled. "I'll try."

He turned back into the parking lot, and she watched him

get into a small, slightly banged-up car. He liked her. Or maybe he thought that she liked him. She looked down at the receipt pressed into her palm and the name he'd scrawled. EVAN SHANA-HAN. She dumped it into her bag. *Evan*, she thought, as she got into her car. She'd always liked that name.

CHAPTER THREE

Back in her room, Rory pulled on her new bathing suit and grabbed her sunglasses. After witnessing that exchange between Mrs. Rule and Isabel in Isabel's room, she decided to skip breakfast. The last thing Rory wanted to do right now was sit across from Mrs. Rule and make conversation.

As she reached the back door, the kitchen door swung open. "Oh, Rory," said Mrs. Rule. "Do you have a minute?"

Rory wheeled around. "Sure," she said.

Mrs. Rule cleared her throat and stepped closer to her. "About what Isabel said upstairs," she said, casting her eyes down to the floor. "I do hope I can count on you to be discreet. Connor said that you would be."

Rory felt a slight pang. It would have been nice for Connor to give her some warning about all this. "Sure, whatever you need," she said.

"Good. My daughter likes to overdramatize, as you probably know. And she loves to paint me as a hypocrite." She tucked a lock of blond hair behind her ear and forced a smile. "You'll understand when you have a daughter."

"Are you okay, Mrs. Rule?"

Mrs. Rule stared at her.

"It seems like you might be going through a rough time." As soon as the words were out, Rory could hear how ridiculous they sounded. She took a step toward the back door, even though escape was unlikely.

"Well, now that you mention it, things have been better," she said. "But it's nothing that other families haven't gone through. And I don't believe in making everyone else aware of your private business."

"Right," Rory said. "There's no need for people to know everything."

Mrs. Rule smiled. "Exactly. I just wish my daughter felt that way." A look of controlled civility came over her face.

"Well, I won't say anything to anyone," Rory said. "Not that I would know who to say anything to."

Mrs. Rule cocked her head and stared at Rory, as if she were trying to put her finger on something that was out of her reach. "My son cares about you a lot," she said, as if it had just occurred to her.

"Thanks." Rory wondered what hidden subtext lay in that statement. Because knowing Mrs. Rule, there had to be some hidden subtext.

"So...you and Connor will be there tonight, then? At the Georgica?" Mrs. Rule asked, abruptly changing tack.

"Sure," Rory said. "And I think Isabel is coming."

"Oh? How did that happen?"

"We were talking about it, and she changed her mind."

Mrs. Rule's shock gave way to mild awe. "Well. That's good to know. Thank you."

"It wasn't anything I did—"

"It starts at six," Mrs. Rule interrupted. She walked back toward the swinging door. "Oh, and Rory?" she asked, turning around. "You do have something nice to wear tonight, right?"

Rory swallowed. "Yes."

"Good. See you later, then."

She pushed through the swinging door, and Rory slowly let out her breath. No matter how vulnerable Mrs. Rule had seemed just now, she was still the same person. With the same priorities.

Rory stepped out the back door and into the soft, early summer morning. A butterfly flitted among the roses. She didn't know what to say to Connor when he woke up. The Connor she'd known up until now would never have pretended not to know such a big detail about his parents' lives. But maybe she didn't know him as well as she thought she did.

"We won't stay long—don't worry," Connor said as he steered the car down the series of long, curving paths that led to the Georgica Club. The main house looked even more foreboding than Rory remembered. Golden light from the setting sun outlined the many eaves of the shingle clubhouse while the front of it was cast in shadow. "We'll just say hi to a few people and leave. Make an appearance."

"I can't believe I agreed to this," Isabel grumbled from the backseat. "I'm sure Thayer and Darwin are going to be here."

"I thought they were your friends," Connor said.

"They are," she said. "We had some issues last summer. And those two hang on to things. For, like, years."

40

"I'll help you deal with them," Rory said. "You want me to tell them off again?"

"That was so awesome," Isabel said. "I'll never forget that. The ballsiest move ever."

Rory looked over her shoulder at Isabel. "Yeah?" she asked.

"Yup," Isabel replied. Then she mouthed something. *I met someone.*

You did? Rory mouthed back.

Yup, Isabel mouthed back, and wiggled her eyebrows in a way that said, *More later.*

They drove up to the main entrance, and a pair of eager valets in white polo shirts ran out to greet them. "Have my parents arrived?" Connor asked the one who opened his door.

"They're waiting for you in the lobby," he replied.

Rory stepped out of Connor's car carefully, then smoothed the back of her sleeveless cowl-necked dress. She'd bought it on sale at Calypso at the end of last summer but had never worn it. Now the back of it was somehow a few inches higher than she remembered. "Can you see my butt?" she asked Isabel as they walked into the club.

Isabel took a step back and scrutinized her. "Nope, but it *is* kind of short."

"Great."

"Relax. I think it's awesome," Isabel added. "Just what this place needs."

Not exactly comforting, Rory thought. Isabel would probably show up naked at the Georgica if someone dared her. She yanked the dress down and felt the blister on her heel throb. At least she'd left the Jack Rogers at home. But high-heeled sandals weren't making anything easier. If only Mrs. Rule hadn't made her feel so preemptively underdressed that morning, she would have worn flats.

In the lobby, the rest of the Rules stood waiting at the check-in desk, looking grim and bored. "What took you guys so long?" Mr. Rule said.

"Sorry," Connor said. "I thought we left right after you."

"Well, we've been waiting here awhile," he said. The cool, collected, youthful vibe he'd projected the night before was gone, Rory noted. The pinched-looking, impatient CEO was back.

"Well, sorry," Connor said under his breath.

"Hello, Isabel," said Mr. Rule. He walked toward his daughter to give her a hug, but Isabel stiffened, as if he were a stranger. "How was graduation?" he asked.

"Fine," she said. "How was that business trip?" Her voice dripped with sarcasm.

Mr. Rule gave a sheepish half smile. "It was fine. You know I wish I could have been there."

"I'm sure," she said curtly.

He nodded in a resigned way. "Well, let's go," he said.

The family began to head toward the exit.

"They're in a great mood," Isabel whispered as she came to walk beside Rory.

Rory didn't say anything. It seemed to her as if Mr. Rule had tried to be nice to Isabel but that she'd been the one to snub him.

They walked outside to the rickety staircase that led down to the pool and the patio, where the party was already in full swing. Men in pastel polos and chinos stood clustered together, while women in brightly patterned shift dresses talked in their own little groups. Before they went down the stairs, Mr. Rule took a step backward so that he was abreast with his wife and curled his arm around her waist. Mrs. Rule stood up straight and threw back her shoulders. Then they descended the staircase together.

"Check it out," Isabel said, discreetly pointing to her parents. "It's like they're Bill and Hillary."

It was true, Rory thought. All the tension she'd sensed in the lobby had vanished, and now they walked down the stairs as close and cozy as if they were a newlywed couple. Mrs. Rule even seemed to lean into her husband's tall, slim body, as if she needed his very help to stay upright. Rory looked over to see if Connor was noticing this, but he seemed to be lost in thought about something, looking off toward the ocean.

"So tell me about this guy you met," she said to Isabel as they walked down the stairs.

"Oh yeah," Isabel said brightly. "I was driving to Two Trees and sort of got into a car accident—"

"A *what?*"

"It wasn't really a car accident; it was a *near* car accident."

"A near car accident?"

"I almost rear-ended someone—*almost.*"

Sloane turned to look at them over her shoulder. "Are you sure that you actually passed your driver's test?" she asked.

"Mind your own business," Isabel said. "Anyway"—she turned back to Rory—"the driver was this really annoying yoga freak who was practically delusional, saying that I'd ruined her car or something, and this guy walked over and started defending me. And he was so sweet. And funny. And he gave me his number."

"Are you gonna call him?"

"I don't know."

"Call him."

"I've never called a guy first."

"But does he have *your* number?" Rory asked.

"No."

"Then you have to call," Rory said. "Or I will for you. You said he was cute, right?"

"Yeah."

"Then go for it."

"Wow, look at you," said Isabel. "Last summer I had to twist your arm to talk to a guy at a party."

"Well, that was last summer," Rory said proudly, casting a glance at Connor, who still looked preoccupied.

"Fine, I'll call him," Isabel said. "Chill."

At the bottom of the stairs, Mr. and Mrs. Rule moved into the crowd; Sloane and Gregory headed toward a group of their friends; and Connor, Isabel, and Rory assessed the party.

"I don't really see anyone yet," Isabel said.

"I'm sure there are some Isabel admirers here. Don't worry," Connor joked. "You guys want something to drink?"

"I'll take a Sprite," said Rory.

"Have him get you something stronger," Isabel advised. "You might need it."

"Not happenin', sis," Connor said. "Do you want a soda?"

"No, thanks," she said, shaking him off.

Connor went to the bar, and Rory watched him go. He still seemed off, but she couldn't figure out why.

Suddenly Isabel grabbed Rory's arm. "Oh god. Look. One o'clock."

"What?"

"Over there. *The Shining* twins," Isabel said, steering Rory's arm so that she faced the right direction.

It was Thayer and Darwin, standing a few yards away, scanning the crowd over their drinks as they chitchatted out of the sides of their mouths. Thayer's glossy chestnut hair had been curled at the ends, like Kate Middleton's, while Darwin's golden-red locks looked suspiciously longer and thicker than they had last summer. Maybe they were extensions, Rory thought. But did real people actually do that? Or was that just a Hollywood thing? Thayer spotted them and gave Isabel a halfhearted wave with the tips of her fingers.

"May as well get this over with," Isabel said.

"You want a wingman?"

"I can take care of it."

Isabel ambled off in the direction of the two girls. Rory looked around again. Nobody seemed to notice that she was standing alone. In fact, nobody seemed to notice her at all. People were too busy giving each other air-kisses and gulping down what looked like tall glasses of iced lemonade. She decided to go in search of Connor, who still hadn't come back from the bar. She found him, drinks in hand, standing beside his parents and an older couple.

"There you are," Connor said when she joined his side. "Rory, this is Mrs. Randall." He gestured to the tall, horse-faced woman in the center of the group. "Mrs. Randall, this is my girl-friend, Rory."

"Oh," Mrs. Randall said with surprise as she shook Rory's hand. "It's nice to meet you. You're from New Jersey, right?"

"Right," Rory said. She was starting to wonder if she had a sign on her back.

"I love New Jersey," said Mrs. Randall. "Some parts of it are so beautiful." Mrs. Randall let go of her hand and turned to speak to Mrs. Rule. "You know, Lucy, I've been meaning to tell you. If you two are ever in the mood to do a bike trip through Burgundy, Mark and I are more than happy to bring you along."

"Oh, we should do that," said Mrs. Rule, clutching Mr. Rule's arm. "I've always wanted to do one of those. It would be such fun."

"Belinda loves her bike trips," said the older, red-nosed man standing next to Mrs. Randall, who Rory assumed was Mr. Randall. "She looks forward to them all year."

"I think Lucy loves the idea of drinking French wine all day more than the actual bicycling," Mr. Rule said.

The Randalls, and Mrs. Rule, laughed appreciatively.

Isabel hadn't been kidding, Rory thought. The Rules really could put on a show.

After a few more minutes of banter, Connor gracefully extracted himself and Rory from the group, and they walked over to the buffet. The ice in her soda had melted, and when she brought it to her lips her front teeth tingled with cold. "If one more person tells me how beautiful New Jersey is, I'm going to lose it," Rory muttered.

"They're just trying to be nice," Connor said.

"So why say that?" Rory asked. "It's not like I created the state or something." They stood in front of the hors d'oeuvres, which were mostly rows of orange-tinted cheese tarts. She picked one up and bit into it. It was even drier than it looked.

"This isn't the most original crowd, I'll give you that," Connor said. "And the Randalls can be a little bit much."

Rory sipped more of her soda, wondering how best to ask what she needed to ask. "Why didn't you tell me that your parents are definitely getting a divorce?"

Connor frowned. "What?"

"Isabel told me."

Connor took a sip of his drink. "Well, for one, it hasn't happened yet."

"But it sounds like it's on its way to happening," she said.

"So? Why is that so important?"

"Because it is. Divorce is a big deal. And I care about you—"

"Then drop it, okay?" He drained his drink. "I'm gonna get another one. You want anything?"

"I'm fine," she said past the knot in her throat.

"Be right back," he said, and walked away.

She watched him go, stung. He'd never spoken to her like that. Not ever.

Standing in front of Thayer and Darwin, Isabel needed a drink. It was clear within the first fifteen seconds of walking up to them that they were still mad at her for blowing them off last summer, and now she was trapped.

"Hey," Thayer said, her trademark blasé in full force. She leaned over—just barely—to give Isabel a hug. "When did you get in?"

"This morning," Isabel said.

Darwin whipped her extralong hair over her shoulder several times, as if begging Isabel to notice her new extensions. "What's up? Did you get that at Blue and Cream?" She nodded at Isabel's dress.

"No, some place in Montecito." Off their confused faces, she added, "Near my school."

"Oh," Thayer said coolly, swirling the ice around in her cranberry juice. "Right."

"It must be weird going to school so far away," Darwin said, her narrow blue eyes flashing. "And I heard the schools aren't as good out there."

"Where'd you hear that?" Isabel asked.

Darwin shrugged, as if this minor detail weren't that important.

"So . . . how was senior year?" asked Isabel. "Thayer got into UPenn," said Darwin. "And I got into Vanderbilt."

"Oh?" said Isabel. "I got into NYU. Tisch School. For drama."

Darwin looked taken aback. "Really?"

"Yep," Isabel said, letting that bomb land nicely. "And what are you guys doing this summer? Just hanging out here at the club?"

"Why? Are you actually going to be here?" Thayer asked, studying the inside of her glass.

"Why does it bother you so much that I hung out with other people last summer?"

"That didn't bother us," Thayer said. "What bothers us is that you think you're too good for this place."

48

"But hey, if you'd rather hang out with people who work at the fruit stands, that's fine with us," Darwin said with a smirk.

Isabel smiled. "You guys aren't snobby at all," she said.

"Look, do whatever you want," Thayer said, sounding bored. "Nobody cares. I think people have already forgotten about you, if you want to know the truth." Thayer spotted someone else in the crowd and waved generously. "Tatiana!" she called. "Hey, sweetie pie."

Before Isabel could say anything, Thayer and Darwin moved off to say hello to Tatiana Gould. She stood looking down at the ground, slowly curling her hand into and out of a fist. So much for trying to do the polite thing, she thought. It was never worth it.

She turned and looked out at the pristine Georgica beach, the same one where she'd met Mike almost exactly a year ago. How lucky she'd been, to find an escape from this place. Now she'd have to find another one. And she didn't have the least idea how to do that.

CHAPTER FOUR

On the ride home, Connor was quiet behind the wheel, and Isabel didn't say a word from the backseat. Rory guessed that things with Thayer and Darwin hadn't gone so well. She stared out the window into the dark, still hurt and confused by Connor's reaction. *Don't overreact*, she thought. *You're blowing this way out of proportion.*

"You want to watch TV for a little while?" Connor asked her when they walked back into the house.

Rory watched Isabel go up the back stairs. "I think I should go spend some time with Fee."

"Okay. G'night, then." He leaned over and gave her a chaste kiss on the cheek. "See you tomorrow."

"Yeah. See you tomorrow."

He went up the back stairs as she went down the stairs. *A kiss on the cheek?* she thought. Something was definitely wrong.

She had a feeling that Fee was still in the same room, despite her promotion. At the closed door at the end of the hall, she raised her hand and rapped lightly.

Fee opened the door. "Hello, dear," she said. "You're just in time for the end of *The Bachelor*." She wore a fluffy white bathrobe with FLM monogrammed above the left breast. She got back onto her bed and tucked her feet in under the covers. "Where on earth do they find these girls?" she said. "They're all a bunch of train wrecks."

Rory sat on the edge of Fee's bed and pulled off her high heels. "That's a nice robe."

"A gift from the Rules," Fee said, looking down at it. She grabbed a cellophane bag of Jordan almonds from the night-stand. "Settling in?"

"It's a little strange not to be working here, if you want to know the truth."

"Ah, you'll get used to the life of leisure," Fee said, then held out the bag. "Want one?"

Rory shook her head. "And it's also a little strange, what's going on here this summer. You know, with the Rules."

Fee nodded. "So Connor told you?"

"Isabel's been a little more clear about it all."

"Truth is, I've seen it coming for a while now. It started right after we went back to the city after last summer. I'd hear them arguing, sometimes so loudly that there was barely a place I could go in the apartment where I wouldn't hear them. And then Mr. Rule would leave for a few days and go to a hotel."

"Would Mrs. Rule talk about it to you?"

Fee selected a baby-blue almond from the bag and popped it in her mouth. "She'd say that he was on a business trip. Then she stopped trying to explain it. It got to the point where she knew that I knew, and there was nothing she could say. Eventually he'd come back, and things'd be fine. And then they'd have another barn burner, and poof! He'd be gone again." She closed the bag of almonds and put it in her nightstand drawer.

"What were they fighting about?" Rory asked.

Fee shrugged. "It was different every time. What kind of tuxedo he should wear to the opera, whether to sell their house in Bedford, what time to have dinner, whether to let the chef go…little things. Suddenly everything was a fight."

"Do you think there was something behind it all? Like, one main reason?" It wasn't exactly an honest question, but she needed to know if Fee had any suspicions.

"Hard to say," Fee said. "It was never the most affectionate marriage. In eighteen years I don't think I ever saw them kiss each other. But they were happy, in their own way. I don't know what happened. It all was so sudden." She opened the nightstand drawer once more and took out the bag of almonds. She popped another in her mouth. "Did Connor mention a reason to you?"

"Nope." Rory looked down. It wasn't a lie. But she was starting to get that pit in her stomach again. "Whatever the reason for it, the Rules seem to want to keep it between them."

"Oh, yes," Fee said. "They want to keep the entire thing between them. It's why she got rid of Bianca. Didn't trust her. She knew that Bianca liked to gossip with some of her friends from the other houses out here, and she didn't want anyone hearing that they were having problems. She's trying to keep as much of this behind closed doors as possible."

"But why? People get divorced all the time. Especially in New York."

Fee clicked off the TV and closed the bag of almonds again. "Because they're perfect, I suppose. They're not supposed to have flaws. Or they don't think they are. Speaking of flaws, how's your mother?"

"She and boy-toy Bryan broke up."

"Again?" Fee asked, arching a brow.

"Yep. But I'm sure they'll be back together again by next week."

Fee shook her head. "At least you have college to look forward to," she said, putting the bag back in her nightstand drawer. "And then, my dear, you can really get on with your life."

"Yeah, I guess so." Rory stood up and went to the door. Then she turned back. "Connor's their favorite, isn't he?"

Fee gave her another skeptical look. "You're just figuring that out now?"

"I mean...because of that he feels very protective of them. Doesn't he?"

"Well, he'd never do anything to disappoint them, that's for sure," Fee said. "He's a good boy. And that's what you love about him, isn't it?"

As much as she wanted to dispute that, she knew that Fee was right. She'd loved that about him last year. There were so few truly good people she'd ever met. But perhaps all of that goodness came with a downside. "Have a good night," she said. "Sleep well."

"You too, dear," said Fee.

As she walked back into the cool, dim hall, she thought about what Fee had just said about getting on with her life. Obviously she'd meant leaving behind her mother and all her drama, but now Rory wondered if it meant leaving the Rules behind, too. She'd always assumed that she and Connor would last forever, or at least through her college years. It had been one of the reasons she'd picked Stanford.

But what if she and Connor weren't meant for forever?

It was just one stupid argument, she told herself as she climbed up the stairs. *Nothing to get all worked up about.*

The next morning, Isabel tapped lightly on Rory's closed bedroom door. "Rory? You up?" If Rory and Connor had spent the night together in her room, then hopefully both of them were up and dressed by now. "Rory?" She knocked again.

"Yeah!" Rory opened the door. Her hair was wet, and she wore a silk blouse and black pants that made her look like she was interviewing at a law firm. "Sorry. Are we supposed to be at breakfast or something? I'm running a little late."

"No, it's fine," Isabel said, breezing into the room. "You can get yourself something from the kitchen if you'd like." She flopped down on the bed. "So the party sucked last night. Thayer and Darwin were just as bitchy and awful as I thought they'd be."

Rory stood at the mirror, raking a brush through her hair. "Can we talk about this later?"

"It wasn't anything that I didn't already expect," Isabel said, disregarding Rory's hurry and yawning into her open hand. "But five minutes with them is totally soul killing. And I've been thinking. I can't—*can't*—spend the summer at the Georgica. I can't. I need to find something else to do."

54

"Like what?"

Isabel bit her lip. "Like a job." She crossed her legs and examined her already-fading tan. "What about at the film festival place? Can you ask if they need someone?"

Rory looked over her shoulder, her brush stuck in her wet hair. "That might be a little tricky. I mean, it's my first day."

"Fine. Then where else?"

"What about something at Calypso? Or Blue and Cream?" Rory ran into the bathroom.

Isabel wrinkled her nose as she mulled this over. "I shop at those places. And Thayer and Darwin go there all the time."

Rory rushed back out of the bathroom with an eyeliner in her hand. "Okay—what about waitressing?"

"*Waitressing?*" Isabel exclaimed. "Seriously?"

"It can be fun," Rory said. "And I'd think there'd be a lot of places out here that still need some help."

"Waitressing…" Isabel muttered. She thought about all the waitstaff that she'd glimpsed in her life. A montage of bad outfits, sneakers, and harried, sweaty faces ran through her mind. Her enthusiasm wilted.

"Yeah, it's probably a bad idea. It's harder than it looks. I mean, physically hard." Rory pulled her wet hair back with an elastic band. "Last night wasn't great for me, either. Connor and I had a weird moment. I told him that I knew about the divorce. He got a little defensive."

"That's because he's in denial. Someone ought to make him face reality."

Rory pulled the elastic out of her hair and shook it loose. "Does this look okay? This outfit?"

"It looks fine," Isabel said, sliding off the bed. "If you're trying to get a job as a paralegal or something."

Rory sighed. "Why don't you call that guy? Maybe he could meet you for coffee or something?"

"You don't have to worry about my day or anything," Isabel said, heading for the door. "I'll be fine."

"Just call him," Rory said. "It's time you got back out there."

Isabel turned around at the doorway. "Are you telling me to ask him out?"

"Yes. You're Isabel Rule. If you can't do this, nobody can."

Isabel thought about this for a moment. "Yeah, you're right," she said, and walked out of the room.

As she made her way through one of the alleys that led from the parking lot to Main Street, Isabel checked her reflection in the window of a jewelry store. She wasn't sure if this was a date or not, but just in case it was, she wanted to make sure she looked decent. Her text had deliberately walked the line—or tried to—between asking him out and saying a quick, friendly hi.

> Hey, thanks for the impromptu defense yesterday. Can I buy you coffee to thank you?

Funny, sweet, and flirty—but not overly so.
Evan wrote back ten minutes later.

> Have to work later but coffee sounds great. Starbucks? Or much cooler, artisanal, single-pour place that I don't know about?

Btw, I HATE the word "artisanal."

She smiled. This guy was good. Possibly even more of a master texter than she was. And funny. Mike hadn't been funny. He'd been too cool and mysterious for that. What a pain in the butt he'd been, she thought as she pulled open the door to Starbucks.

Her eyes scanned the long line in front of the counter, and then she saw Evan coming toward her. He was taller than she remembered, with a mop of dark tawny hair and a build that was just on the right side of gangly. Not her usual type, but she didn't quite know what her type was anymore. "Hey. I got here early, so I took a wild guess." He handed her an iced green tea latte.

"Thanks," she said, more delighted than she expected to be. "I love these."

"You do?" His eyes were large and green and alive with mischief, as if he was in on some joke that she didn't know about. He wiped his brow in an exaggerated way. "Phew."

"Didn't you get something?"

He held up a bottle of water. "I don't do the hard stuff."

"Got it," she said, smiling. "Well…" She took in the line snaking in front of the counter. "Should we leave, then?"

"Please." He ran to the door and held it open for her as she walked out. *So he has manners*, she thought. Mike had never done something like that.

They stepped outside onto the street. Isabel searched for something witty to say, but her mind was a blank. "That place was crazy," she said, at a loss for anything better.

"I have a theory about Starbucks," he said as they started

57

walking toward Newtown Lane. "That it's only contributed to world anxiety."

"How so?" she asked.

"Think about it. Before Starbucks, people made coffee at home. Now they leave the house, wait in line for it, pay three times as much as it costs to make it, and wonder why they're in a bad mood and can't sleep. Doesn't make any sense."

"So you're against all fast-food places?" she countered.

"I have no argument with Cinnabon. No argument at all."

She laughed. "But you can only find them in airports."

"That's what's so great about them. I'm all about the combo Burger King slash Pizza Huts. They're the best. No other smell like it in the world."

"Ugh, gross," Isabel said.

"What? Obviously you don't appreciate fine cuisine."

"I guess not." She laughed again, and then she worried that she was laughing too much. "Thanks again for yesterday. That was really cool of you to help me out."

"No problem. I love sticking it to the Man. Or in this case, the Yogi." As they walked past BookHampton, he craned his head to see what was in the window. "Sorry, I have a physical reaction when I see an actual bookstore," he said. "And I mean something that doesn't look like it belongs in a strip mall next to a Costco."

"You want to go in?"

He glanced at the store, looked at her, and then took her hand. "Let's do it. Before they're extinct."

They walked into the store. She watched as Evan appraised

the tables and shelves with an expert eye, taking everything in. "Not bad," he said.

"What are you looking for?" she asked.

"Oh, here we go," he said, walking over to the film-and-television section. He surveyed the books on the shelf and then began pulling one book after another out of the tightly packed row. "These are great," he said. "They'll remind me to stay focused."

"Focused on what?" she asked. She looked at the books piling up in his arms. One was on independent film in the nineties. Another was titled *Classical Hollywood Storytelling.* The last book was about writing for television.

"My roommate, Jeff, and I are writing a screenplay," he explained. "My roommate from school."

"Where do you go?"

"Providence College." He walked to the register and put his books on the counter.

"Is that where you're from?" she asked.

"No. I'm from Wilton, Connecticut. I like to say it's small-town living at its smallest." He paid the salesclerk. "We're writing a comedy. But don't ask me to tell you what it's about. Nothing ever sounds funny when you describe it."

"So you're writing a comedy that's not that funny," Isabel teased.

"No, it's just...our sense of humor is a little weird. Jeff and I make these shorts that we put up on YouTube, and they barely make sense to *us* most of the time. Thanks, man," he said to the cashier, and waved. He grabbed his bag of books and they headed toward the door. "But what we really want to do is write for *SNL*. When we graduate, you know. The screenplay would just be a writing sample."

"*SNL?*"

"*Saturday Night Live.*"

"Oh." It was hard not to be impressed by Evan's ambition. None of the guys she'd dated had ever wanted to write for *Saturday Night Live*. Or do anything right after they graduated.

"What do you want to do?" he asked, holding the door open for her as they left.

"I want to be an actress. I'm going to Tisch in the fall."

"That's cool," he said. "I can see how you'd be good at that."

"How can you see that?" Isabel asked.

"You're gorgeous, to begin with," he said. He gave her a sheepish smile and looked away. "Sorry. I know that probably sounded cheesy."

"No, it didn't," she said, feeling her heart swell with the compliment. "It was nice."

"Thanks," he said. He shook his head and sighed. "Yeah. So that wasn't embarrassing. Anyway..."

"I'll change the subject. How's that?" she asked.

"Great idea," he said, blushing. Isabel couldn't believe how charming that looked.

"Why are you out here if you're writing a screenplay?" she asked.

"We were gonna live in the city this summer and find jobs there. But then Jeff's uncle told us we could use his guesthouse in Sag Harbor. And rents in New York are pretty ridiculous so,…we're working there." He pointed across the street at the Baybreeze Café.

"You're working there?" she asked.

"Yeah. Why?"

The Baybreeze Café, once the Hamptons' hippest eatery, was one of the few places on Main Street that had refused to keep up with its newer, fancier retail neighbors. Its awning was still an ancient forest green, and its signage—big white bubble letters that reeked of the eighties—proudly defied chic. Isabel had never actually gone in there, and nobody she knew had, either.

"We heard that the guy who started *Saturday Night Live* eats there sometimes—"

"He does?" Isabel asked. "I hate to tell you this, but that place hasn't been cool for decades. Nobody goes there except tourists and people who don't have a clue about the real Hamptons. Sorry."

"Wow," Evan said. "Talk about shooting down a dream. And what are *you* doing this summer?"

"You mean for work?" she asked tentatively.

"You don't really need to get a summer job, right?" he asked. "That's the vibe I'm getting."

"Why would you say that?"

"The riding pants yesterday kind of tipped me off."

"Oh." She thought quickly. "Well. Yeah. I'm not out here just for the summer, if that's what you mean. My family has a house here."

"That's cool," he said. "And I didn't mean to embarrass you."

"You didn't," she said.

"It's just that I heard that the summerhouse people sort of keep to themselves," Evan said as they crossed Main Street. "Like, there are the people who come out here to work for the summer, and then the people who come out here to *not* work for the summer. And the two of them don't really hang out."

"That's a little simplistic, don't you think?" Isabel countered.

"Or maybe I'm just full of shit," Evan said, and laughed.

She laughed, too.

They reached the curb and stopped in front of the restaurant windows. "There's Jeff," he said, pointing to a short, muscular guy with a blond buzz cut and blue eyes.

The guy waved to them and turned around, pretending to drop his pants. "Hey, stop it!" Evan yelled.

Jeff looked over his shoulder, grinned, and went back to folding napkins.

"He's the worst waiter in the history of the universe," Evan went on. "And I'm a close second. Luckily the manager seems pretty desperate. One of the waitresses never showed up. I guess that happens a lot around here in the summer. But the people who work here are pretty cool."

She peered in the window. Two girls chatted with each other as they folded napkins and set out silverware. They looked a bit older than Isabel but not too old. *I could be friends with them,* she thought. Even better, neither of them were as pretty as she was.

Evan's friend Jeff seemed a little geeky, but people looked like they were actually having fun, and wasn't that what she wanted for this summer? To have a fun place to escape to during the day? Being around Evan all day wouldn't hurt, either, she thought. The only downside she could see was the very drab uniform: black jeans and a black polo. But there were ways around that.

"So if that other waitress never showed up," she asked, "do you think your manager's looking to hire someone?"

"Why? You know someone who's interested?"

"Yeah," she said, looking right at him. "Me."

"You?"

"Uh-huh. Not that I have any experience." She batted her eyes. "But that shouldn't be too big a deal, right?"

Evan's eyes seemed to light up. "Stay here," he said, pulling open the door to the restaurant. "I'll go get Bill."

He disappeared into the restaurant, leaving her alone with her thoughts. If this worked, and she actually got a job here, this would definitely qualify as the most random thing she'd ever done. Everyone in her life was bound to think that this was either crazy or kind of embarrassing. Naturally, this made working here even more attractive. And there was always the added benefit of working alongside Evan. He would definitely make it a good time, and possibly more.

Evan opened the door and gestured for her to come inside. Isabel stepped into the restaurant, feeling the sudden attention of the rest of the waitstaff.

"This is Bill," he said, leading her over to a stocky man with beady eyes and a thick, seventies-style mustache. The scowl on his face was like a sucker punch to her confidence. He seemed to be chewing something. "Bill, this is Isabel."

"So you don't have experience?" Bill asked, eyeing her closely.

"Yes," Isabel said. "I mean, no."

Bill looked her up and down. "You know how to add?"

"Yes."

"You own a watch?"

"Right here," she said, holding up her hand.

"You got somewhere of your own to stay out here? You're not gonna have to leave in the middle of the summer because you had a fight with somebody?"

"I have somewhere to stay," she said.

"Fine," Bill said grudgingly. "We'll start you off at lunch. You can shadow Evan for a coupla days. After that, if you don't get the hang of things..." He made a burping sound and slashed the air with his hand. "*Finito*. And this isn't a fashion show." He pointed at her peasant blouse and jean skirt. "Black jeans, black polo."

"Actually, about that," Isabel said. "Isn't black a little depressing? Especially for lunch?"

"Eleven o'clock tomorrow," Bill grunted, and then thrust a menu covered in green leather at her. "Take this home. Learn it. Cover to cover. No excuses." Then he turned around and lumbered back to the kitchen.

"Looks like you won him over," Evan said.

"That was winning him over?" she asked.

"Yeah. He practically fell in love."

"Too bad he's not my type." She grinned.

"Oh yeah?" Evan asked. He smiled at her in a way that made her blush.

"I'll see you tomorrow, then," she said coyly.

"Guess so," he said. "See ya."

As she walked to the door she felt Evan's eyes on her, following her. She'd forgotten how much fun it was to flirt. Of course, she'd had her rusty moments, but she hadn't lost her touch. And Evan turned out to be a worthy sparring partner. He was smart and funny, and there was something sexy about his green eyes and quick wit. All she needed to do was survive her first day of work, and she had a feeling that her dry spell would be a thing of the past.

CHAPTER FIVE

"Here's what we're trying to accomplish at the East End Fest," said Nina Montalban Sanders from across her cluttered architect's desk. Her voice was slow and her words perfectly enunciated, and as she talked she petted her long, shiny black hair. "We want to celebrate the Hamptons' history as an artists' colony," she went on. "To bring back the time when creative geniuses like Jackson Pollock and Willem de Kooning and Andy Warhol lived and worked here. When this was a place of artistic refuge. Before it became a place about money and real estate and Gwyneth and P. Diddy."

Rory noticed Nina's perfectly manicured nails and her gold drop earrings in the shape of obelisks. As one of the directors of the East End Festival, a new nine-day festival of independent film, music, and digital entertainment, Nina was exactly the kind of Stanford alum Rory hoped she'd be one day—stylish, put together, but with a strong artistic soul. The application process to be her summer intern had involved multiple phone interviews, e-mails, and letters of recommendation, but now that Rory was here she knew that it had been worth all the work.

"That's the whole idea behind the festival," Nina continued. "Reestablishing the Hamptons' artist cred. Getting back to its creative roots by featuring cutting-edge art and music and film." Nina leaned back in her sleek postmodern chair. "Sort of like Coachella meets South by Southwest meets..."

"The Cannes Film Festival?" Rory offered.

"Exactly," Nina said, holding up a finger.

Rory glanced up at the bulletin board behind Nina, where black-and-white portraits of Jean-Luc Godard, Patti Smith, and Samuel Beckett were tacked up among handwritten lists and bullet-pointed memos. She'd always meant to get into Samuel Beckett but for some reason had never gotten around to it.

"Opening night is August fifteenth," Nina went on, "so we should have all the entries finalized by now." She touched a key on her computer keyboard, and her screen lit up. "That's funny. We don't. Shorts has one more open slot."

"Shorts?" Rory asked. "You mean short films?"

"Someone must have dropped out." Nina blinked a few times. "Right now I have my hands full with the opening gala, so what if you select the last one?"

"Sure," Rory said, so excited she could barely speak.

"Wonderful. And let me say something else. I know that summer internships can sometimes be disappointing for people. But you are not going to be sitting around answering phones and running to get coffee. You are going to be a vital part of the process here, Rory. We don't have assistants, so our interns get to do everything. You're going to learn a lot here."

"Great," Rory said. She couldn't stop smiling.

"Good," said Nina. "So a few technical things. Since I'm going to be in meetings for most of the day, I'd love it if you could answer my phone. If I get a call from my partner—his name is Troy—it always comes through."

Rory scribbled *Troy* on her pad.

"And then I have a dinner reservation that I'd love for you to reschedule for later tonight at Nick and Toni's. Around nine would be perfect."

"I can do that," Rory said.

"And, this is very important. At exactly noon today, I need to register for Revolution."

"Revolution?" Rory asked.

"Oh." Nina smiled gently—apparently this was a foolish question. "It's a spin studio. You've never heard of it?"

Rory shook her head.

"Well, I'm kind of addicted to it," Nina said delicately, placing a lock of hair gently behind one ear. "And so is everyone else around here. Which is why you have to register a week early to get into Kiera's class on Saturday mornings. And the only time you can get in is when they put up the new schedule on Mondays at noon. I would do it myself, except I'm going to be in a meeting then. It's really easy. You go to their website and type in my full name and password—it's *revolution*—and you hit a button to register a bike. It couldn't be simpler."

"I'm sure I can figure it out," Rory said. She wrote down the words *Revolution* and *twelve noon*.

"Great," said Nina, tapping her small hands palms down on the desk. "Well, then I think we're all set. Oh, and one more thing. I heard that you're staying with Lucy and Larry Rule."

Rory tried to remember if that had come up in her phone interview with Nina. "Yes, I am."

"They're quite the power couple out here," Nina remarked. It was unclear whether she was giving them a compliment.

"Yeah, I guess you could say they are."

Nina's phone trilled. Rory reached for it, but Nina held up her hand and answered. "Yes? Be right there." She replaced the phone in its cradle. "Another fund-raising meeting," she said with a knowing roll of her eyes. "Well, that's it, then. Go get settled in."

"Okay," Rory said, standing up. "And I just wanted to say... I'm really glad to be here."

Nina smiled broadly. "I'm glad you're here, too, Rory. Good luck."

Rory walked back to her desk and sat down. Her cubicle was cramped, but it had a decent desktop computer and her own landline. It also had a pair of futuristic-looking padded headphones that were already plugged into the monitor. Rory guessed that these were for watching the submissions. She'd never had a job before where she needed a computer and a phone, let alone fancy headphones. She thought for a moment about calling Sophie or Trish and chatting for a while, but she didn't want to be caught slacking on her first day.

There was a creak as the person in the cubicle next to her wheeled his or her chair back a few inches. A girl a year or two older than her with curly auburn hair and deliberately large, tortoiseshell glasses faced her. "Hi," she said. "I'm Amelia."

"I'm Rory."

"Are you actually doing anything here? Or just waiting for

people to notice you?" Her stare was almost as blunt as her question.

"It's my first day," Rory said, "so I'm not sure yet."

"I've been here since last week," she said drily. "And I've been doing nothing. *Nada*. Unless you count the crossword. But then again, that's how all these internships go. You think you're going to be rolling up your sleeves and having an impact and all that, and you just end up sitting around texting all day." She squinted at Rory. "How old are you?"

"Eighteen," Rory said. "I just graduated."

"First internship?" Amelia pressed.

Rory nodded.

"This is my *third*," Amelia said.

"If they're all so lame, then why do you keep doing them?" Rory asked.

Amelia looked this way and that and wheeled her chair closer to Rory. "I have a film," she said in a half whisper. "A short. I heard that if an intern submits something they like, they'll get behind it. Include it in the lineup."

"Oh?" Rory said. Nobody had told her about this.

"They don't really advertise it, but it's sort of a known thing," she said. "I figure a summer of boredom is worth it if it helps me with my career. But now I just have to get up the nerve to tell my boss that it's on the server." Amelia pointed behind Rory. "It's Luis. He's the one with the Che-Guevara-goes-Fifth-Avenue facial hair."

Rory turned to see an attractive dark-haired man with a revolutionary's beard and carefully coiffed hair sitting in a glass-walled office.

"I'm not sure he knows that I'm his assistant," Amelia added.

"Well, good luck," Rory said. "That's really exciting."

"Who's *your* boss?"

"Nina," Rory said.

"Oh, yeah," Amelia said knowingly. "She's the one in charge of shorts, I think."

"Is she?" Rory said. She didn't want to seem too knowledgeable about it.

The muffled chime of a cell phone could be heard behind the cubicle wall.

"Oh, that's me." Amelia wheeled herself out of sight, leaving Rory alone at her desk.

Rory clicked onto the server and opened the folder marked SUBMISSIONS—SHORTS. She scrolled down the list of titles and directors and found Amelia's right away.

A slight wave of jealousy rippled through her. Even though her films were all documentaries, she still wished she could submit something. Looking at Amelia's name now, she couldn't tell if she wanted her film to be good, so that she could recommend it, or if she wanted it to be terrible, because of her less-than-pleasant attitude. She decided to watch some of the other shorts first, just to have some context.

The first one she watched was entirely silent and involved a man walking down a highway with a dog, trying to hitchhike. When it was done Rory dropped it in the REJECTION folder with only a shred of guilt. *I could make something better than this*, she thought. She went on to the second one, which was marginally better, but not by much.

There was another creak of wheels, and soon Amelia poked her head into Rory's space again. "I'm gonna go out and get something to eat," Amelia said. "Wanna come?"

"No, thanks," Rory said. The less she was around Amelia's negative attitude, the better.

Amelia got up and left. Rory went back to her movies. About five minutes later, she realized that she was hungry. She looked at the clock at the top of her screen: 12:10. *Time for lunch*, she thought. And then her eyes fell onto her notepad.

Revolution, twelve noon.

Her heart stopped. She'd forgotten all about Nina's spin class.

With a few clicks of the keyboard, she found the website. She typed in Nina's name and *revolution* to log in and clicked on the schedule. The Saturday morning class was full.

Rory picked up the phone and dialed the number on her screen.

"Hello, Revolution," said the woman on the other end.

"Yes, hi, is your Saturday morning class full?" Rory asked, trying not to sound panicked.

"It is. Would you like to be put on the waiting list?"

"Actually, is there any way you could fit one more person in there? You see, my boss asked me to register her, and I totally forgot, and it would just be for this one time, not a regular habit or anything—"

"I'm sorry, but there's only the waiting list," the woman said. "Do you want me to put her on it or not?"

Nina didn't strike Rory as the type of woman who liked to

72

wait. Especially when there was a good chance that it would be for nothing. "That's okay. I'll call back."

Rory hung up. It was her first day and already she'd done something wrong. She got up and slowly walked to Nina's office. Through the glass wall she could see Nina and Luis deep in conversation. Great, Rory thought. There would be a witness to all this.

Nina waved her in. "What is it, Rory?" she asked.

Rory took a deep breath. Luis was staring at her.

"I started watching the submissions, and I...well...I forgot to register you for the spin class. I'm so sorry."

Nina hesitated, as if the words were still sinking in. "I didn't get into the class?" she asked in a toneless voice.

"I can't believe I forgot. I got so wrapped up in watching those submissions I think it just slipped my mind."

Nina was about to speak, when Luis shook his head quickly, as if signaling Nina to rein it in. The cloud passed from Nina's face, and soon she seemed utterly content. "That's okay," Nina said nicely. "Really. No worries."

Rory glanced at the photo of Samuel Beckett. His craggy, weathered face seemed to be looking down at her, furious with disapproval.

"Are you sure? I really am sorry."

Nina held up her hand. "Completely fine. No big deal." She looked at Luis and smiled. "By the way, this is our codirector, Luis Sandoval. Luis, this is Rory McShane."

"Hello, Rory," Luis said in a smooth baritone, extending his hand. "It's a great pleasure to meet you."

"Uh, thanks," she said, momentarily frazzled by his attractiveness.

"I've met Lucy and Larry Rule before," Luis said. "But I doubt they'd remember me. I know how social they are."

"Um, sure," Rory said. She wasn't sure why Luis was bringing up the Rules during this awkward moment, but at least he was being friendly. She turned back to Nina. "I'm really sorry, once again."

"It's okay," Nina said, glancing at Luis.

"Nothing to be upset about," Luis chimed in. "Oh, and tell Gregory I said hi. We have some mutual friends."

"I will." Rory backed up toward the door.

"I'll let you know if I need anything else," Nina said. She waved. "Bye, Rory."

That had gone so much more smoothly than she'd expected. But Rory couldn't shake the feeling that there was a reason for Nina's easygoing reaction. A reason she couldn't quite put her finger on.

Isabel carried the last pair of black jeans from her closet to the bed, where she carefully laid them down next to the other five pairs she'd already bought. Even though she hadn't started her job yet, it couldn't hurt to get her uniform together.

"What's all this?" Rory asked as she walked in.

"Tell me, which do you like better?" Isabel asked. "The ebony AG's or the metallic black J. Brands?"

"Did somebody die?" Rory asked.

"I got a job." Isabel tossed her hair over her shoulder and did

74

a little happy dance. "*You* are looking at the Hamptons' newest waitress."

Rory looked shocked. "Really?"

"Yep. And this is my ugly uniform."

"Wow," Rory said. "What place is it?"

"The Baybreeze Café."

Rory had no reaction.

"The place on Main Street?" Isabel prompted. "Near the movie theater?"

"Oh," Rory said, clearly still mystified.

"It's good practice for New York. I mean, all actors do in the beginning is wait tables."

"Do you think you'll need to do that?"

"Maybe," Isabel said, annoyed. "I thought you wanted me to get a job."

Rory lay back on Isabel's pink duvet and covered her face with her hands. "Actually, I'll switch with you. Right now."

"What happened?" Isabel asked.

"My boss asked me to do one thing, and I messed it up."

"What was that?"

"Register her for a spin class at Revolution. And I completely forgot."

Isabel sat down next to Rory and pried her hands away from her face. "It was a *spin* class."

"I know," Rory said. She sat up on her elbows. "But she went to Stanford. I was hoping that she might be able to put in a good word for me with the film department. You know, help me get into some of the advanced classes."

"Is that why you took the job?" Isabel asked, trying to keep a straight face. Rory could be too much of a goody-goody sometimes.

"No, of course not," Rory said, blowing a stray dark curl out of her face. "But I thought it might help. Until I messed up the spin class."

"Well, try to let it go," Isabel said, patting her shoulder. "Pretty soon she'll see what an awesome assistant she has for the summer."

"Thanks," Rory said.

"Wanna grab dinner tonight?" Isabel asked. "Just you and me?" She smiled. "I could tell you about my coffee date with Evan."

"Yeah, sure—" Rory began, and then Connor appeared in the doorway.

"Hey," he said, stepping into the room. "Can I come in, or are you guys talking about top secret girl stuff?"

"How 'bout knocking first and then asking?" Isabel said.

"Hey," Rory said as she got up from the bed and went to give Connor a hug.

Isabel watched them kiss each other on the lips. It was still strange to see them together, and not just because Connor was her brother. Last summer Rory had been the one without a boyfriend, and she'd been the one having a passionate summer fling. Now it seemed as if their roles had reversed. Never in a million years would she have seen that coming.

"Hey, how was your first day?" he asked Rory in an intimate murmur.

76

"Not bad. I'll tell you about it later. How was yours?" she murmured back.

"Pretty good. Just an orientation for the teachers."

"I can't believe you're teaching sailing again," Isabel broke in. "Don't you ever get tired of it?"

"At least I have a job, unlike some people," Connor said.

"*Au contraire, mon frère.* I have a job. I got one today. At the Baybreeze Café."

"Doing what?" Connor asked skeptically. "Eating?"

"Waiting tables."

"But you don't know anything about waitressing."

"So? I'll learn."

"Mom is going to freak out when she hears about that."

"What makes you think I'm going to tell her?"

Connor wiggled his eyebrows, as if to say *Okay, fine, you win,* and turned his attention back to Rory. "You wanna get some dinner tonight?"

"Oh, um…" Rory cast a glance over at Isabel. "What if Isabel comes?"

Connor hesitated.

"No, that's okay," Isabel was quick to say. "You guys go. I'll be fine."

"Are you sure?" Rory asked. "I thought you wanted to go out."

"No, it's cool," she said, walking into her closet. "I have to figure out my work wardrobe." *Yeah, I wanted to go out, but not with my brother,* she wanted to say. She dug through her hangers, listening to them talk to each other in an annoying lovey-dovey tone. She was disappointed in Rory. Someone with a little more guy

77

experience would have known that it was okay to say no to your boyfriend every once in a while.

When she was sure they'd left the room, she left the safety of her closet and sat down at her desk. She flipped open her laptop and began an e-mail to Mr. Knox.

So my parents want us to pretend to all their friends that they're still together. Even though my dad has his own place and he's never even here. And my friend Rory would rather spend every waking minute with my brother...just as I'd thought.

She paused with her hand above the keys. It sounded like she was writing in her journal, for God's sakes. Mr. Knox wasn't going to care about any of this. But he asked her to keep in touch. And he was, after all, her dad. Better start treating him like it, she thought. Before he drifted out of her life, too.

"So remember that other sailing teacher I told you about last summer? The one who'd talk about himself in the third person sometimes? Like he was a hip-hop star?" Flickering light from the votive candle between them made Connor's eyes a deep indigo.

"Yeah," Rory said, reaching for the bread basket. "Don't tell me he's there again."

"Yup. The guy couldn't tack if his life depended on it. His parents must have donated more money to the club." He grabbed a piece of bread and dipped it in the dish of greenish olive oil on the table. "So now I gotta listen to him all day long."

"Maybe *you* should start talking about yourself in the third person," Rory joked. "Just to get him back."

"Who says I don't? Have you met C-Dog yet?"

Rory laughed. "C-Dog? Are you serious?"

"Totally. You should have known me in high school."

"I'm starting to be glad I didn't," she teased him. She opened her menu. So far the tension that she'd felt between them last night seemed to be over, thank god.

"Man, I feel like a burger," Connor said, reading his menu.

"I'm gonna have one. And I'm gonna have fries."

"Good. Then I can steal some," Connor said.

"Order some. You don't always have to eat so healthy. It's okay to have some fun once in a while."

"Hey, I can have fun," he said, reaching for her hand. "I can have *a lot* of fun."

"Uh-huh," she said, squeezing his hand right back. "So…I had my first day of work."

"How'd it go?"

"Great. My boss is pretty awesome. She's this really cool mix of stylish and artistic. And she wants to give me all kinds of responsibility, too. But I kind of messed up."

"How so?" Connor asked, looking back down at his menu.

"She asked me to register her in a spin class. At some place where it's so popular you have to do it, like, six days early. But I got so caught up in watching these short films that it slipped my mind. And then by the time I remembered, the class was full. I was so annoyed with myself."

"Yeah, I can see why," Connor mused, reading his menu.

"What?" she asked, wondering if she'd heard him wrong.

Connor looked up at her. "I just said, I can see why you felt bad."

"So you think that was a stupid thing to do, then?"

"If she seemed upset," Connor said, turning the menu over and scanning the desserts, "then I can see why you felt bad."

"She didn't seem that upset, weirdly."

"That's good," Connor said. "I guess you got lucky."

"But you think she *should* have been upset?"

"I'm not saying that," he said. "But I can see why you felt bad. It's kind of a dumb thing to do. Right?"

"Gee, thanks for the vote of confidence," she said.

"I'm not judging you," Connor said. "I'm just saying that I can understand why you felt bad. *I* would feel bad."

"Maybe that's not what I want to hear right now," she said. "Maybe it would be nice for you to say that I *shouldn't* feel bad, and that it's not such a big deal."

Connor sighed and put down his menu. "It's not a big deal. I'm just saying—hey, when did you get so sensitive?"

"And when did you get so...so..." She tried to think of the right word to describe it. "Forget it."

Connor peered closer at her. "Ror. What's going on? What's wrong?"

"Nothing," Rory said, focusing on her menu. "Let's talk about something else." She remembered the time they'd been eating with his friends at USC and she'd mispronounced the name of the French critic Michel Foucault. She'd called him "Fu-KALT." There'd been a pall over the table as Connor's

80

friends looked at one another, silently reacting to her naïveté. She'd known instantly that she'd made a mistake. But Connor didn't rush to her defense or hold her hand. His manners seemed to go on pause as he looked at her from his spot across the table, slightly uncomfortable, and stayed quiet. It had been mortifying, infuriating. *How could he do that?* she'd thought. She felt the same way right now.

"I think I will have the burger," Connor said, closing his menu.

"Great," Rory said, too annoyed to look at him.

"What are you going to have?"

"What's going on with you?" Rory asked, looking him straight in the eye.

"What's going on with me?" Connor asked. "What's going on with *you?*"

"Connor?" A female voice made them look up. A petite dark-haired girl with a fringe of bangs and doe-like brown eyes stood next to their table.

"Augusta?" Connor said.

"Oh my god!" she exclaimed. "I thought it was you!"

She threw her arms around Connor, sending his face straight into her chest.

Rory watched as Connor tried to hug her back.

"What are you doing here?" Connor asked when she pulled away.

"My dad rented a place here for the summer—oh, it's so fantastic to see you!" The girl's voice held a faint English accent, which made Rory like her even less. "Guess who's here with me! Caleb, Dylan, and Nico!"

"No way!" Connor exclaimed.

"They all came out for the week! It's like a reunion!" Finally the girl turned to acknowledge Rory.

"Oh, this is my girlfriend, Rory," Connor said. "Rory, this is Augusta Rapton. We went to St. Paul's together."

"Hello," the girl said as she offered Rory her small hand. "It's so lovely to meet you."

"Hi," Rory said, feeling as dainty as a lumberjack as she shook this girl's hand. Augusta was more put together than a model in *Lucky*. Her bangs, black vintage-looking dress, slouchy ankle boots, and oversize cardigan all screamed urban cool.

"So you guys aren't living in London anymore?" Connor asked.

"My dad wanted to be in the States this summer," she explained. "I think because he knows how much I like New York."

"Augusta goes to Columbia," Connor explained.

"Oh," said Rory, pretending that this was fascinating information. Hopefully this chitchat wouldn't go on much longer.

"Wait," Augusta said. "Come join us! We have a huge table. What do you think?" Augusta's heavily lined eyes stayed fixed on Connor.

"Uh...I don't know...Rory? What do you think? It could be fun."

Rory hesitated for a moment, and then she realized that Connor was serious. "Sure," she said quietly.

"Great," Connor said, standing up. "Lead the way."

This isn't happening, Rory thought as they got up. *This was supposed to be* our *time.*

"I haven't seen these guys in almost three years," he said to her over his shoulder. "Isn't this funny?"

"Yeah, it's really funny," she said, trying to sound enthusiastic.

"You'll love them," Connor said.

"Right," Rory said, pretending to smile. She was pretty sure she wouldn't, if these people were anything like his college friends. At a table in the corner sat a group of two guys and a girl watching them approach. Rory took a deep breath and remembered her mantra from USC: *No matter what, don't look like you're having a bad time.*

"Hey!" Augusta called out to them. "Guess who's joining us?"

"Hey, man!" said one of the guys. He wore a red-and-black-patterned Baja hoodie and had a well-manicured soul patch. "What is up?"

Connor leaned over to give the guy a bro-shake. "Hey, Caleb!"

"Connie!" said the other guy, who was smaller than Caleb with black hair. He wore a polo shirt.

"CR," said the girl, who had long blond curls and a laid-back demeanor. "How's it hangin'?"

The guy with the soul patch slapped Connor on the back. "Good to see you, man. How's Cali?"

"It's awesome. How's Duke?"

"Forget Duke, I transferred to Brown, man," said the guy, touching his soul patch. "It's so much more my speed."

"Rory, this is Caleb," Connor said. "Caleb, this is Rory. My girlfriend."

"Peace," Caleb said, shaking her hand.

"Uh, peace," Rory replied.

Rory watched Connor turn to the black-haired guy. "Hey, man, this is Rory," Connor said, introducing her.

"Hi, Nico," Rory said.

The girl with long blond curls burst into coarse laughter.

"Uh, *that's* Nico," Connor said, pointing to the blond girl. "*He's* Dylan."

"Oh, sorry," Rory said. "Hi." She turned to Nico. "Hi."

"Heyyyy," Nico drawled, touching Rory's hand lightly before turning her attention back to Connor. "So what's up, Connie? Are you still at USC?"

Before long, "Connie" was regaling them with stories about Hollywood hipsters, Santa Monica yoga worshippers, and the occasional celebrity sighting. Rory flipped through the menu and tried to keep her cool. *So he ran into some friends*, she thought. *It's bound to happen. This* is *his stomping grounds. Not yours.*

But their unpleasant exchange about her job still lingered. Maybe she'd just been supersensitive. It was hard to know. Regardless, this was their third tense moment since she'd arrived. In nine months they hadn't had one argument. Now after three days together, they seemed to be getting on each other's nerves.

"Hey, Rory, did you hear that?" Connor asked, his face alight with laughter. "Caleb was saying that he has family in New Jersey."

"Oh yeah?"

"Yeah," Caleb said. "I think New Jersey's cool, man. It gets a bad rap. But there are some awesome parts of it."

Connor reached across the table and took her hand. "New Jersey has to be beautiful," he said, looking into her eyes.

She smiled for all of his friends to see. For a moment, her doubts about them disappeared.

Then it hit her: *Connor and I are just like his parents,* she thought. *Pretending to be the perfect couple, when inside, we're really not.*

CHAPTER SIX

"I'd like the Bridgehampton Cobb," the woman said over the din of the lunch crowd, "but can I get that with avocado instead of bacon?"

Isabel scribbled something that she hoped would remind her of this on her small lined pad. "Uh, I'm not sure. I'll find out."

"*Unless* the bacon is nitrate-free," the woman said, rearranging her bracelets. "In that case I'll take the bacon. Do you know if it's nitrate-free?"

"I don't," said Isabel, scribbling again. "I'll check."

"And I'd like some bread with that," the woman went on, plucking at her diamond pendant necklace. "But *only* the pretzel bread. If you don't have any, then nothing."

Isabel flipped the page and scribbled the word *pretzels*. "Pretzels, okay."

"No, pretzel *bread*," the woman corrected, her smile beginning to wear thin. "And some more iced tea. What do you want, Penny?" she asked, turning to her friend.

"How is the pasta special done?" The woman's friend was younger, in her thirties, and she had the sinewy, half-starved look of a serious Pilates fan. "Do they use chicken broth? Because I'm vegan."

Isabel scribbled the word *vegan* on the pad. "Um, I'm not sure. I can find out."

"I'll have that but only if the chef can use veggie broth," the friend said. "Otherwise I'll have the garbanzo bean pancake. With no raita."

"Ry-ta?" Isabel asked.

"*Raita*," the woman said in a sharp voice. "The yogurt dressing that's right here?" she said, pointing to the menu.

"Oh, sorry, it's my first day," Isabel said. "I'll take care of it."

The women traded looks. Isabel turned to leave.

"Excuse me?" the first woman said. "Don't you want the menus?"

"Oh, right." Isabel snatched them out of their hands. On her way to the kitchen she almost collided with a customer threading his way between tables. "Sorry," she muttered. She glanced at the clock on the wall. 12:22. She'd been at work for less than an hour, but it already felt like three days. The other waitress who was supposed to work today had sprained her foot at a club the night before, which had left her, Evan, and the manager, Bill, to handle the crowd. This also meant that aside from the first ten minutes, during which Isabel followed Evan around as he took orders, there'd been no "shadowing." Rory, it turned out, had been right about waitressing. She wasn't prepared at all. This job was hell.

In her peripheral vision she spotted an arm frantically waving at her. It was attached to a middle-aged, balding man who looked vaguely familiar.

"Yes?" she asked, approaching his table.

"Where's my French dip?" he demanded. "I ordered it twenty minutes ago."

Had she taken an order for a French dip? None of this was ringing a bell. "Let me check," she said.

"And another Arnold Palmer!" he yelled after her.

She raced toward the computer. On her way she passed Evan, who was bent over a table, taking an order. He glanced at her and raised his eyebrows. *You doin' all right?* his look seemed to say. She smiled bravely and gave him a thumbs-up. She scanned the computer for the French dip, saw nothing, and typed it in. Then she flipped through her pad to add the two women's lunch orders. But they'd had a lot of questions—hadn't they? Now she couldn't remember any of them. She flipped through her pad to see if anything jogged her memory. Phrases like *tuna gluten-free* and *vegan avocado* jumped out at her.

"How's it going?" Bill asked. Somehow he'd sneaked up behind her, so close to her that she could smell his tobacco breath. "You got this under control?"

"Sure. Is our bacon nitrate-free?"

"Who the hell wants to know?" Bill asked.

Before Isabel could formulate an answer, Evan swooped in. "Those women at table twelve wanted me to tell you to forget the bacon, just do avocado," he said, his eyes gleaming. "And the pretzel bread."

Oh my god, I love you, she thought. "Oh," she said casually. "Perfect."

Bill grunted and stalked off toward the kitchen, leaving them alone.

88

"Um, did they say what their order was by any chance?"

"Cobb salad and the pasta special. Which *is* vegan, by the way."

"Thank you," she said, and let out a deep breath. "This is so crazy. I feel like I'm at war."

"It'll be over soon," he said. He put a hand on Isabel's shoulder, and she almost jumped from the electricity that shot down her arm. "And you're doing great. My first day doing this I almost dropped a bowl of chili in somebody's lap."

Isabel laughed.

"As long as you don't scorch anyone's balls, I'd say you're crushing this."

"Thanks," she said, still aware of his hand on her arm.

"What do you say to some ice cream when we're done?" he asked.

"Sure," she said. "Sounds good."

Before she could say anything, he bolted in the direction of a table. She watched him check in on a couple of customers, feeling a new burst of energy. *He likes me*, she thought. *He definitely likes me.*

"Hey, Amelia," Rory said, wheeling her chair far enough out of her cubicle so she could see Amelia huddled over her cell phone, furiously texting someone. A tall iced coffee sat on her desk, slowly creating a puddle. "Amelia. Hey."

Amelia put down her phone and looked over her shoulder. "What's up?"

"I just watched your short."

Amelia's quizzical face relaxed into a smile. "Yeah?"

"It's really good."

Amelia got up from her chair, took Rory's arm, and walked

her into an empty conference room down the hall. She shut the door. "You think so?" she asked. "Seriously?"

"Yeah. I don't know how you did that. The editing's awesome."

"It's just Final Cut Pro."

"I couldn't make anything look that good on Final Cut Pro."

"Sure you could." She folded her arms. "Do you think I have a shot?"

"I would say you do. But I haven't seen all of them."

Rory didn't want to say that she hadn't expected much when she clicked on Amelia's film a few minutes before. But almost as soon as Amelia's film started, she found herself waking up—and forgetting the hour and a half of terrible, muddled, badly edited rip-offs of Godard and Scorsese and Spielberg and Rohmer that she'd just sat through.

"I love how simple the story is," she said. "The little girl trying to find the flower she dropped in Central Park. It's so cute. And so beautifully shot. And I love that you didn't even need to use dialogue. So many of these other films are so cluttered with stuff. They're hard to watch."

"So you think I should say something?" Amelia asked breathlessly. "'Cause I've been trying to get up the guts for days."

Rory thought for a moment. "Let me say something to Nina. That way you don't have to speak for yourself."

"Really?" Amelia exclaimed. "Oh my god. That would be so cool of you."

"I wouldn't do it if I didn't think it was good."

"And hey, if there's anything I can do for you—"

"It's really nothing," Rory said. "Let me see what happens."

Nina was alone in her office, going through a pile of what looked like gilt-edged invitations. Rory knocked on the door.

"Yes, Rory?" Nina said, smoothing her dark hair.

"Hope I'm not interrupting, but I just saw a short I really liked. I think it would be a great option for the last slot."

Nina touched her fingers to her forehead, as if she were warding off a headache. "Yeah? Which one is it?"

"*Flower Child* by Amelia Daniels. She's actually an intern here."

Nina looked up. "She is?"

"She sits next to me. I think she's Luis's intern. But of all the ones I've seen, it's definitely the best. I was really impressed."

"Huh," Nina said, playing with a gold bangle around her wrist. "I'll have to look at it. And by the way, I have a question." Nina cocked her head. "Do you think the Rules would be interested in being on our board?"

"The Rules?" she asked, slightly blindsided.

"Well, I know that they're big supporters of the arts, and I'm thinking, what if we were to invite them to the opening night party? It's going to be a very star-studded crowd. I can put them at Alec and Hilaria's table."

"Alec and Hilaria?" Rory asked.

"Alec Baldwin and his wife," Nina said testily. "If they care about that sort of thing. I mean, I can seat them anywhere they like. And if they have a good time, then maybe they'd want to be involved with the festival on a more regular basis. What do you think?"

Rory hesitated. There was something manipulative about

this. Now the comments Luis had made the day before about knowing the Rules made sense. "I'm not sure what sorts of… causes they're into. But I can check." As soon as she said it, she knew that it had been a mistake.

"Great," Nina said. "And I'll take a look at Amelia's short. You did say it was Amelia's, right?"

"Right."

When Rory got back to her desk, Amelia was waiting for her with an expectant look on her face. "So? What'd she say?"

"She said she'd watch it."

Amelia stood up and threw her arms around Rory. "Thank you!" she shrieked. "Oh my god. That's amazing. Can I buy you lunch? Or anything you want?"

"All I did was say that I liked it," Rory said. "I wouldn't get my hopes up too high."

"Oh please," Amelia said, waving her off. "I'm just so happy I didn't have to say something myself. I hate having to push myself onto people. The world's most overpriced turkey sandwich is on me, 'kay?"

Rory shrugged. She felt uneasy, but she wasn't sure why. "Sure."

At three forty-five, the last two customers finally paid their check and walked out the door, and Isabel leaned against the bar, breathing a great sigh of relief. Her feet ached as if she'd run a marathon barefoot, and her arms felt rubbery from carrying so many trays. But the day had been a triumph. Only two people had complained about her to Bill, and to her enormous surprise she hadn't dropped anything, except a leather checkbook holding several credit cards that had gone flying under different tables.

Bill ambled over to her. "So, you can't take an order to save your life, and you seriously pissed off one of our best customers," he said, shoving a stack of trays on the bar, "but all in all, you did okay."

"Thanks," she said.

"So, take this again," he said, giving her the menu once more. "And actually look at it this time."

"Okay."

Bill shook his head at her apparent idiocy and walked away.

"Good job, rookie," Evan said, his eyes lit up and smiling. "Not that I didn't think you could handle it, but not having any time to actually train...I'm impressed."

"I told you I was a quick study," she said.

"Yeah, you definitely are." He paused a moment, studying her face. "So. What'll it be? Chocolate-chip ice cream or a shot of vodka?"

"What about both?" she joked. She flashed him her biggest smile. She wasn't sure whether it was the way he was looking at her or the immense relief coursing through her body, but suddenly she wanted to grab Evan and kiss him right here and now.

"First, lemme show you how to clock out," he said, taking her hand.

She slid her hand into his. "So someone is actually showing me how to do something around here?" she teased.

"Believe it or not."

He pulled her toward the back of the restaurant, past the

kitchen and the line cooks cleaning up. Bill seemed to be in his office with his door closed. A small room marked STAFF ONLY was right off the hall. They stepped inside. She'd been inside the staff room for a few minutes before the start of lunch service. It was a tiny room, only big enough to hold a narrow bench, a few lockers, and a clumsy-looking machine on the wall with an old-fashioned clock built into it.

"Which slip is yours?" Evan asked, gesturing to the row of slips slotted into tiny cubbies next to the machine.

Isabel leaned in close to him as she pulled out her slip. Her arm brushed his, sending a small shock through her system.

"Okay, you dip it into the machine," he said. "Here, I'll show you," he said, taking it from her. As his fingers touched hers, she couldn't resist holding on to the slip, allowing their hands to make contact for as long as possible. She looked up at him, holding her breath.

He smiled and leaned in closer to her. When his lips pressed against hers, soft and rough at the same time, she remembered all that she'd been missing these past nine months.

Dry spell officially over, she thought, as her hands circled his neck.

CHAPTER SEVEN

As soon as she could hear Rory's dilapidated car chugging its way up the gravel drive, Isabel sprang from her chaise by the pool, shoved her feet into her flip-flops, and ran to the back door.

"Hey," Rory said, slinging her purse over her shoulder. "What's up?"

"I need to talk to you," Isabel said, grabbing Rory's arm and dragging her into the house. *"Right now."*

"Can I at least go to the bathroom?" Rory asked.

"No," Isabel said, dragging Rory down the hall to her room. She opened Rory's door and ushered them both inside.

"Okay," Rory said, sitting down on her bed and kicking off her flats. "What the hell happened?"

"I kissed someone," Isabel said. "That guy I told you about. We kissed." She let out a small shriek.

Rory jumped. "Okay," she said tentatively. "That's good."

"God, I feel like such a *dork*," Isabel said. "Look at me. It's like I'm in sixth grade all over again. But I can't stop thinking about him."

"All right, back up. Start at the beginning. I thought you had work today."

"I did," Isabel said, tossing some hair over her shoulder. "And you were right—waitressing *is* hell. But luckily, Evan—his name is Evan—he works there, too."

Rory stopped massaging her heel. "Wait. Evan works at the restaurant? Is that why you got a job there? Because of him?"

"It's not *why* I got a job there," Isabel said, bristling at Rory's tone. "But it's where I got the idea. He was telling me how much fun it was to work there and how cool the people who worked there were, and I was totally looking for something to do anyway and—"

Rory put her head in her hands.

"What? What is that for?"

"Nothing," Rory said, shaking her head. "Go on."

"Anyway, so, I had this feeling that he liked me after our coffee date," Isabel said, pacing the room, "which I haven't even told you about, by the way, but it went really well, and then today, at work, which was a *nightmare*, he was so sweet and was constantly coming up to me and saving my butt—seriously—and then when lunch was finally over, and he was telling me how well I'd done, he took me into the back to show me how to clock out and he kissed me. Right there. Right in the back!"

Rory's face was blank.

"And it was a really good kiss. You know, I wasn't sure how it would be, or what would happen, but it was really good."

"That's great," Rory said, her face still blank.

"Why aren't you happy for me?" Isabel asked.

"I am happy for you," Rory said, standing up. "I'm just letting it all sink in." She went into the bathroom and emerged with a hairbrush in her hand.

"Thanks," Isabel said. "Now I need you to meet him."

"What?" Rory froze with the hairbrush in midair.

"Because what if he's bad news and I can't see it? Like Mike?"

Rory sat down on her perfectly made bed. "Don't you think you'd be able to tell this time?"

"I don't know...." Isabel flopped down next to her. "I mean, I *think* I'd be able to tell now, but I don't trust myself anymore. I need a second opinion." She grabbed Rory's arms. "Please? You saw through all of Mike's stuff. Right from the beginning."

"A blind man could have seen through Mike's stuff from the beginning," Rory answered. "Fine. When?"

"I was thinking tonight."

"Tonight?" Rory blurted.

"Yeah. We sort of talked about that I *might* go see a movie and that if I'm still out then I *might* text him after he's done with the dinner shift—"

"So we now have to go see a movie?" Rory asked.

"No, we can just say we did," Isabel said. *"Duh."* She stood up. "I'm gonna go lie down. See you in a bit." She left Rory's room, feeling slightly hurt that Rory was so averse to her plan. And it didn't help that Rory had been so unexcited for her about the news. It was so unfair. Last summer she'd practically done a jig when Landon asked Rory out. She'd never pegged Rory as the competitive type.

But it didn't matter, she thought, taking the stairs two at a time.

97

So what if she felt like an amateur? It was fun to feel this excited again. There was life after Mike. She knew that there would be.

Rory carried her paper plate over to one of the booths and sat down. The pizza joint was almost empty of customers, except for her and Isabel and a couple in their twenties with a toddler asleep in a stroller. The neon clock on the wall read 9:25. A radio played classic rock from behind the counter, where one forlorn employee halfheartedly stretched some dough into a pie.

"Don't you think this is going to look a little bit obvious?" Rory asked. "I feel like I'm wearing a sign on my chest that says SECOND OPINION."

"He thinks we were hanging out anyway," Isabel said, sitting across from her. She lifted a greasy slice to her lips for a tentative bite. "It's cool. Don't worry about it."

Rory shrugged and took a bite of her sausage and onion. As much as she wanted to help Isabel avoid another dating disaster, part of her wished she could have stayed at home. That way she and Connor might have been able to regroup after last night's dinner. Connor had talked nonstop with his St. Paul friends and Rory had sat at the end of the table, trying to seem interested in the time Nico almost got suspended for throwing a party in her room, or the time Caleb snuck off campus to go to a Phish concert. When Connor finally noticed that she'd gotten quiet he tried to change the subject to Stanford, but it was so obvious it made her cringe. *Don't*, she wanted to say. *Don't make it worse.* Then Augusta interrupted and turned the subject back to St. Paul's, which had almost been a relief.

When they left she kept waiting for him to say something

98

like *Hey, I'm sure that was kind of boring for you* or *I hope you didn't feel left out* or *Sorry our romantic dinner got hijacked by my friends.* But he only talked more about his friends and their boarding school misadventures until she began to think that she probably had no right to expect an apology. Lately things with Connor had gotten so confusing. There seemed be a disconnect between what she thought he might do, and what he actually did. She hadn't remembered that being the case last summer.

At her door she'd kissed him good-night.

"Long day?" he'd asked, smiling.

"Yeah, really long," she'd said, trying to smile back.

"Okay," he'd said, and kissed her again. Then she'd gone inside and shut the door.

Now she wondered if a little time alone with him tonight would have erased last night from memory. Unfortunately, she hadn't had a chance to find out. Isabel, still hyped up from her big kiss, had hung out with them in the kitchen during dinner, and then had bluntly told Connor that he wasn't invited along on this fact-finding mission.

Connor didn't care. "You guys have a good time," he said. "I'm going to go to bed early."

"But we should be back in an hour," Rory said. "You're going to bed before then?"

"I'm gonna get up early in the morning and run," he explained. "You guys have fun." He kissed her on the cheek.

So two nights in a row of not being together, Rory thought. She hoped this guy Isabel was so crazy about was worth all this trouble.

"Oh, wait, here he is," Isabel said, wiping her hands with a napkin.

Rory looked over at the door. A tall, slim guy with messy blondish-brownish hair walked into the restaurant. He had the gentle quality and slightly awkward gait of someone who'd always been taller than his friends, which was a point in his favor, Rory thought. As he approached their table, he smiled broadly. *And he's not afraid to show that he likes her,* Rory thought. *Another point in his favor.*

"Hey," he said.

"Hi," Isabel said and gave a short little wave. She seemed nervous. "How was the dinner shift?"

"Man, if you thought lunch today was bad," he said to Isabel, sliding into the booth next to her, "tonight was like the Attack of the On-the-Siders. Everything *on the side.* I think Bill needs to rethink his sauces." He gave Rory a friendly smile. "Hi," he said, holding out his hand. "I'm Evan."

"I'm Rory." She shook his hand and became aware that he had very attractive green eyes.

"You guys just saw a movie?" Evan asked.

Rory and Isabel both nodded.

"Which one?"

Rory waited for Isabel to take the fib.

"That one with Tom Cruise," Isabel answered vaguely.

"Oh yeah? Was it good?" Evan asked.

Isabel seemed to be drawing a blank, so Rory stepped in. "It was okay. Not as good as the one last year."

"Rory's staying with me for the summer," Isabel put in, neatly changing the subject.

"Oh yeah? Where from?" Evan asked, picking up Isabel's discarded straw wrapper.

"New Jersey," Rory answered. "And please, don't tell me it's beautiful."

Evan chuckled. "You've been hearing that a lot, I take it."

"Constantly. It seems like everyone I speak to lately thinks New Jersey is gorgeous."

"My dad's from New Jersey," Evan said. "Parsippany. Which is not the most gorgeous place in the world."

"I'm sort of close to there. Stillwater. In Sussex County."

"*Still*-water?" Evan asked, amused. "Wasn't that the name of the band in *Almost Famous*?"

"Yup."

"I love that movie," Evan said.

"Me, too." Rory looked across the table at Isabel, who was nervously popping her straw up and down in her drink. *Time to rein it in*, she thought. "Isabel said she had a great first day at work," Rory said.

"She did," Evan said, turning his attention to Isabel. "And she didn't even have time to train."

Isabel beamed. "I messed up a little bit," she conceded. "But yeah, it went okay. My feet are pretty sore, though."

"Get used to that," Rory said.

"You wait tables, too?" Evan asked her.

"Not right now, but I do at home. Have been for a few years. There's a pizza place in my town—"

"I do, too," Evan said, holding up his hand for a high five. "Every day after school."

"Me, too." Rory gave him a high-five and then glanced at Isabel across the table one more time.

"Rory's dating my brother," Isabel said, somewhat bluntly.

"Oh," Evan said, as if this were incredibly interesting.

Rory felt herself almost blush. "But Isabel and I were friends before." She paused. Isabel looked like she was waiting for Rory to elaborate. "We've been dating since the end of last summer," she added.

"Oh," Evan repeated again as if this was incredibly interesting. "So you're out here spending time with Isabel and her brother?"

"And I'm interning at the East End Festival," she said, wanting to get off the subject of Connor. "I'm working on the film end of things."

"No way," Evan said, lighting up. "I was thinking of submitting a short to them. But I know I missed the deadline."

"Yeah, I think they just finalized the lineup," Rory said, thinking of Amelia's film. "But I'm sure your short is great." She cast a glance at Isabel, who was still watching them quietly, with an inscrutable expression. *Stop talking to this guy,* she thought. But it was so easy. So much easier than it had been talking to Connor.

Isabel put her hand on Evan's arm, subtly but effectively turning his attention toward her. "I'd love to see it," she said, fixing him with a meaningful look that Rory recognized. "Maybe you can show it to me sometime?"

"Sure," Evan said. "Anytime. Of course, you might have to have a crash course in comedy before you see it. So you can appreciate its genius. Just kidding."

Isabel giggled. Evan stretched his arm around the back of her chair.

Rory took this as her cue to get really interested in her pizza.

As she ate, Isabel and Evan started talking about the restaurant. It was clear that Isabel's interest in him was mutual. Evan had a silly grin on his face the entire time they talked, and he edged himself closer to her every few minutes. Isabel, for her part, had slipped into the role of coquette pretty easily. It was nice to see her so happy again.

Finally the guy behind the counter announced that he was closing, and the three of them got to their feet. Evan walked them to the parking lot. A bright, creamy moon shone down over the tops of the cars.

"Well, thanks for texting me," Evan said. "It was nice to hang out for a while."

"Yeah," Isabel said. "I guess I'll see you tomorrow."

"Yeah. See you tomorrow."

Rory walked straight ahead to the car while the two of them hung behind. She was pretty sure that they kissed, but she didn't hear anything, and she didn't want to turn around to find out.

When they got in the car, Isabel paused with her hands on the wheel in the dark. "So...what'd you think?" she asked, staring straight ahead through the windshield, as if she was too embarrassed to look Rory in the face.

"I think he's great," Rory said.

"Really?" Isabel asked, whipping her head around to face Rory. "You *do*?"

"Yeah. I do. He's like the anti-Mike. He's awesome."

Isabel started the car. "I totally knew it," she said, backing out of the spot. "I got a great vibe off him from the moment we met. I wanted to be sure."

Isabel pulled onto Main Street. "Hey, I don't want to put you on the spot or anything," Isabel said, "but are things okay with you and Connor?"

"Yeah, sure, things are fine," Rory said. "Why?"

"You seem kind of down tonight. Thought you guys might have had a fight."

I wish, Rory thought. At least there'd be a chance of making up. "Nope," she said. "No fight."

Isabel glanced at her, and even in the darkened car, Rory could see the concern in her eyes. "Things aren't winding down between you guys, are they?"

Rory was jarred by Isabel's choice of words. *Winding down* had a pretty terrible ring to it. And she wondered for the first time if that was what Isabel secretly wanted. "No. Not at all. We ran into some of his boarding school friends last night at dinner. So it was kind of a weird night."

"Ugh, *those* people," Isabel snorted. "No wonder."

They didn't say anything else on their way home. Rory wanted to ask Isabel if she could see evidence of things winding down, or if she felt that things might be winding down, or, even more to the point, if she *wanted* things to be winding down, but she stayed quiet. No sense in looking like an obsessive freak, Rory thought. Or in creating a self-fulfilling prophecy.

When they got back into the house, Rory went up to Connor's room to see if he was still up. It was dark under his closed bedroom door. He'd gone to bed, just as he'd said. It wasn't a surprise, but she went to bed feeling slightly rejected anyway.

CHAPTER EIGHT

The following Saturday morning, Rory walked into the kitchen to grab a late breakfast and found Mrs. Rule at the kitchen table, huddled over her laptop. Her first instinct was to blurt out a reason for leaving and bolt back to her room, but she knew that it was too late to duck out. She'd managed to avoid running into Mrs. Rule alone since her second day here, almost a week ago. But apparently her lucky streak was over. "Morning," Rory said, heading toward the refrigerator. "I'm getting kind of a late start today."

"Well, it's Saturday," Mrs. Rule said. She closed her computer and took a sip from a mug on the table. In the morning light streaming through the windows, her face looked slightly older and more lined than it had recently. As far as Rory knew, Mr. Rule hadn't set foot in the house since the weekend before. She wondered if his absence was beginning to take a toll. "So. What do you and Connor have planned for today?" she asked.

"Not much. He's teaching this morning. I was just going to hang out at the beach." Rory took out a sleeve of bagels from the bread drawer.

"Well, I was going to go into town. If Sloane were here I'd ask her to come with me, but she's in the city."

There was something needy in Mrs. Rule's tone. And for most of Rory's life, needy had been too hard to resist. "Do you want some company?" Rory asked, in a tone so bright and cheery that it surprised even her.

"That would be wonderful," Mrs. Rule said. "How about we leave in about fifteen minutes."

"Sure."

"And you *are* going to..." Mrs. Rule lowered her gaze.

Rory looked down at her khaki shorts and lavender V-neck T-shirt. "I'll change," Rory said, trying to smile.

A few minutes later, Rory sat in the Land Rover, her hands folded primly in the lap of her ivory sundress. Mrs. Rule flipped through the channels of her satellite radio. Lily Pond Lane was deserted as always. That seemed to be the real mark of wealth, Rory thought. No cars passing, no kids playing, nobody puttering in their front yards or schlepping bags from Stop & Shop and Costco up their driveways. Just blacktop, blue sky, hedges, and perfectly silent, enormous homes.

"How's your job so far?" Mrs. Rule asked, finally settling on a station of Brazilian samba music.

"Great. My boss is giving me lots of responsibility. I'm helping her select the shorts for the competition."

Mrs. Rule didn't say anything in reply so Rory asked, "Did you work before you got married?"

"Yes, I did," said Mrs. Rule, turning left onto Ocean Road. "I worked at *Seventeen* for a year or two, and then at *Mademoiselle*, in the fashion department. But it wasn't because I needed to. My father thought I should. So it didn't look too obvious that I was looking for a husband."

"Did you like working?"

"Very much," Mrs. Rule said. "But it wasn't something I wanted to do forever."

"So you don't miss it, then?" Rory asked.

"No, I don't miss it," she said. She pulled up to the stop sign behind Town Pond.

"About my job, actually," Rory said delicately. "My boss wanted to know if you and Mr. Rule would like to come to their opening night party."

"Opening night for what?" Mrs. Rule asked, tapping her fingers on the steering wheel.

"For the festival. It's August fifteenth. It's supposed to be a really fun event. Should I tell them to send you an invitation?"

Mrs. Rule sighed, as if this was one of countless demands on their time and attention. "I don't know if that's exactly our cup of tea, but I suppose it's fine. Have them send it. And speaking of parties," Mrs. Rule continued, swinging the car onto Main Street, "I want to get your opinion on something. I'm thinking of having a birthday party. Not for Larry—I did that last year as you know, and he wasn't so happy about it. This one would be for my birthday. Larry and I are only a week apart. I'm July twenty-sixth."

Rory tried to muster a smile. Besides the fact that Mr. Rule probably had no real desire to give his estranged wife a birthday party at a house he was no longer living in, their kids would doubtless have to play along again with the Rules' charade of togetherness. That couldn't be a good thing. "I guess that sounds like fun," Rory said, trying to be enthusiastic.

"Maybe it would be nice for the family to have something to lift our spirits," Mrs. Rule said.

And show everyone in East Hampton that absolutely nothing is wrong, Rory thought. "Yeah, maybe."

"I think it'll be just what we need," Mrs. Rule said, taking the ticket from the machine in the parking lot entrance. "The kids love it when I throw a party."

"Then do it," Rory said. "Why not?"

Mrs. Rule glanced at Rory with uncertainty. "You think so?"

"Sure. And I'm happy to help with it if you need—"

"That's not why I'm telling you about it," Mrs. Rule said. She swung the car into a spot. "You know, I'd like to apologize for last summer. For some of the things I did and said. I'm afraid I wasn't very...open-minded."

Rory tried not to look too surprised. "Oh. Okay."

"Because now I can see how important you are to my son," Mrs. Rule continued. Her normally glacial eyes had gone soft. "You're a good influence on him. He needs that. Especially now."

"Thank you," Rory said.

"You're a good influence on Isabel, too. And about Isabel..." Mrs. Rule turned off the ignition and looked right into Rory's eyes. The penetrating stare was back. "Is there anything she's not telling me about? Anything I should know?"

Rory swallowed. It wasn't clear if Mrs. Rule suspected a new job, or a new boyfriend, or both. "No. I mean, nothing I know of..." she said, letting her voice trail off.

"All right, then," Mrs. Rule opened the car door. "Let's start at Christopher Fischer. I need some new cashmere."

Rory grabbed her purse and got out of the car. All this time, she'd wanted Mrs. Rule to accept her. But now that it had finally happened, she felt anything but relief.

CHAPTER NINE

Ten days into her new summer job, Isabel made a wonderful discovery: She sort of knew what she was doing. When customers asked what raita was, she could explain it to them. When they wanted to know the best way to order the vegan wrap—with the black bean tapenade or with the low-fat Chinese dressing—she told them. Best of all, waiting tables turned out to be one of those activities, like horseback riding or shopping, that completely occupied her brain. When she was working, there was no massive family secret that she had to carry and no sense of being a third wheel around Rory and Connor. She was too busy to think about anything except remembering that a certain customer didn't want pickles or had a terrible peanut allergy. It was mindless work, in the best way.

Best of all, there was Evan. By the third day, it was clear that something was officially going on between them, even though they hadn't kissed since that night they'd met up at the pizza place. After work they'd discreetly slip away for ice cream or just to take a walk down Main Street. It wasn't actual dating, but it was mutually understood hang-out time, which was practically the same thing. The physical stuff could come later. After everything that had happened with Mike, Isabel was fine with that.

It didn't sound as if Evan had been gifted with the easiest childhood. His father had taken off when Evan was six. This left him; his younger brother, Sam; and their mom on their own, until his mom married a guy named Phil, who owned a gourmet Italian food shop. Phil was a rumpled, good-natured guy who instilled in his stepsons a deep work ethic and respect for food. Unfortunately Phil was better at sourcing prosciutto and making homemade ravioli than he was at managing a business. When Evan's mom found out that he was deeply in debt, the marriage fell apart.

"But it's all okay," Evan said to Isabel one afternoon, a few days after she'd started work, as they walked down Main Street. "The funny thing is, my mom is happier now than she's ever been in her life, even though she's alone. And Sammy seems happier. He went through a tough period with all of it, but now things have straightened out. He's gotten through it okay. So it's all kind of wasted energy to be mad or resentful, you know?" The late afternoon sun lit up the tips of his hair and his eyelashes. *This was more than Mike ever told me about himself,* Isabel thought. *At least up until the last day I ever saw him.*

"So, my parents are getting a divorce," she said.

"Oh, that sucks," he said. He put his hand on her forearm. "I'm sorry."

Goose bumps rose up on her skin from his touch. "And my mom wants to pretend it's not happening," she went on. "It's like we all have to live in a fantasy. They've got this whole act going on in front of their friends. It's so gross to watch." She drank the rest of her iced latte. "You ever wish you didn't know something?"

"All the time. The words to every Justin Bieber song, for starters."

"Excuse me?"

"Jeff's uncle has a twelve-year-old daughter," he explained.

"Oh," she said.

"Divorce is tough. But you just have to keep living your life. Remember that it's not about you."

But it is about me, she thought.

"My mom's terrified I'm now going to be a waitress for the rest of my life," she said. "She thinks that this is, like, a career move, or something." She let herself accidentally brush up against Evan as they squeezed past a crowd of people on the sidewalk.

Evan stopped walking and turned toward her. Right there, on a sun-dappled stretch of Main Street, right in front of Tiffany's, he leaned down and kissed her.

At first she wanted to pull away. She'd never kissed anyone on Main Street before, in all the eighteen summers she'd spent here. But she'd been waiting too long for Evan to make another move. She circled her arms around his neck and pressed herself close to his firm, lanky torso. His lips were soft but insistent, and the kiss built so quickly that she had to pull away, slightly out of breath.

"Whoa," she whispered. "In broad daylight, no less."

He smiled at her. "I've been wanting to do that for, like, weeks."

"We haven't known each other for weeks."

"Well, it's felt like that," he said. His hands still held her tightly around the waist.

Even after their PDA kiss, they kept their romance a secret from the other waitstaff. Jeff, Evan's roommate, was the only person who knew that they were a couple. Jeff was the perfect foil for Evan. Short and thick, where Evan was tall and slim, Jeff was fussier than Baybreeze's worst customers. He claimed to suffer from OCD, Tourette's, and IBS, though for this last condition Evan believed that Jeff's junk-food diet was mostly to blame. "He's like a really neurotic Owen Wilson," Evan always said about him, and it was true. Jeff never went anywhere without a vial of Purell. Sometimes Isabel would look over and see Jeff hovering around a customer's table, trying to work up the nerve to clear dirty dishes. "For the love of Mike, stop dancing around and do it," Bill would bark at him. "You wanna get fired?"

"It's so…disgusting," Jeff would say, marveling at the idea of it.

The other waitresses, Sadie and Nicole, weren't really friend material. Both of them were going into their junior year at college, which meant that Isabel might as well have been six years old to them. Sadie was from Port Chester, went to Colgate, and loved clubbing. She was the one who had sprained her foot. Nicole was from Piscataway, New Jersey. Like Sadie, she was a seasoned pro at waiting tables. She memorized every order without writing down a word, no matter how many changes a customer made to a dish. Isabel would watch, amazed, as Nicole typed several orders into the computer from memory. "You get used to it," she'd say, and then stalk off.

A few days after Isabel and Evan's sidewalk kiss, Sadie finally deemed Isabel worthy of conversation.

"So I'm having a birthday thing tonight," she half said, half yawned as she sidled up beside Isabel at the pass-through. "Everyone's invited. Even *those* weirdos," she said, nodding to the two busboys, Marcus and Warren, who cleared tables and filled water glasses with silent, unhappy efficiency.

Isabel flinched at the dubious honor of being included along with weirdos. "Where are you doing it?" she asked.

"The Ripcurl. Out in Montauk."

Isabel's heart stopped for a moment.

"It's a really cool place," Sadie went on. "Lots of cute guys. Oh, and don't worry. They don't card." She winked, as if she knew what had happened the last time Isabel had gone to the Ripcurl. Then she grabbed her orders—a Reuben with fries and a tuna melt with a garden salad—and headed back out to the floor.

Isabel stayed at the pass-through, even after her turkey burger had been shoved in front of her by one of the line cooks. The Ripcurl. Mike. Suddenly she remembered everything about that night they'd gone there—how his snotty friend Leelee had denied her a drink, how she'd heard about Mike's older, model girlfriend, how they'd fought in the parking lot, and then how they'd gone back to his place and slept together. For a place she'd been to once, for approximately an hour, it had way too many associations.

"Hey, are you going to Sadie's birthday thing tonight?" she asked Evan as soon as she could corner him for a second.

"I think so," he said. "Not that she'd show up for my birthday party in a million years."

"I'm not a big fan of the place where she's doing it. It's kind of cheesy. Lots of guys in baggy white button-downs."

"Then we have to go. I love the baggy button-down."

She laughed. "You're right. Let's go."

She knew that she was overreacting, but it didn't stop her from trying to recruit Rory to go with her.

"I can't," Rory said later that afternoon, as they took a walk with Trixie down the beach. "Connor's having his St. Paul's friends over tonight to make lobster rolls."

"Then you have to come," Isabel said. "Don't tell me you want to hang out with those dweebs."

"I'm trying to make an effort. You know how it is."

And you're definitely not making an effort with me, Isabel wanted to add.

Rory picked up a stick and hurled it down the beach, sending Trixie dashing to get it. "What exactly is freaking you out about going to the Ripcurl?"

"Weird memories, I guess. It's where Mike's friend works. We went there one night. The night we slept together the first time. But I'm sure it'll be fine."

"Of course it'll be fine. And you could always tell Evan about Mike. If you wanted to. I'm sure he'd understand."

"No," Isabel said. "There's no reason to do that. It's not like Mike is a thing. He's in the past."

Rory gave Isabel a sidelong glance. She seemed to want to make a comment about this, but restrained herself. "Maybe you, me, Connor, and Evan can have dinner sometime. How about that?"

"I don't usually have my brother hang out with the guy I'm dating."

"He'll be nice, I promise," Rory said. "And I think he and Evan would really hit it off." She grabbed the stick from Trixie. "And if I can get Connor to hang out with Evan instead of Augusta Rapton, then I'm all for it."

"I hear that."

Later that night, Isabel met Evan and Jeff at the restaurant after the dinner shift. They piled into Evan's forest-green Saab and drove east toward Montauk.

"It's right here," Isabel said, pointing out the turn.

Evan pulled into the driveway. Apparently the Ripcurl's popularity had only increased, judging from the bumper-to-bumper line of luxury SUVs and convertible sports cars in the drive.

"Dude, look at the aloha shirts on those guys," Evan said, pointing to the valets. "We should have gotten jobs here, just to wear those shirts."

"You need shoulders for an aloha shirt," said Jeff. "Which you don't have."

"I have shoulders." Evan turned to Isabel. "Do I not have shoulders?"

"Watch out!" Isabel yelled. "You're about to hit that Porsche."

They finally inched their way up to the valet.

"Aloha, welcome to the Ripcurl," he said as she opened the car door.

"Aloha," Evan replied.

Isabel stepped out of the car and looked at the line of people waiting outside the closed doors. A small part of her hoped that they wouldn't get in.

"So let me guess," said Jeff, as they walked to the entrance. "This place has a surfing motif."

"You got it," Isabel said.

"Why aren't we surfers, man?" Jeff asked Evan. "That's where we went wrong in life."

"Would you like me better if I were a surfer?" Evan asked her, snaking an arm around Isabel's waist.

"No," she said. "Absolutely not."

"See?" Evan said.

"Whatever," Jeff said. "I still feel like it reflects badly on our manhood."

The bouncer at the door stopped them with his hand. "The line starts there," he said, pointing into the distance.

"We're here for Sadie Klein's birthday," Evan said.

Without a word, the bouncer unhooked the velvet rope and ushered them inside.

"So Sadie's got some clout around here," Evan said.

"Yeah, who knew?" Jeff said.

Inside, the crowd was so thick that they could barely move through the front room. Isabel's memory of bankers in baggy white button-downs turned out to be completely wrong. The crowd was much more Brooklyn hipster than Wall Street analyst, and as she and Evan and Jeff made their way through the different rooms, she felt the kind of joy that only being in a really cool, really exclusive bar can give.

"Where do you think she is?" Evan asked, scanning the people draped along the rattan-frame sofas and clustered around the bar.

"Maybe check outside?" Isabel suggested. "I think there's a patio straight ahead."

Evan fought his way through the room until Isabel felt a rush of cool air on her face and smelled briny sea air. Outside, the patio was almost as packed as the rest of the Ripcurl. Japanese lanterns in shades of pink and lavender hung over long picnic tables stocked with girls sipping tropical drinks in bright pastel colors. Guys in dark jeans and jackets circled around their tables, waiting to make their move. A few had already done so, and out of these, most had found seats near Sadie, who held court at a table on the opposite side of the patio.

"There she is," Isabel said, grabbing Evan's arm. "I see her."

"Wow. She really is kind of popular," Jeff said behind her.

"I'm not so sure that's a good thing," said Evan.

They moved toward the table, single file, and as Isabel passed one of the tables, someone with thick dark hair, tan forearms, and a familiar slouch caught her eye. Her heart leaped into her throat. It was Mike. He sat with his hands wrapped around a Stella Artois, chatting with his friend Gordy and his roommate Esteban. He hadn't seen her, but she felt the urge to turn and run anyway.

"I have to go to the bathroom," she said. She tugged on Evan's hand.

"Okay," Evan said, looking over his shoulder.

"Be right back." With one last glance in Mike's direction, she pivoted around and walked back into the club.

He didn't see you, she thought as she pushed her way through the crowd toward the bathroom. *He has no idea you're here.*

But unless he decided to leave soon, he was going to see her, eventually. And they were probably going to have to speak. She felt the contents of her stomach shift around. If she didn't get to the bathroom pretty soon, there was a good chance she might throw up right in the middle of the Ripcurl.

She'd almost reached the hall that led to the bathrooms when she felt a tap on the shoulder. She turned around.

Mike stood in front of her. "I thought that was you," he said.

He stood closer to her than she would have liked, and when someone pushed up against him from behind, his hand brushed against hers.

She didn't speak. Couldn't speak.

"It's nice to see you," he added. He seemed almost as nervous as she was. "You look great."

Words still eluded her. In the dim light, his liquid brown eyes were even more mesmerizing than she remembered. His hair was longer, which made him look older, more mysterious. His lips, however, were just as full and inviting as they'd been last summer. Had he kissed anyone since then? she wondered.

"I'm here for someone's birthday," she said, pulling herself together. "With my boyfriend. We're here together."

Mike nodded, as if she'd just told him the time.

"He's out on the patio," she continued. "With his friend. I'm with him."

Another person brushed past them, and they stumbled toward each other. When their arms touched she felt an actual current jump his skin and go through hers.

"So. Yeah," she said. "I should probably get back to them—"

Mike smiled. "How's your summer been so far?" he asked.

"Good," she said. "Fun. I'm waitressing."

"You are?" he asked.

"Yeah. It's great," she said, tossing some hair over her shoulder. She waited a beat. "How's yours?"

"Good. I'm working at the surf shop in Montauk. It's pretty cool." He ran a hand through his hair. "Surfing as much as I can. You know."

She could feel herself being pulled toward him, as if his torso were one gigantic magnet. If she didn't leave quickly, she was going to be in trouble. "That's great. I should probably get back—"

"I've been thinking about you," he said.

"You've been thinking about me?" she repeated.

"I had a feeling you were back in town." He touched her arm. "I wanted to call you."

She shook her head.

"I miss you," he blurted. "I want you to give me a second chance." He paused. "I think I deserve that."

She blinked, letting this sink in. "You want what?" she asked. "I don't hear from you all year, and now you miss me? And you deserve a second chance?" Her breath started to come fast. "Are you *kidding* me?"

"Isabel, I wanted to call you. Of course I did. But you blew me off pretty hard that last day. I don't know if you remember—"

"I think I had a right to blow you off," she said.

"Okay, I was a jerk," he said. "I know that. I've had nine months to think about that." A wounded look appeared in his eyes. "But if you give me another chance, I'd do better this time."

The words made something melt inside her. She pictured herself taking one small step, throwing her arms around his neck, and kissing him hard on the mouth. It would be so easy, so simple. And standing in front of him, she could feel that this was exactly what she wanted to do.

But then her anger returned. "It's too late. I'm with somebody now." She stepped backward into the hall. "Good-bye, Mike." She felt dizzy. She needed to throw some cold water on her face. She turned to go.

"Isabel," Mike said, but she kept walking.

In the ladies' room she locked herself in a stall and put her palm on the door to steady herself. Her heart rose and dipped, as if she were in the middle of turbulence. It almost didn't seem real that she'd seen him. There were too many crazy things that had come out of his mouth. She'd need the entire night to process them all. Alone, and definitely not here.

She left the ladies' room and made it back to the patio. Mike's seat at the table was empty. Sadie was sitting down, carousing with some guy wearing too much hair gel. Evan and Jeff sat beside her.

Isabel waved to Sadie and then leaned close to Evan. "I have to go," she announced. "Like, now."

"What happened?" Evan asked.

"I don't feel well," she said. "I think it's something I ate."

Evan studied her face for a moment, as if he wasn't sure he believed her. "Are you sure?"

"I'm positive. Hey, Sadie," she called over to the birthday girl. "I have to take off."

Sadie looked over her shoulder, gave Isabel a flimsy wave, and went back to talking to her admirer.

"Okay, then I guess we have to go," Evan said. "Dude, I'm going to take Isabel home. You want to come or stay here?"

Jeff picked his hand up from the table and began wiping it on his pant leg. "Ugh. This table's covered with something sticky."

As they stood up to say their good-byes to Sadie, Isabel snuck a glimpse of Mike's table. He'd sat down again and now had his back to her. He probably would leave her alone the rest of the night if she stayed, but she didn't want to take any chances.

"All right, let's go," Evan said, guiding Isabel in front of them with his hand on the small of her back.

She felt Mike's eyes on her as she passed his table. A small voice inside her begged her to turn around and make eye contact. *This isn't what you want*, it said. *You still care.*

But then Evan's hand sought hers as they reached the inside of the club, safe from Mike's gaze, and she knew without any doubt that she'd done the right thing.

JULY

CHAPTER TEN

"I don't see why we have to do a double date," Connor said as they walked down the beach. "It's not like I want to get buddy-buddy with the guy who's dating my sister."

"You don't have to get buddy-buddy with him; you just have to meet him," Rory said, braiding her fingers with his. "And he's really cool."

Beside them the waves drew in on themselves, built to a crescendo, and then crashed downward, collapsing into foam. Up ahead, Main Beach was starting to thin out now, as the sun grew weaker and the wind began to feel chilly.

"So this was your idea?" Connor asked.

"Uh-huh," she said breezily.

"Too bad Caleb and Nico and those guys went back to the city," Connor said. "Maybe Augusta could join?"

She tried to check her irritation. "Maybe not. It's a double date, you know?" She'd spent plenty of time with Augusta over the past couple of weeks. Besides the endless dinner the first night they'd run into her, she'd come over to make lobster rolls;

she'd met them at the beach to hang out on a hot, lazy Sunday; and she'd invited them over to her house in Bridgehampton to play badminton, which they hadn't done but which still annoyed Rory every time she thought about it.

"You don't like Augusta that much," Connor said, his voice hovering between serious and teasing.

"I like her fine," Rory said. "But why does she have to be part of a double date? Wouldn't she be a fifth wheel?"

"I don't think Augusta could be a fifth wheel if she tried."

"Well, if you want her to come so badly, then invite her."

"Whoa," Connor said. "What's that for?"

Rory looked out at a pack of gulls swooping close to the water. She hadn't meant that last bit to be said out loud. "Sorry," she said. "It's only that you and I aren't alone that much anymore."

"But I want to be alone with you," Connor said. "Wasn't I just saying that I don't want to go to this tonight?"

Rory hugged herself against the wind. "Yeah," she said. "But this is about Isabel. I think your opinion is really important to her. Believe it or not."

Connor kept his face turned away from her, his eyes on the ocean. It had been like this so many times over the past couple of weeks. They'd be talking about nothing, just having a conversation, and then out of nowhere she'd say something that would annoy him, or he'd say something that would hurt her feelings, and before she knew it she'd be reaching for his hand or trying to engage him with a smile, and he'd be gone, lost within himself, silent and unreachable.

So here was the real truth about relationships, Rory thought. You could be with your boyfriend on a beach at sunset, holding his hand, feeling awe at his handsome profile, and still feel as lonely as you'd ever felt in your life.

Isabel sat in the front seat of Evan's car, looking out at the bluish twilight as they drove past open fields.

"So Jeff and I are thinking of doing another YouTube piece this weekend," he said. "Probably me interviewing random people on the street. Jeff will shoot it. But I think I'll need someone else to be in it, playing my assistant. What about it? Do you want to do it?"

Isabel realized that she'd missed most of the question. "I'm sorry, what'd you say?"

"I said I'm gonna be doing another YouTube piece with Jeff," Evan said. "And I asked you if you wanted to be in it."

"Oh, sure," she said. "That'd be great."

Evan gave her a curious look. "Is something on your mind? Are you stressed about me meeting your brother?"

"Oh no," she said. "He'll love you. And even if he doesn't… you look sexy with that shirt on."

Evan looked down at his striped oxford. "Is it baggy enough for you?"

"Totally," she said. *Good save*, she thought. She had to stop zoning out, or else it wasn't going to be a fun dinner. And she needed this to be a fun dinner. For the past ten days, ever since she'd run into Mike at the Ripcurl, her mind had been taken over—commandeered, actually—by thoughts of him. It was starting to get annoying. She'd be at work, putting in her lunch orders, and suddenly she'd remember the electric sensation of Mike's wrist brushing against her own. Or she'd be telling someone the specials, and she'd get a whiff of his scent that night—beer, salty ocean water, that peppermint bodywash he liked to use. Or she'd be with Evan, and thoughts of being with Mike—taking off his shirt, kissing his neck—would make her completely deaf to what he was saying. And then she'd need to have him repeat things, like she was some kind of airhead. Evan was starting to think she was a little out of it, she could tell. *Get it together,* she told herself in the car. *That guy is old, old news.*

It made even less sense that she was thinking so much about Mike because things with Evan were going so well. He'd finally started inviting her over to his house toward the end of June. But it wasn't her favorite place to hang out. Jeff's uncle's guesthouse was more of a storage facility for his uncle's collection of mid-century modern furniture than a dwelling for guests. One couldn't walk through the living room without banging a knee into an ottoman or a coffee table. There was almost nowhere to stand, but many, many places to sit. A depressing bare lightbulb hung from the center of the living-room ceiling over the furniture, which was upholstered in green felt or orange fabric. The bathroom was only wide enough for a toilet and a shower, and there was just one real bedroom, which happened to be Evan's—but only for the month of June.

"We switch off having the bedroom and being out here," Evan had explained on her first visit, pointing to a tangerine-colored futon with a tangle of blankets and a pillow that lay smack in the middle of the living-room floor.

128

"Oh," Isabel had said, scrutinizing the futon. "So this will be where you'll sleep next month?" Her fantasies of spending alone time with Evan—the kind of alone time she'd spent with Mike in his tiny but private bedroom—instantly trickled away.

"Yeah," Evan said, kicking the futon. "It's not so bad. And Jeff is a pretty solid sleeper so it's not like he's up and walking around."

On this particular July evening, however, Jeff was at work, so they'd made themselves at home in the tiny, mildew-smelling back bedroom. They'd just graduated from making out to doing other, more serious things, and as she lay in Evan's arms, kissing him, he started to take off her shirt. Thoughts of Mike shot back into her brain with a force that made her sit up.

"You okay?" Evan asked.

Isabel hugged her knees, feeling stupid. "I had this boyfriend last summer," she said, looking down at the chocolate-colored bedspread.

"And?" Evan asked.

He had a different chest than you, she wanted to say. Mike's chest had been well-muscled, sturdy, smooth. Evan's was longer and thinner and paler, with a central tuft of chest hair. It wasn't less attractive than Mike's. But it was different. "It's nothing," she said. "Just my own weirdness."

"Do I need to break his knees?" Evan asked.

Isabel gave him a bewildered look.

"Man, that sounded macho, didn't it?" Evan said. She laughed.

Now, in the car, she drummed her nails on the car door and gazed out at a lonely vegetable stand, closed up for the night. It wasn't Mike's stand, but it looked just like it. "Would you ever want to try surfing?" she asked.

"I tried it once," he said, turning onto Montauk Highway. "I thought the skin was gonna get permanently scraped off my ribs from all the paddling. And I have no balance. But if you want to teach me, then I'm more than interested."

"Good to know," she sighed.

"Oh, I've been meaning to tell you," Connor said from across the table. "My dad wants me to stay over at his place this weekend. Would you have a problem with that?"

Rory looked up from the overpriced menu. Isabel and Evan were late, and the restaurant was strangely empty. "You mean for the Fourth?" she asked. "Sure. Okay. We don't have plans for it anyway, right?"

"I mean, I think he wanted me to come by myself," he said. "You know, for some father-son bonding." Connor grabbed his water and took a quick sip, as if he was eager to look away from her stare.

"So we wouldn't spend the Fourth together?" she asked.

Connor shrugged. "Is there something that you really wanted to do? I remember last year you stayed at home."

Yeah, but we hung out together, she thought. It had been the night they'd first kissed. "If that's what you want," she said.

"It's not what I want; it's what my dad wants," Connor said.

"Well, exactly."

Connor smiled. "What's that supposed to mean?"

"You don't always have to do what your parents want you to

do," she said. "It's like you always have to be the good kid. You don't have to be that way."

"He's just asked me to hang out for a couple of nights. Why is it a character flaw if I go?"

"It's not a character flaw. I'm just pointing something out."

"I think you're blowing this out of proportion," he said, annoyed. "It's a couple of days."

Rory twisted her napkin in her lap. "Fine. Go. Have fun."

He cocked his head and gave her a pained look. "Are you just saying that?"

"No, it's fine," she lied. "Go to your dad's house. You're right, it's a couple of days." She saw Isabel and Evan coming toward them.

"Hey, you guys!" Isabel called, waving.

Quickly Rory waved back, hoping that her fake smile was convincing. Connor turned around and waved, too, as friendly and graciously as possible. *Here we go again*, she thought. *The fake happy couple.*

Evan had the same open smile that she'd seen at the pizza place. "Hey, sorry we're late," he said. "It's all Isabel's fault." His green eyes twinkled.

"It's because someone drives like they're a senior citizen," Isabel said, socking him in the upper arm.

Evan sat down across from her. Once again, Rory noticed how attractive his eyes were.

"Hey, man, I'm Evan," Evan said, extending his hand toward Connor.

"Connor," said Connor. "Isabel's told me a lot about you."

"She has?" Evan asked, amused.

"Not too much, don't worry," Connor said. "I am the older brother, after all. I get very little info."

Isabel gave Rory a look. *How are you guys doing?* it seemed to ask.

Rory gave her a half smile, which she hoped conveyed, *Not great.*

"So...where are you from again?" Connor asked.

"Wilton, Connecticut."

"I think I had a guy on my floor at St. Paul's who was from there," Connor said.

"St. Paul's?" Evan asked.

"It's a boarding school," Connor said.

"Oh," Evan said, a bit self-conscious.

"Connor goes to USC," Isabel pointed out. "He used to be a big swimming star."

"Are you into sports?" Connor asked.

Evan shook his head. "Not so much. I tried playing basketball, but I found myself getting beaten up a lot."

Connor was quiet.

"Why does everyone think that because a guy is tall, he has to be amazing at basketball?" Rory asked, breaking the silence.

"Where were you, like, three years ago?" Evan asked. "I could have used you then."

"Hey, what are you guys doing for the Fourth?" Isabel asked, changing the subject.

Rory glanced at Connor, to see if he was willing to answer.

"I'm spending it at Dad's," Connor said.

"You *are*?" Isabel asked.

"I'm sure you're invited."

"No, thanks," Isabel said abruptly. "Are you going, too?" she asked Rory.

Rory shook her head.

"Dad wants it to be just family, I think," Connor put in. "At least, that's how he made it sound."

Isabel arched an eyebrow. "So Rory's not invited?"

Rory lowered her eyes to the table. She could feel Evan watching the three of them closely.

"It's not up to me," Connor said.

"Then you're hanging out with us," Isabel said to Rory, tipping her head to include Evan. "Once we figure out what we're doing, that is." Isabel threw a dark, shaming look in Connor's direction.

"So does everyone know what they want?" Rory asked, eager to move on. As she glanced down at her menu, she made eye contact with Evan. She was startled to find sympathy in his gaze. Then she looked away.

Isabel walked with Evan back to his car, even though she was getting a ride home with Connor and Rory. She'd been distracted for most of the dinner, thinking about Mike, and now she felt disoriented, as if she'd shown up late to a class and had no idea what anyone was talking about. Plus, she'd felt a strange energy whizzing back and forth across the table, as if the four of them had been engaged in an intense bout of doubles Ping-Pong. "Thanks for doing that," she said. "I think my brother really liked you."

"You think so?" Evan said. "I couldn't tell. He seemed a little weird toward your friend, though. Did you pick up on that?"

"Rory?"

"Yeah. He seemed...well, they both seemed like they'd been kind of bugged at each other. You didn't notice that?"

"Not really," she said.

When they got to his car she stepped closer to him, cuing him to put his arms around her. But he didn't. In the moonlight his eyes held a new, unfamiliar distance.

"Well, see you tomorrow," he said. "Sleep tight."

"I will," she said. "You, too."

He rubbed her shoulders and then got into his car. It was hard not to feel a little bit rejected as the door shut. But she knew that she sort of deserved it.

When she got in the backseat of Connor's car, Rory turned around in the shotgun seat. "Evan's so cool," she gushed. "Did he have a good time?"

Isabel slammed the door closed, and Connor started the engine. "Yup," she said. "He did."

As they took off in the dark, Isabel clutched the door handle in frustration. Evan *was* cool, she thought. And if she didn't get herself together and stop thinking about Mike, she was going to lose him.

CHAPTER ELEVEN

Rejecting people all day long had to be bad karma, Rory thought as she cut and pasted yet another filmmaker's name and address into a form rejection on East End Festival letterhead. WE APPRECIATE YOUR INTEREST IN THE EAST END FESTIVAL, BUT DUE TO THE OVERWHELMING AMOUNT OF SUBMISSIONS IN YOUR CATEGORY, WE ARE UNABLE TO ACCEPT YOUR FILM AT THIS TIME....She wondered how she'd feel if she got one of these letters. Probably the same as she'd felt that morning watching Connor pack his bag for his dad's house. She'd sat on his bed, watching him open drawers and dump clothes into a gym bag, trying to act as if she hadn't stayed up most of the night before, wondering if she'd been too nitpicky at dinner.

"What do you guys have planned for the Fourth tomorrow?" she asked, hoping she didn't sound too interested.

"Something mellow, I'm sure," Connor said. "It's not like my dad's gonna be at the Georgica. I think he'll have some friends over. Grill some steaks." He placed a suspiciously hefty pile of T-shirts in the bag. "You and Isabel gonna do something?"

"Me and Isabel and Evan," she corrected him. It was a cheap shot, bringing up another guy, but she couldn't help it.

Connor continued to pack his bag. "He seems like a nice guy," he said. "You'll have a lot more fun with them." He glanced at the Swiss army knife on the end table but didn't pack it.

"Yeah, probably," she said, feigning a smile.

After her tenth form letter, she started to feel tired. She closed the file, and then closed her eyes, letting herself drift off to sleep, her chin on her hand. Then she smelled the familiar scent of vanilla-and-musk perfume wafting over from somewhere close by.

"Rory, do you have a moment?" she asked.

Rory jerked herself upright. Nina hovered over Rory. She blinked groggily. "Sure, what do you need?"

Nina didn't seem to notice Rory's drowsiness. Instead she wore an oddly giddy smile as she stood by Rory's chair, hand on her narrow hip. "We heard back from the Rules. They RSVP'd yes to the gala."

"Oh, that's great," Rory said, unsure how happy she was supposed to be about this piece of news.

"Between you and me," Nina said in a conspiratorial voice, leaning closer, "everyone on the fund-raising committee is *beside* themselves that they're coming."

"Oh." For some reason this made her feel less than excited. "Wonderful."

"And Andrea?" Nina asked, leaning over toward Amelia's cubicle.

"You mean Amelia?" Rory heard Amelia say.

"Sorry, *Amelia*," Nina said with a bashful smile. "I just wanted you to know that we all voted to include *Flower Child* in our shorts selection. Congratulations."

"Really?" Amelia cried. From the other side of the cubicle, it sounded as if she'd almost fallen out of her chair. "Are you serious?"

"Yes, we all loved it," Nina said, her brown eyes gleaming. "And you can thank Rory for bringing it to our attention. She clearly has good taste." Then Nina clip-clopped off down the hall.

Amelia sprang up over the cubicle wall. "I can't believe it," she said. "That actually *happened*. Thank you."

"I didn't do anything. They obviously liked your movie."

"Who are the Rules?" Amelia asked, with a skeptical arch of her brow.

"These people I'm staying with," she said. "My boyfriend's parents."

"They sound pretty important."

"They have a lot of money," Rory said.

Amelia snorted. "Of course they do."

"What does that mean?"

"I've lived here all my life," Amelia said. "Not in East Hampton—on the North Fork. But whatever. Same diff. And there's no question—money means everything around here."

"So you're saying that's why they chose your film?" Rory asked.

"Depends. What did you promise them about these people you're staying with?"

"Nothing," Rory said. "I didn't promise them anything."

Amelia thought for a moment and then waved her hand.

"Ah, forget it," she said. "You're right. I should be happy. At least one of these dumb internships actually turned into something." Then she popped out of sight.

Rory turned back toward her computer. She knew that Amelia was probably right. Living with the Rules seemed to give her clout here, in a way she couldn't have foreseen. But she hadn't "promised" Nina and Luis a thing. If they wanted to put Amelia's short in the lineup, that was their choice. Her conscience was clear. And she would make sure it stayed that way.

"I can't believe he left you alone on the Fourth," Isabel said the next day as they sat in bumper-to-bumper traffic on Montauk Highway, headed east. "That is so not cool."

"What am I gonna do?" Rory asked. "Force him to hang out with me?"

Isabel leaned her head out of the window, trying to assess the traffic situation. The smell of cold fried chicken wafted from the backseat, making her stomach grumble. Fee had packed them a three-course picnic dinner for the fireworks that night, but Isabel was hungry enough to break into it now. "Maybe we should have left earlier," Isabel said. "I think everyone in the world is trying to get to Montauk right now."

"Do you think there'll be any spaces left?" Rory asked.

"It's a beach. It's not like they can close it off." Isabel slammed her foot on the accelerator as the car in front of them lurched forward, then slammed her foot on the brake as soon as the car slowed down.

"Has Connor always been like this?" Rory asked. "You know, the perfect son?"

"I made it pretty easy for him," Isabel said.

"The funny thing is, that's what I liked about him last summer—his goodness," Rory said. "I knew that he'd always do the right thing. I could trust that about him."

"Yeah, but a person's best quality can be their worst quality," Isabel said. "You ever notice that? Like with Evan. He's so sweet, he's so considerate, he's so open about how he feels about me."

"So all those things are his worst qualities?" Rory asked.

Isabel gave Rory a look. "Sometimes I think he's too open, too nice. It can be a little bit...boring."

"Maybe you don't know what it's like to be with someone who doesn't play with your head," Rory said.

"I *knew* you'd say that," Isabel said.

"No, I'm listening. What about all that is bad?"

"I saw Mike," Isabel said bluntly. "At the Ripcurl that night. I didn't want to tell you, because I was afraid you'd think I'd be into him again. And I'm not."

"Uh-huh," Rory said cautiously.

"But there was more...I don't know, *heat* in the five minutes I was standing in front of him talking than there is when I'm actually hooking up with Evan."

"But you're not into Mike," Rory said in a deadpan voice.

"No, I'm not. He wanted me to give him a second chance, and I said no."

Rory looked impressed. "Good for you."

"But I think about him," Isabel said. "I've been trying not to. But I do."

The car ahead of them finally began moving again. Isabel lurched forward and turned up Rihanna on the radio. The sun was setting fast, and straight ahead, toward the east, the sky was awash with pinks and lavenders.

"I get it," Rory said. "There's no perfect package. You date a guy who's good to his parents? Then he wants to hang out with them on major holidays instead of with you."

Isabel laughed. "If only he knew the real reason for the divorce," she said. "Maybe I should tell him."

"But didn't your mom make you promise not to?"

"Forget my mom," Isabel said. "She's so caught up in denial it would probably do her good."

"But what about me?" Rory asked.

"What about you? You'll just pretend that you didn't know anything about it."

"But I don't think I could do that," Rory said.

Isabel was quiet. "Fine. I won't say anything. Even though he deserves to know."

Rory didn't know what to say to this. She figured it was best not to say anything and simply pat Isabel's arm, to let her know that she understood.

By the time they got to the beach, most of the sand was covered with blankets and towels and beach chairs. A few scattered bonfires sent halos of light into the twilight. Dogs loped around on the beach, while their owners roasted marshmallows in the flames. It was unabashedly romantic, and Rory felt an acute sense that she'd be a third wheel around Evan and Isabel tonight. "Looks like this is our best bet," Rory said, pointing to a patch of sand in the glow of someone's bonfire.

Isabel lay the blanket down, then placed the shopping bag

she'd been carrying in the center of it. She pulled out a bottle of Cristal and two plastic glasses.

"You stole *another* bottle of champagne from your parents?" Rory asked.

"They have so many they'd never even notice."

"What about cops?" Rory asked, looking around.

"Oh please," Isabel said impatiently. She popped open the bottle behind the shopping bag and poured two glasses—one for herself and one for Rory. Then they clinked glasses. "To letting go of expectations," she said.

"Yeah," Rory said simply, and brought the glass to her lips. The sweet and tangy drink sizzled on her tongue. She'd never cared for champagne that much, but tonight it tasted simply delicious. *One year ago tonight I kissed Connor for the first time*, she thought. *And now I'm back out here, and he's hanging with his dad.*

"Want some more?" Isabel asked, tipping the golden bottle toward her.

"I think I'm okay," she said.

Isabel downed her glass, then poured herself another. "I'm gonna try to tell Evan where we are over text," she said, taking out her phone. "Maybe he'll bring Jeff. You might like him," she said, winking.

"Things aren't that dire yet," Rory said.

They opened the cardboard picnic box that Fee had packed and tore into the fried chicken and homemade coleslaw. Somewhere in the distance someone was playing Jack Johnson on a boom box. Rory felt a pleasant mellowness come over her. Even if things were hard with Connor, she was damn lucky to be here. And at least she had an amazing friend in Isabel.

As it got darker, Isabel continued to check her phone. "No text back," she said. "Maybe I'll get up and do a quick recon, see if he's here. I'll be back in a minute."

"Okay." Rory lay on her back on the blanket and stared up at the sky. It suddenly seemed obvious, lying there with the canopy of stars above her, that things with Connor had changed, and not for the better. *We probably need to break up*, she thought, and a deep sadness welled up in her chest. Things had been so good between them for the entire school year. They'd survived being three thousand miles apart. And now, after a few weeks of being in the same house together, they couldn't make it work. How pathetic was that?

"Hey," said a familiar voice. "Are you having a moment? Or can I join you?"

She sat up on her forearms as Evan crouched down in front of her.

"You looked like you were communing with the heavens or something," he said. "Or maybe you were about to fall asleep, I couldn't tell."

"Hi," she said. "Isabel went to look for you."

"Oh yeah? I walked around this whole beach looking for her," he said. He sat down a few inches from her on the blanket. "I figure if I stay put, at least one of us has a fighting shot." He wore a hoodie that was the same olive green as his eyes and dark jeans that made his long legs look even longer.

"You want some food? We have a ton here."

"Nah, I'm good. Had the shrimp diavolo at work." He rubbed his stomach. "I think Bill is secretly trying to poison us. Is Connor…"

"At his dad's house," Rory supplied.

"Right," Evan said. "He seems like a cool guy."

"Yeah, he is," she said. She stared out at the waves. It was dark enough now that she could barely see them. "He is a cool guy," she repeated, as if willing herself to believe it.

"But…" Evan said.

Rory turned to look at him.

"It sounds like there was a *but* at the end of that sentence," Evan clarified.

"I just don't know if we're cool together. You know what I mean?" It was a relief to say this out loud, even to her friend's boyfriend. "It's probably my fault. I probably screwed it up somehow."

"Why do you say that?"

She shrugged. "If I tell you something, will you promise not to laugh?"

"I promise."

"He's my first boyfriend," she said. "I've never been in a relationship before." She dug her bare feet into the still-warm sand, holding her breath for his response.

"Can I tell *you* something, if you promise not to laugh?" he said.

"Okay." She gave him a sidelong glance, and in the light of the bonfire his eyes glowed.

"I didn't have *my* first girlfriend until freshman year of college."

"What? You didn't have a girlfriend at *all*?"

"Well, I thought I had girlfriends, but they all turned out to be dating other people on closer inspection. You know, they hadn't gotten the memo that *we* were actually dating. So it was all a little one-sided."

She laughed, and for a moment her head was so crowded and jumbly that it was hard to process a thought. When one finally came it was so direct and so certain that it made her catch her breath: *I like him. I like Isabel's boyfriend. I definitely, absolutely, no-holds-barred like him.*

"Well, I won't tell your secret, if you won't tell mine," she said playfully.

Evan's eyes were fixed on her in the flickering light from the bonfire. "I won't," he said, and something unsaid seemed to pass between them. It was probably ridiculous to even consider, but she wondered if Evan might like her, too.

"Hey, guys." Isabel plopped down on the blanket. "So you made it," she said to Evan, leaning over to give him a hug. "I figured you had to be here. I must have schlepped up and down the entire beach."

"Hey, beautiful," Evan said.

Rory looked away as they kissed. The first firework exploded above them, lighting up the night sky in whites, blues, and reds.

Time to get ahold of yourself, she thought. *You don't really like him. You're just lonely and bored.*

But if that's all it was, just being lonely and bored, she thought, it wouldn't feel this bad to hear them kiss.

CHAPTER TWELVE

"I think I should tell the caterers we want to do a pasta, a fish, and maybe a beef tenderloin," Mrs. Rule said, addressing Rory over her shoulder. "What do you think?"

"Great," Rory said, because it sounded like Mrs. Rule needed to hear that. "All of those sound great." She trailed behind Mrs. Rule through the prepared food aisle at Citarella carrying a basket, in case she was here to help with any grocery shopping. But like last week's shopping expedition, she had the distinct feeling that she was here to keep Mrs. Rule company, for reasons she still didn't understand.

"I always do this before I give a party," said Mrs. Rule, gesturing to the glassed-in case of crab cakes and grilled salmon and Kobe beef burgers on display. "It's the only way that I can really get a sense of what I want before I figure out the menu. Excuse me."

The man in chef's whites behind the case walked up to her.

"I'd like a taste of that soy-ginger seared beef," she said, pointing. Rory noted the she did not say *please.*

"Hmmm," she said, nibbling on the tiny toothpick-sized portion of beef. "Would you like to try some?" Before Rory could answer, Mrs. Rule faced the man behind the counter again. "Another one for my friend."

Mrs. Rule passed her the toothpick, and Rory popped the entire piece of beef in her mouth before she could remember to nibble. "Good," she said, swallowing.

Mrs. Rule clasped her tanned hands under her chin and thought deeply. "The flavors...I don't know. They're so...ethnic. Maybe we should do something like the Kobe burgers."

"So you're really going to go ahead with this party?" Rory asked.

"Of course. The invitations were sent out this morning," said Mrs. Rule, turning to the man behind the counter. "The Kobe burger, please."

"Is the family excited about it?" she asked tentatively.

Mrs. Rule nibbled half the burger sample and tossed the rest in the trash. "Why wouldn't they be? Well, one person isn't. And I think you know who I'm talking about." She walked farther down the case. "Kelly Quinlan tells me that Isabel's turned her back on all her old friends. She's waitressing at a glorified diner. Her father says that she ignores his e-mails and phone calls and invitations to go stay with him. Which is fine; she doesn't need to do that if she doesn't want to," Mrs. Rule said lightly, pulling her handbag strap farther up her shoulder, "but she should at least write him back. And I can't talk to her. She doesn't listen to me. But she listens to you. You're the *only* one she listens to."

Rory wanted to say that Isabel listened to absolutely no one, including her.

"I'd like you to tell her that she's made her point, whatever that is, and that it's done. She needs to be part of this family, instead of constantly running off and spending time with… with…" Mrs. Rule shook her head, as if Evan and Isabel's fellow waiters eluded description. "You know what I'm saying."

"But I think she's happy," Rory said. "I think she likes being a waitress."

"I've known Isabel a little bit longer than you have," Mrs. Rule said. "And I can tell you that she doesn't like being a waitress. She likes making me angry. It was obvious when she told me about it." She drummed her nails on the glass case, drilling in her point. "It's a boy, isn't it?" Mrs. Rule asked. "There's a boy involved in all this."

Rory looked down and blushed. *Damn it*, she thought.

"I knew it," Mrs. Rule said. "It's always about a boy." She shook her head. Rory waited for her to say something else, but nothing came. "Anyway, will you please say something to her for me?"

"I'll see what I can do," Rory said, hoping that would put an end to the interrogation.

"Thank you," she said. "Now, let's go over to the Golden Pear and see what they have. Unless there's anything you need here?"

Rory shook her head. She loved how Mrs. Rule pretended to care about other people's needs, even hers.

"I'm thinking that you should learn some paddle tennis this summer," Mrs. Rule remarked. "How would you like that?"

Rory wanted to say that she wouldn't like it all, but she smiled and nodded. "Sounds great," she said, with a sinking heart.

Isabel sat cross-legged on the kitchen chair, one eye on the flat screen as she picked at her pasta primavera. Her mom was out with Sloane for a girls' dinner, and Gregory was back in the city, being their father's business slave. Connor was still at their dad's house. She'd had an especially long day at work—there'd been an influx of late arrivals, some of them so exacting in their orders that she'd almost invited them to go back to the kitchen and cook the food themselves. She put down her fork and massaged the balls of her feet. At least Evan had been so cute today. Giving her little smiles as they passed each other between tables, telling her how pretty she looked when she came in, and then kissing her good-bye in the back room, when anyone could have walked in and caught them. She was starting to think that she was utterly wrong about the two of them. Maybe they did make sense together after all.

Rory walked in and grabbed a plate to serve herself from the platter Mickey had left out on the counter.

"Long day?" Rory asked.

"The longest. But I think I was also kind of tired from last night. What time did we get home from the beach?"

"I think it was after midnight," Rory said. "Thank god I didn't have work today."

"So…what'd you and Evan talk about when I was gone?" Isabel asked.

"Oh, nothing that important," Rory said. "Just chatted 'til you showed up."

"He's really talented," Isabel said, grinning. "And sweet. And adorable." She pushed her plate away. "I take back everything I said last night in the car. I'm really into him."

"Oh?" Rory looked back down at her plate. "Cool."

"He's so funny and so quick and so smart and so...gentlemanly," Isabel said. "He holds the door open for me when we go into places. Mike never did that."

"That's great," Rory said, staring at her food.

"He never leaves my side when we're in a crowded place together. He asks about my day."

"That's amazing," Rory said, poking at some pasta with her fork.

"And I can tell he really respects me," Isabel said. "I was sort of worried, because things have started off so slow. But now, I know that that's a good thing. And I can tell that he really likes you, too."

"He does?" Rory asked, looking up from her plate.

"Yeah. He doesn't know that many people here, and I think he'd like to be friends with you. You know, hang out sometime, even if I'm not there. Would you be into that?"

Rory kept her eyes on the food. "Sure."

"I'll give him your number, then."

Rory stood up suddenly and took her plate to the sink.

"You're not hungry?" Isabel asked.

"I had a pretty big lunch. Your mom and I went out for a while."

"You *did*?" Isabel said.

"I think she wanted to talk to someone about this party she's planning." Rory walked back to the table. "She also wanted to know if you're seeing someone."

Isabel rolled her eyes. "She would."

"I told her I didn't know. I don't think she believed me."

"Right. Because it's all about the guy that I'm seeing. *He's* the problem."

"So Mike wasn't a problem?" Rory teased.

"Mike was a waste of time, that's what he was."

The swinging door opened, and Connor entered with his duffel bag. It had only been two days, but he seemed thinner, more drawn, than before he'd left. Isabel wondered if her dad had any food at his house.

He looked from one to the other of them and slowly put his bag on the floor. "Hey," he said. "What's everyone doing?"

"Eating," Isabel said. "What does it look like?"

Rory didn't move. "You're back early."

"Yeah, well, there are only so many conversations you can have with your dad about sand traps and business school." Connor walked over to Rory and put his arms around her.

Isabel watched Rory kiss him back, but as slightly as possible.

"So you guys went out to Montauk last night," he said. "How was it? Fun?"

"Yeah, it was nice," Rory said.

"I still can't believe you went off to Dad's house and left Rory here alone," Isabel said casually. "Talk about rude."

"Isabel, don't," Rory said.

"No, it is. Totally rude."

"I'm not the only one," Connor said, his face darkening. "Dad said he's sent you, like, four e-mails asking you to come by. And you haven't responded to one of them. Now who's being rude?"

"I don't owe Dad a thing," Isabel said.

"How can you say that? Do you hear how crazy that is?" Connor's face was turning slightly pink. "He's your father."

"Hate to say it, but you're living in a fantasy world, Con," Isabel said. "It's time to wake up."

"What the hell are you talking about?" Connor asked.

"Okay, okay," Rory said, coming to Connor's side. "Everyone calm down."

"I'm totally calm," Isabel said coolly. She stood up and barged out of the room, letting the door swing back and forth in vast, rapid motions in her wake.

Rory stood across from Connor, wondering how to explain Isabel's comment to him.

"Every time I think she's getting better, it's like she does a one eighty all over again," he said, looking at the swinging door. "How much longer is she going to act like this? Like everyone in the world is against her?"

Rory gently took his arm. "She's only saying that stuff because she cares about you."

"Huh? Where do you get that?" Connor asked.

"It's a little hard to explain," she said.

"Whatever," Connor said, shaking his head. He let out a deep breath, and the flushed color went out of his face. "I've been trying to figure out my sister for years. When am I going to learn that I can't? She *wants* to be misunderstood. It's her whole reason for living." He ran a hand through his hair and smiled ruefully.

"So, how was it at your dad's house?" she asked, hoping to get off the subject of Isabel.

"Good," Connor said, dropping into a chair. "But a little weird, too. He's turned into some kind of groovy bachelor dude. It's a little bizarre."

"Huh."

"You really wouldn't have had a good time," he said. He put his arms around her. "I'm sorry I left you all alone."

"I haven't been all alone," she said, nestling herself into his shoulder. "Isabel has been here. And your mom."

"My mom?" Connor asked.

"Yeah. Now all of a sudden we're best buddies."

"I told you she likes you."

"I'm not sure if I want to be best buddies with your mom, Connor," she said. "No offense."

"That's okay," he said, touching her cheek. He gazed into her eyes. "You look really pretty."

They kissed, but there was no more light, rubbery feeling in the backs of her knees. She didn't feel her stomach turn over. It was almost routine, as if they were an old married couple. She held the kiss for as long as she could, and then she pulled away.

"Do you want to go upstairs? Help me unpack?" he asked, pulling her closer to him.

An image of Evan flickered across her mind. *No*, she wanted to say. *I don't.*

But this was her boyfriend, who was finally back with her, finally paying attention to her. She owed it to him, and to herself, to do whatever she could to make this work.

"Sure," she said. "But just for a little while. I have work tomorrow."

He picked up his bag and took her by the hand. "I really did miss you, Ror," he said, with more earnest feeling than she'd seen from him in weeks.

"I missed you, too," she said, and in that moment, she believed it.

CHAPTER THIRTEEN

"Now, where do you think the Rules would rather sit?" Nina asked, pointing at the seating chart on her desk. "We could put them at Alec Baldwin's table, which will also have the director of the festival, an editor from *Vanity Fair*, and the society columnist from *Dan's Papers*, or..."

Rory politely covered a yawn with her hand and wondered when she'd become the Rules' social director. Nina apparently seemed to think their seating at the opening night gala to be a matter of supreme importance. This was their third conversation about it.

"I think wherever you want to put them is fine," Rory said. "I'm sure they'll have a good time either way."

"But would you say they'd rather sit with celebrities or with more artistic people?"

Neither, Rory wanted to say. "Artistic people," she said.

"Great," Nina said. "I'll put them with Lou Reed and Laurie Anderson," she said. "They know who they are, right?"

Rory knew that they probably didn't, but she nodded anyway.

"Before I go, can I ask you if there's anything else I can do? All the rejection letters have gone out. Was there anything else you want me to do right now?"

"No, no," Nina said, still studying the seating charts. "I'll let you know. Maybe I'll ask you about the Rules' dietary restrictions at some point. But for right now, we're okay."

Rory walked out of her office, muttering, "Can't wait."

"What was that about?" Amelia asked when Rory returned to her desk. She was busy making laminated ID tags. In the past few days she'd gone from being completely ignored to receiving constant tasks from Luis.

"Nina wanted me to look at the seating chart again," Rory said.

"For your boyfriend's parents?" Amelia asked, smirking.

"Yup."

"Wow. She must have called you in four other times."

"Two, actually," Rory said. "And it's not like I'm enjoying it."

"She must be expecting quite a windfall out of them," Amelia said. "I don't think they're paying that much attention to anyone else coming."

"It's kind of gross, if you ask me," Rory said.

"Well, that's the Hamptons," Amelia said. "It's all about over-the-top butt kissing for money."

Rory felt a prickle of irritation. Amelia had little to complain about. At least she was getting something out of this whole situation. And she wasn't being asked her opinion constantly on how to make the Rules happy.

Suddenly her phone beeped in her bag, and she reached down to pull it out. It was a text from a 203 number.

Hey, I'm off today. Meet for lunch? ☺ EVAN

Isabel must have given him her cell number. She wondered if Isabel knew he'd be asking her to have lunch. But if she'd given Evan the number, would she really care?

Sounds good, she wrote. **Where?**

When she got to Main Beach, Evan was waiting for her in the agreed-upon place, in the shady veranda in front of the snack bar. He was dressed in board shorts and a Quiksilver T-shirt, and even though his clothes looked slightly out of place on him—he didn't have the kind of frame that really showed off beachwear, like Connor did—he still looked extremely cute. As she walked from the crowded parking lot, waving at him, she felt her stomach churn.

"How 'bout I treat you to a cheeseburger?" he said. "It's the least I can do for you coming to meet me so last minute."

"Great."

Once they got their food, they sat down on one of the long benches on the snack bar veranda. The beach was scattered with young moms and nannies shepherding their kids to the water and back.

"It's nice to have the day off," Evan said, unwrapping his burger. "I don't think I've been in the water more than a couple times since I got here."

"That's too bad. That's the whole point of coming out here."

Evan chuckled. "Well, depends on who you are, I guess. Not everyone gets to go to the beach every day."

"That's true."

"I guess you do," Evan said. "Seeing as you're staying in a house on the beach."

"You'd be surprised," Rory said. "Sometimes days go by when I don't get down there. And last summer I didn't spend that much time on the beach, either. But that was a different situation."

"What was last summer?" he asked.

Chewing her burger, she realized that Evan still didn't know the backstory of her and the Rules. "I worked for Isabel's family last year," she said.

"Oh yeah?" Evan said. "Doing what?"

"Whatever needed to be done. Mostly errands and groceries and picking up people from the train, that kind of thing." She wiped her fingers with a napkin. "That's how Isabel and I became friends. But you want to know the weird thing? I almost miss those days. Because now it's like I'm part of this family, and that's even harder. At least last summer I knew who I was. Now they've let me in, but I still don't belong."

Evan sat very still, seemingly hanging on every word she was saying.

"I don't know why I'm telling you this," she murmured.

"No, it makes sense. Not belonging is never a lot of fun." He fixed his eyes on the beach and the churning Atlantic beyond. "I feel like that with Isabel sometimes. On one hand, it's great. I know she likes me and wants to be with me. But then I can feel like an alien half the time, too."

"As far as I can tell, you're not an alien."

"I know, but I can still feel like one. And it's not like the

157

waitress thing changes much. She might think she can slum it at the restaurant, but she's got Ralph Lauren radiating out of her pores. In the best way."

"I know," Rory said. "In the very best way."

"And that's great, and she's such a nice person, but half the time I'm wondering what the hell she's doing with me."

Rory scratched a mosquito bite on her knee. "Sure," she said, unsure of where this conversation was headed.

"And what she's doing at the restaurant. Everyone likes her; don't get me wrong. But we all know she's not really one of us. Jeff calls her the Preppy Princess. Luckily I haven't been inside her house yet. Then I'm sure I'd really freak out."

"But does that matter to you?" Rory asked, edging closer to him. "What she comes from? Because believe me, she wishes she didn't come from it. I know that."

"I think that's the reason we get along," he said. "I've wanted to get out of Wilton since I was, like, two. But now I know that East Hampton isn't necessarily any better." They were sitting so close now that his elbow almost tapped the side of her arm. "You know what I mean?"

"Yeah, I do," she said. She was quiet for a moment, lulled into silence by the waves and the gulls overhead and the sun beating down. She thought about how eager she'd been to leave Stillwater and come back here. There wasn't any pressure to say anything more.

"How much more time do you have?" Evan finally asked. "You want to go down to the water for a minute? Dip our feet in?"

"Sure."

They threw away their burger wrappers and napkins and, still sipping their drinks, walked across the beach. At the shore, a wave traveled up the sand and covered both her feet. It was numbingly, but wonderfully, cold.

"That feels good," Evan said.

"I know," Rory said.

Another wave kissed her toes. The wind made her wet feet feel even colder. A larger wave came charging up the sand and spilled over her feet, her calves, and up to her knees. She howled with the force of the cold and reached for his arm to steady herself. "Aaaaah!" she yelled.

Evan put his arm around her waist to keep her upright. "Stay with it!" he cried.

"It's too cold!" she yelled.

She leaned against him, laughing, and turned to look up at him. She caught a view of his green eyes and his golden lashes, and then before she knew it, he leaned down to kiss her.

She knew the right thing to do was to pull away, but she couldn't. As soon as his lips touched hers, she was kissing him right back. It felt completely natural. Expected, almost. When the wave pulled away, she remembered to do the same.

"Whoa," Evan said. "I'm sorry. Oh man, I'm sorry."

"That's okay," she said. "I should probably go. I mean, we should probably go."

"Yeah," Evan said.

She walked ahead of him across the sand toward the parking lot. There was no way that she could look him in the eye right now. If she was lucky, she'd manage to say good-bye to him and get back in her car without having to do it at all.

"Rory, hey," he said, trotting up behind her. "Hey, I really am sorry. I don't know what happened. I felt something, but maybe it was just me."

"It wasn't just you," she said, barely meeting his eye. "But we can't do this. We really can't do this."

"I'm not a player."

"I know you're not," she said. "And I'm not, either."

"Right," he said. "I sort of got that already."

They were almost at the snack bar. She didn't slow down her pace. She wanted to go straight to her car, get inside, and peel out of the parking lot like Danica Patrick.

"So we'll never mention this again," she said, still barely looking at him. "It'll be like it never happened."

"Agreed," he said.

"It'll be our weird, awful little secret."

"Fine."

She slipped on the flip-flops she'd left buried in the sand near the snack bar and walked into the parking lot.

"Rory, can you stop for a second?" he asked.

She turned around.

"It was a mistake, but I don't regret it, if that makes any sense." He looked unsteady on his feet, as if he wasn't quite ready to say good-bye.

She needed a sip of water. Her head was starting to feel swimmy. "Evan, please don't say anything," she said. "Except see you later. That's really the only appropriate thing to say."

"Okay. See you later."

"Bye."

She turned and marched across the sunbaked asphalt to her car. She'd think about this later, when she had the calmness—and the distance—to analyze and obsess about it. But not now. Now she just needed to get out of here.

She got into the hot car and shut the door. *No,* she thought. *I'm going to obsess about this now. I'm a terrible friend. A. Terrible. Friend.*

She put the key in the ignition and pulled out of the parking lot. She would have to pretend that it hadn't happened. That was the only answer. And she could do that. She'd done that with a lot of things in her life. True, most of them had had to do with her mom's behavior and not her own, but at least she had practice.

The Honda jerked a little as she touched the gas. Maybe, she thought, this was a sign that she and Connor really could work things out; maybe she just needed to try a little bit harder, like she'd had to do this year in AP Calculus. Yes, that was the only way to put this out of her mind. Focus on Connor. And pretend that this had never happened.

CHAPTER FOURTEEN

"What do you recommend for a salad? The Shinnecock Tossed or the Apaquogue Apple and Brie?"

"Definitely the apple and Brie," Isabel said. "But not with the raspberry vinaigrette. Go for the regular balsamic."

The customer, a cherubic-faced young mom with a baby strapped to her chest, smiled with gratitude. "That's what I'll have, then," she said, and handed Isabel her menu. "And an iced tea."

Isabel took the menu, not bothering to write down the order. "Great, coming right up," she said, and walked back to the kitchen.

Anytime Evan wasn't at work the day felt slower. Nicole and Sadie were way too efficient and focused to goof off with her. And Bill, the manager, was definitely not a barrel of laughs. It was going to be a long afternoon.

She went to the computer and typed in the apple and Brie salad and iced tea. In her peripheral vision, she noticed the front door of the restaurant open. She glanced at her watch. It was one thirty. They served lunch for another hour. *Please, God,* she thought. *Don't let there be any more customers. Make this one be the last.*

She glanced up to see who had the audacity to sit themselves down in her section, and nearly dropped the menu on the floor. Mike sat at the table in the corner, across from an older man. Marcus the busboy stood over them, pouring them glasses of ice water. It was all perfectly normal, except Mike had invaded her work space. And now she was going to have to speak to him again.

Chin up, shoulders back, she strode over to their table with as much poise and professionalism as she could muster. All she needed to do was act completely natural. If he was here on purpose, to see her, then she would deal with that as best as she knew how.

"Hi, Mike," she said, coming to stand at their table. She smoothed her ponytail back over her shoulder and bravely looked Mike in the eye.

"Isabel?" Mike asked. He looked slightly incredulous.

"What can I get you?" she asked, in as dignified a way as she could.

"So this is where you're working?" he asked.

"And I'm supposed to believe this is a coincidence?" she replied. Mike looked across the table at his friend as if trying to communicate his surprise, and then back at her. "This is my cousin Tony."

"Hi," said the older man. He faintly resembled Mike with his shaggy dark hair and cleft chin.

"Hello there," she said, forcing herself to smile. "Okay, what'd you like?"

"A Miller Lite," Tony said.

"A Miller Lite, sure," she said. This time she needed her pad. She scribbled down the drink order. "And for you?" she asked Mike.

"Uh…a Diet Coke."

"Diet…Coke," she repeated, scribbling that down as well. "Got it. I'll be right back."

"How's the boyfriend?" Mike asked.

She checked to see if he was being sarcastic, but he seemed completely serious.

"He's fine," she said. "He's not here today, but—"

"Oh, so he works here. That's cool."

Isabel narrowed her eyes. Was there any subtext to that? She couldn't tell. "Yeah, it is cool. It's a lot of fun to work with the person you're going out with."

Mike laughed. "Yeah, well, Tony wouldn't necessarily agree to that, now would you?" he said.

His cousin laughed.

Isabel stayed rooted to the spot, on guard for any innuendo or hints of jealousy. But there didn't seem to be any at all. In fact, Mike seemed entirely neutral about her, as if she were simply an old friend. It was kind of annoying.

"Do you guys know what you'd like?" she asked.

"Oh, yeah, I'll have the Reuben," Mike said.

"I'll go with the tuna melt," said his cousin.

She wrote down the orders, and they handed her the menus. Isabel watched to see if Mike tried to touch her fingers or her hands as he handed her his menu, but he didn't. He could have been any other customer ordering lunch.

"Anything else?" she asked, looking at Mike.

"Nope, I think that's it for now," he said. He looked at her more closely. "Is there something else we should get?"

"No, no. I'll be right back."

She walked back to the kitchen, feeling a little self-conscious. The last time she'd seen Mike he'd practically professed his love to her. Now he was acting like she was some ancient acquaintance, or worse, a regular waitress. It didn't make any sense.

At the computer, Sadie sidled up beside Isabel. "Who is *that*?" she asked, nodding in the direction of Mike. "He is *hot*."

"You want his table? It's all yours," Isabel said, putting in his order.

"No, you take him," Sadie said. "You seem like you could use a fling."

Isabel was about to tell Sadie that she was already dating someone—someone Sadie knew pretty well—but she decided against it. "Thanks, I'll keep that in mind," she said.

When she brought out their orders, Mike and his cousin were deep in conversation.

"Oh, that looks good," said Mike as she placed the Reuben in front of him.

"It's one of our specialties," she said brightly.

She placed the tuna melt in front of his cousin. "Anything else?"

"I think we're okay," Mike said.

She turned to leave.

"Oh, Isabel," Mike said.

165

She turned around, eager to hear what he had to say.

"Can I have some extra Russian dressing?" he asked.

This had to be a joke, she thought. But from the dead-serious look on Mike's face, it apparently wasn't. "No problem," she said.

Where was his passion? she thought, stomping back to the pass-through. Where was his ardor? What had happened to him thinking about her? Wanting her? Missing her? Thinking that he would do better, if given a second chance? That had only been a couple of weeks ago. Now he was asking her for Russian dressing like she was nobody.

She grabbed the bottle of dressing, glug-glugged some into a small ramekin, and brought it back to the table. "Here," she said, setting it down with a thud. "Here's your dressing."

"What's wrong?" Mike asked.

"Nothing," she said. "Why should there be anything wrong?"

Tony and Mike exchanged a wary glance.

She went back to the computer and printed out their bill. As soon as Marcus cleared their plates, she placed it on the table. "Whenever you're ready," she said with gritted teeth.

She busied herself with three other tables until she remembered Mike and checked to see if he was still there. They were gone. When she opened the leather checkbook, she saw that he'd left her a 50 percent tip.

"Here," she said to Sadie as she coasted by. She pressed the checkbook into her hands. "Take it. My gift to you."

"Is this from the hot guy?" Sadie asked, a rapacious look in her eye.

No, from the total asshole, she wanted to say.

She was still in a foul mood that night when Rory joined her in the kitchen for dinner. "I heard you saw Evan today," she said, picking at her salad. "How was that?"

Rory stopped in her tracks for a moment, as if she'd forgotten something.

"What?" Isabel asked.

"Oh, nothing." Rory sat down and served herself some Cobb salad from the bowl on the counter. "Yeah, we met for lunch. Kind of randomly."

"That's cool," Isabel said, flicking through channels on the flat screen. "He said you guys had a good time."

"He said that?" Rory asked.

She seems jumpy tonight, Isabel thought, watching Rory shovel food into her mouth. "Yeah. Sounds like you had a better day than I did. Guess who came into the restaurant? Mike. And it wasn't even on purpose. He was there to have lunch."

"Did you want it to be on purpose?" Rory asked.

"The whole point," Isabel said, trying not to sound irritated, "is that he made this big declaration at the Ripcurl, and today, it was like I was any old waitress at any old diner. He didn't say a thing to me. It was like he'd never laid eyes on me before."

"Maybe he didn't think he could say anything to you. Like, it wouldn't be okay, at your place of work."

"Whatever," Isabel said, all pretense at not getting annoyed now gone. "He's over me now. Or he was drunk that night at the Ripcurl."

"But I thought things were going so well with Evan. Do you *want* Mike to still be into you?"

Isabel put her head in her hands. "No," she said. "I'm done with Mike. Once and for all. I said it before, and I'll say it again. That guy is a big waste of time."

"Isabel?" her mother called on the intercom. "Can you come up here, please?"

Isabel dropped her fork on her plate and stood up. "Yes!" she called out. "What does she want now?" she murmured to Rory.

"Good luck," Rory said, in a way that got under Isabel's skin.

Isabel went up the stairs, getting more furious at being summoned with every step. She went to her mother's bedroom door. "Yes?" she asked.

"What do you think of this dress?" her mother asked. "Be honest." She stood in the center of her room, in front of her full-length mirror. Her hand was on her hip, modeling a body-fitting tangerine-colored dress with a deep V-neck.

"What's that for?" Isabel asked.

"The party," Mrs. Rule said. "You know I'm throwing a party for my birthday."

"And you know that I'm not going," Isabel said.

"Isabel, please don't," she said.

"Why do you insist on these parties? That nobody wants you to have?"

"Because I enjoy it," she said. "Some of us enjoy serving hamburgers and fries, and some of us enjoy throwing parties. Now." She turned in front of Isabel. "Tell me. What do you think?"

Isabel gazed at the dress. "That one's nice," she conceded.

"Thank you. And just so you know, you can bring your new boyfriend. He's invited."

168

"How do you know I have a boyfriend?"

Her mother gave her a look. "I may be a little distracted these days, but I'm not an idiot."

"When are you going to give it up?" Isabel asked. "All this work? All this running around to make sure nobody suspects anything is wrong with us? Aren't you tired of the lie?"

Her mother sighed. "Here we go again. Saint Isabel lecturing me on how to live."

Isabel turned to leave. "I'm in a hurry. I have to get in the shower."

"What's his name?" her mother asked, arching a brow.

"Evan."

"Great. Then tell Evan he's expected here at a party on the twenty-sixth."

"This is all going to blow up in your face, sooner or later," Isabel said. "I hope you know that." Before her mom could respond, Isabel stalked out of the room and shut the door. She felt mean and small and petty, but at least she was being honest. It was more than she could say for anyone else in this family.

She sat down at her laptop and flipped up the cover. Her in-box stared back at her. Three e-mails, and no response at all from Mr. Knox. *Where did you go?* she wanted to write. *What happened to you? How could you just disappear on me?*

She slammed the laptop closed. This was what fathers did, she thought ruefully. They disappeared. She shouldn't have even been surprised.

CHAPTER FIFTEEN

Rory woke up on the morning of Mrs. Rule's party to the sound of enormous trucks screeching to a stop in front of the house. These had to be the tables and chairs. She lay there, too tired to get up, listening to the men begin to unload their cargo with curses and jokes. Mrs. Rule intended to throw the party of the summer, and there would be many more trucks and lots more cursing before the day was over. Beside her Connor slept peacefully on his side, facing away from her, oblivious to the noise. She reached out and lightly touched his shoulder. "Connor," she whispered.

He didn't move.

She leaned over and kissed his shoulder. He moved just a little and groaned slightly, turning around to face her. Then he wrapped an arm around her and pulled her to his chest. "Hmm, hmmm," he murmured, pressing her close, so close that it was hard for her to breathe.

Ever since the kiss with Evan on the beach, she'd made a point of spending the night in Connor's room. She'd made a point of spending other quality time with him as well—dinners, walks on the beach, playing tennis, riding their bikes to the movie theater on Main Street. She also made sure to avoid the subject of his parents. With a little bit of effort—*her* effort, really—they'd become a couple again. She felt proud of herself for her dedication, as if she'd received an A on a term paper she'd worked on for months. But there were still things that were out of her control. His tendency to hang out with people she couldn't stand was one of them.

The night before, Augusta had come bowling with them. It had been Connor's idea. Augusta was as silly and annoying as ever, prattling on constantly about the time they'd locked some friend of theirs out of one of the St. Paul's dorms, or something else equally stupid. *How can he stand these people?* she wondered. *What does he see in them?* A few minutes of hanging out with Augusta, and Rory was back to thinking about Evan.

Did he still like her? Did he think about her? Did he feel guilty about the kiss, or would he do it again if he had the chance? Sometimes the not knowing made her want to scream. She'd find herself staring at the few texts they'd sent each other before their lunch date, dissecting them, trying to read any hidden meaning in the words. Finally she'd tell herself to *stop*, because it didn't matter anyway—he was Isabel's boyfriend, unavailable, not even a possibility, for so many reasons. And she already felt terrible about the kiss. It had turned her into something she'd never thought she'd become in a million years: a cheater. She'd never done that to anybody, and even now it seemed so out of character, so unlike her, so against everything she stood for, that most of the time she couldn't believe she'd done it at all. When Isabel came back from seeing him, Rory would hold her breath, half expecting that she'd found out about the kiss, until it was clear that he hadn't said anything. And each time she knew he'd stayed quiet, she wondered how he felt. It was torture.

She glanced at her watch and disentangled herself from Connor's grasp.

"Hey," she whispered. "I gotta go."

Connor blinked his eyes open. "'Kay," he said, releasing her easily.

"I'll see you at breakfast," she said.

Connor kept his eyes closed, happy to fall back asleep. As she tiptoed out of the room, opening the door as slowly as possible and checking to make sure that Mrs. Rule's door was shut, she felt a slight weariness. Connor never spent the night in her room. He didn't take her out. If they went somewhere alone, it was her idea. Yes, they were on good terms again, but it seemed as if she was doing all the work. And as much as she didn't want to admit that, it was becoming harder and harder to ignore.

Isabel opened her eyes and realized with a start that she was still at Evan's. She didn't recognize it in daylight. White morning light streamed in through the spaces between the venetian blinds, making the green felt–upholstered chairs look even more depressing. On her cheek she could feel a dried thread of drool, along with the imprint of Jeff's uncle's scratchy, basket-weave pillow. Her head ached. Besides being worried about having completely broken her curfew, she felt a general distaste at having fallen asleep in her clothes.

Beside her Evan lay fully clothed, his mouth slightly open, a content look on his face. The tube TV on its stand flickered silently with static.

"Hey," she said, touching him on the shoulder. "Wake up."

Evan shifted groggily and opened one eye like a cat. "What time is it?" he asked.

She grabbed her watch. "It's around eight. I really need to go."

Evan yawned lazily and stretched. "Not yet," he said with a smile.

"No, now," she said, getting up.

Evan propped himself up on his elbows and looked around the room. "Damn, that movie must have been boring."

"I think I was just tired." She started dashing around the room, collecting her phone, bracelets, keys, and lipstick, which she'd left in various corners.

"Sorry that this is sort of my bedroom for now," he said. "I know it's kind of lame."

"That's okay," she said.

"I can talk to Jeff about working something out. There's gotta be something of mine that he wants."

"Really, it's not a big deal," she lied. More than once last night, Jeff had stomped out of his bedroom, walked past them on the way to the kitchen, grabbed a beer from the refrigerator six feet away, and then passed them again. Usually when they were in the middle of kissing.

"I thought you said he'd be out," Isabel had whispered at one point.

"I know, but he doesn't go anywhere without me," Evan had said. "Yo, dude!" he yelled down the hall. "Stay in your room!"

Eventually they gave up on trying to kiss and just watched a movie instead. As she snacked from a bowl filled with Veggie Pirate's Booty and drank a random sports drink she'd found in Evan's fridge, Isabel's thoughts turned to Mike. The sting of his snub at the restaurant had worn off, and she was back to fantasizing. She wondered what he was doing now, who he was with, if he still thought about her, and what would have happened if she'd kissed him at the Ripcurl that first night. She'd closed her eyes, thinking about him—those golden arms, that thick dark hair, those intense, searching, slightly wounded eyes, staring hard at her mouth.

Now she stumbled through the room, still groggy, trying not to bump her shin against the low coffee table. Thankfully she didn't have work today and could go home and take a nap.

"So what time's your mom's party tonight?" Evan asked, standing up.

"Oh, probably around seven."

"Do I need to put on a tie?"

"You *have* a tie?"

"Of course." Evan looked a little hurt at the implication that he didn't.

"You don't have to wear a tie, but a button-down would be good. A nice one. My mom is into clothes. Like, freakishly so." She walked up to him and gave him a chaste kiss on the cheek. "Morning breath," she explained.

"Right," said Evan.

Isabel thought he looked a little let down, but she never liked to kiss anyone before brushing her teeth. "See you tonight."

"See you," he said.

Rory was toasting a bagel in the kitchen when Isabel walked in.

"I need to find something for this stupid party tonight," Isabel said, sipping from a takeout cup of coffee. "Want to come with me to town?"

"I thought you weren't going to the party," Rory said.

"I'm going for an hour," Isabel said. "Evan's coming. Then we'll probably take off and go somewhere."

"Evan's coming?" Rory asked, taking out her bagel. This was interesting.

"Yeah. I figured I'd bite the bullet and invite him."

Rory thought quickly—she'd been planning on wearing jeans and a nice top. But now that Evan was coming, something a bit dressier might be better. "I'll go with you," she said.

Twenty minutes later, they were in Scoop NYC, rifling through the racks.

"I spent the night with Evan last night," Isabel announced.

"You *did?*"

"But only in the technical sense," Isabel said. "I fell asleep there by accident. Luckily my mom was too busy with the florists to even notice me coming in this morning."

"So was it fun?" Rory asked.

"Sort of," Isabel said. "But the guy doesn't even have his own bedroom. He's crashing in the living room right now. On a futon. His roommate came out, like, four times to get stuff

175

from the kitchen while we were making out. It was kind of a bummer."

Rory didn't want to think too hard about Isabel and Evan making out. "I'm sure Evan was embarrassed by that."

"Maybe, but I mean, come on. You know, Mike wasn't the best boyfriend in the world, I'll give you that. But at least he had his own room," Isabel said, taking three dresses to the fitting rooms.

Rory wondered why Isabel was bringing up Mike but decided to let it go. While Isabel was in the fitting room, a text came through on Rory's phone. It was from Connor.

Turned out to be a half day for me. Where r u? Wanna get
a bite?

Sure, she wrote back. With Isabel now. We're at Scoop.
Meet you in 15, Connor texted back.

Rory looked longingly at a cute electric-blue silk halter dress with purple beading along the bodice, hanging on a mannequin. It was four hundred dollars. Evan would think it was pretty; there was no doubt in her mind.

"Ugh, none of these work," Isabel said, emerging from the fitting room with an armful of dresses. She handed the salesgirl the balled-up dresses and then stopped in front of the manne-quin. "What about that one?" she said, pointing to the blue-and-purple-beaded dress.

"It's cute," Rory concurred.

"Lemme try it," she said.

The salesgirl removed it from the mannequin and gave it to Isabel.

A few minutes later, Rory watched as Isabel bought the electric-blue dress. Rory had told her it looked beautiful on her, but as Isabel casually handed her credit card to the salesgirl, Rory felt a pang. Things came so easily to her sometimes. It wasn't fair.

"Connor wants to meet us for lunch," Rory said as they walked out of the store into the hot afternoon.

"Okay," Isabel said.

Groups of tourists walking four abreast roamed the sidewalks, eating ice cream and window-shopping. Almost every store had a small American flag hanging above the window. Connor appeared from around the corner.

"There he is," Isabel said, pointing.

"Hey!" Rory called out. "This place is a zoo. Look at all these people."

"I rode my bike," Connor said. "It was my only hope."

"Where should we eat?" Isabel asked. "I'm starving."

"Mom asked me to go to Citarella and pick up a few things," Connor said.

"That's fine," said Rory. "We can grab sandwiches there."

They crossed Main Street and walked over to Citarella, where a stream of people continuously entered and exited its doors. Inside, the store was more packed than Rory had ever seen it. The line to pay snaked around the perimeter, and all the aisles were thick with shoppers.

They were on their way over to the sandwich counter when a petite, fortyish woman with a sleek brown bob and meticulously plucked eyebrows came over to them. She tapped Isabel excitedly on the shoulder. "Isabel!" she exclaimed. "Connor! Hello, you two!" The woman gave Isabel a hug. "How are you? We haven't seen you in ages!"

"Hi, Mrs. Quinlan," Isabel said politely. She turned to Rory. "This is Thayer's mom," she explained.

"Your mom tells me that you got some kind of job?" she asked, looking at both Connor and Isabel for confirmation of this.

"You know Isabel," Connor cut in. "She really likes to keep busy."

Fortunately Mrs. Quinlan seemed too scattered to catch Connor's evasion. "Isn't this place packed today?" she asked, looking around. "I came in to get some pancetta, and I don't think I'm going to get out for hours. Thayer's here," she said, craning her head to find her daughter in the crowd. "Well, she was just here. Oh, there she is. Thayer!" she called. "Look who's here!"

Rory turned to see Thayer coming toward them. She wore a belted linen dress with a horseshoe pattern and her usual expression of blasé ennui above it all.

"Hey," she said coolly.

Isabel tossed some blond hair over her shoulder and stiffened. "Hey," she replied.

"You need to come over one of these days," Mrs. Quinlan said to Isabel, oblivious to the coolness between the two girls. "We have a whole new kitchen now."

"Sure," Isabel said.

"Unless you're too busy working," Thayer said with an audible smugness. "Aren't you waiting tables? Or is that just a rumor?"

"No, it's not a rumor," Isabel said bravely.

"I heard you got into UPenn," Connor broke in, trying to change the subject.

"Yeah?" Thayer said.

"Some buddies of mine from St. Paul's go there. Let me know if you want their e-mails."

"Thanks," she said. "And is everything all right with your dad?"

"My dad?" Connor asked. "What do you mean?"

"Honey, don't bother them with that now," Mrs. Quinlan said in her raspy voice, looking embarrassed. "We should really get in line."

"I'm just asking. You were the one who told me about it," she said to her mom.

Mrs. Quinlan smiled. "I finally got my real estate license," she explained. "And the place on Gibson Lane in Sagaponack that was empty for years? Well, I heard there was a new tenant."

"Your *dad*," Thayer said, with obvious relish. "What's he doing there?"

Everyone was silent. Rory looked from Connor to Isabel, wondering who was going to take up the challenge.

"He and my mom are separated," Isabel said flatly. "And they're probably getting a divorce. Like, any minute. Anything else you want to know?"

Thayer smiled as if she'd expected this answer all along. Mrs. Quinlan looked anxious. "We really need to get back home, honey. Your father's probably starving." She put her hand on Isabel's shoulder again. "It was so good to run into you, sweetie. Really. Come by anytime. We'd love it."

Rory looked over at Connor. His eyes looked like they were

179

boring holes into his sister's face, and his lips were pursed and thin, almost drained of color.

"Okay," Thayer said, with the barest smirk. "It was great seeing you, Connor. And sorry, I've forgotten your name."

"Rory," she said.

"Right, *Rory*," Thayer said. "See ya."

Mother and daughter walked away toward the back of the line, leaving the three of them alone near the smoked-fish display. Connor immediately walked off toward the doors, leaving both Rory and Isabel in his wake.

"Where's he going?" Isabel asked.

Rory shook her head. "No clue."

They followed him out of the store and found him speed walking down the street, wading through a crowd of families, strollers, and dogs.

"Connor, calm down," Isabel said.

He wheeled around. "Are you crazy?" he asked. "What is wrong with you? Why would you say that?"

"Because it's the truth," Isabel said. "It's not like people aren't going to find out."

"But why would you hand it to them like that on a silver platter? Why not send an e-mail around the town with the whole story? Don't you know how fast that's going to get around? Right before the party tonight?"

"Connor, calm down," Rory said.

"They obviously knew something was up," Isabel said. "Why do you have this obsession with defending Mom and Dad?"

"Because I care about this family."

"Connor, let it go. Drop the perfect-son routine. You're not

180

going to get any points." She lowered her voice. "And you know that Mom had an affair. Don't you?"

Connor's eyes flashed. "What the hell does *that* have to do with anything?"

"It has everything to do with *everything*," Isabel said. "They screwed up, and now they're too chickenshit to come out to the world and admit all their mistakes. So they're trying to recruit all of us to bail them out. It's sick."

"You would believe the worst about them," Connor said, turning away.

"I don't have to believe it." Isabel's voice turned flinty. "I have *proof*."

"You have proof?" he asked, disgust lacing his voice. "Like what?"

Isabel darted her eyes at Rory.

Connor turned toward Rory. "Do you know something about this?"

"No," Rory said, looking down. "I don't know anything."

"Then why did she look at you like that?"

"Isabel's just trying to be honest," Rory said. "She's not trying to cause trouble or be crazy or any of that other stuff you think."

"What do you mean, be honest?" he said. "What do you know?"

"N-nothing," she said.

"Stop being so immature," Isabel said. "She didn't do anything."

"She's my girlfriend. She's supposed to be on my side," Connor said. He turned back to Rory. "I don't get it. What is it you know about all this?"

"She knows nothing, okay?" Isabel cut in. "But even if I were to tell you, you wouldn't be able to hear it. You're in too much denial."

"Right, *I'm* in denial," Connor said. "You want to know why you can't hang on to any of your friends? Because you alienate everyone in your life. You push people away. And you don't even see it."

Rory's stomach ached, and her head felt light. "Connor, don't be mad. Come on."

"No, I think I need to be alone for a little bit," he said, stepping away from her outstretched hand. "I'll see you later." He crossed Main Street just as the light was about to turn, and headed down Newtown Lane. Then he slipped into an alley toward the parking lot and was gone.

"Well, that was interesting," Isabel said.

"Why *did* you say that to Thayer, in front of him? You must have known that he was going to freak out."

"Connor needs to face reality. And if you're not going to make him do that, then it may as well be me."

"Not everyone needs to be improved, Isabel. Sometimes people are getting by the best way they can."

"Oh, come off it, Ror," Isabel said. "I know you're not happy. It's so obvious. But you're just like him. Always wanting to put on this perfect display."

"Maybe I'm just trying to make things work."

"No, maybe you're a *doormat*," Isabel said.

"A doormat?" Rory asked.

"Yeah. I don't know what happened to you. Last summer

you were so kick-ass. You did your own thing. I looked up to you. You didn't care about changing who you were for a guy. Now you have a boyfriend, and it's like you've become a robot."

"Lay off me, okay?" Rory snapped. "I'm sick of watching you act like a spoiled brat. Yeah, okay, you've been dealt a rough hand. So have I. And you don't see me taking it out on the entire world."

Rory watched as Isabel set her face in the same disgusted, haughty, and totally over-it stare that she'd given Rory the first day they met. "Fine," she spat. "I'm out of here."

She crossed the street with her head held high, swinging her shopping bag like she didn't have a care in the world. She was so much like her mother, Rory realized. Both of them always needing to have the last word. Both of them so lonely, but always pushing people away.

CHAPTER SIXTEEN

Isabel threw the shopping bag in the car. She barely noticed as her new dress spilled across the backseat in folds of blue silk and then finally slipped down onto the floor of the car. She pulled out of the lot and turned east on Montauk Highway, speeding toward Amagansett. The words *spoiled brat* rang in her head, making her grip the steering wheel. So that was what Rory thought of her. At least it was better than being a coward. Rory and Connor deserved each other.

She drove through Amagansett without stopping. She wasn't sure where she was headed, except that to go in the other direction, toward home, would feel like defeat. Eventually the shops and the homes fell away, and the road became pure highway, just blue sky and green trees on either side of her, a straight shot toward Montauk and the farthest end of Long Island. Ditch Plains would make her feel better. She was pretty sure that she had a suit in the trunk. The pink-painted structure of Buford's Lobster Shack appeared on her right and then vanished behind her. Another reason to think of Mike. All of this was his fault. If he'd only been a decent guy to her last summer, then maybe she wouldn't have taken the news about Mr. Knox so hard. She had Evan, she remembered, but she wasn't sure that she wanted him anymore.

She reached Montauk and drove through town, toward the nondescript street that led to the permitless parking lot for Ditch Plains. She changed into her suit lying down on the backseat, grabbed a towel from the trunk, and got out. The ocean breeze was cool in the midday sun, and as she headed toward the sound of pounding surf, she felt her breath start to come more easily. Ditch Plains looked exactly the same. The pebbled beach looked inviting, filled with young children and couples and dogs. A flock of surfers floated on top of their boards in the lineup, waiting their turn.

She wished now that she had a board and her wet suit. Today would be perfect for surfing. And then she remembered—Mike worked in the surfboard store in town. He would rent her a board, maybe even for free. He certainly owed her that.

She turned on her heels and walked back to her car, ignoring the voice that told her that this was a really, really bad idea. She drove into town and pulled over at the first surfboard store she saw. From her parked car she could see the panoply of wet suits hanging above the open door and the stack of neon-colored shortboards leaning against the store window. This had to be the one. Now if only she knew exactly what to say to him. Or what she wanted him to say to her.

She got out of the car, and realized with a start that she was still wearing only her bikini and flip-flops. *Whatever,* she thought. That very first day they'd met he'd seen her topless, so what did it matter now? She slammed the door and made her way toward the store. She hoped this place had a bathroom.

The store was narrow and deep and crowded with racks of wet suits, stacks of surfboards, and snowboards hanging on the walls. She pulled off her sunglasses and blinked as her eyes adjusted to the dim interior. Sublime played on the speakers, and the air was thick with the smell of brand-new neoprene and cocoa-butter suntan lotion.

"Can I help you?" Mike stepped out from behind a rack of wet suits and brushed a wavy lock of hair out of his eyes. At the sight of her, he stopped short. "Isabel," he said. "Hi."

"I need a surfboard," she said without preamble. "And a wet suit. To rent, if you have it."

His eyes traveled the length of her half-naked body. "Where are you surfing?"

"Ditch Plains. I forgot my stuff."

"Okay. You want a shortboard?"

"Sure," she said. A blast of air-conditioning hit her from up high, and she put her arms around herself. The last thing she needed was to have crazy headlights in front of Mike right now.

"You cold?" he asked. "You want a rash guard?"

"I'm okay. Just the board and the wet suit. And do you have a bathroom?"

"Yeah, it's in back," he said, pointing.

She marched to the back of the store, past another sales clerk who sat behind the counter, engrossed in a game on his iPhone. She guessed that the door in the wall led to the bathroom, and she was right. The walls were covered with stickers advertising boards, wet suits, and surf wax, and the sink and toilet looked like they hadn't been cleaned in several years. It reminded her of that first time she'd gone to Mike's house and hid in the bathroom during his surprise party. The mess had been appalling, and also weirdly sexy. *If only I'd known*, she thought, running some water over her face. Of course his place of work would be just as filthy. Why had she come here? She was so confused. All she wanted to do right now was go home. This had been a mistake.

When she emerged from the bathroom, the other sales clerk was gone, and Mike was waiting for her at the counter with a wet suit and yellow shortboard. "I think this should be it," he said. "What do you think?"

She avoided his gaze and looked at the merchandise. "Looks good." She pulled out her credit card and handed it to him. "Here."

Mike took her card and then looked at her closely, cocking his head. "Isabel, are you all right?"

"Yeah. Why?"

"You seem like you're having a pretty bad day, that's all."

"Maybe I am."

"You want to tell me about it?" he asked, swiping her card.

"Not especially."

He didn't seem fazed.

"Stuff with my family," she admitted.

"Like what?" he asked.

"Do you really think that I'm going to confide in you?"

"Well, you're here, right?" he asked, giving her a knowing smile.

"I needed a board and a wet suit," she said evenly.

"Right," Mike said. "Of course. Well, don't let me keep you, then." He handed her the credit-card slip to sign.

"So *now* you want me to be your friend?" she asked. "*Now* you're interested in chitchat?"

"Well, you came in, didn't you?"

"Not because I needed to talk to you," she said.

"Right. So this was all just an accident."

"No more of an accident than you coming into my restaurant," she said. She signed the credit-card slip.

"Actually, that *was* an accident. My cousin Tony happens to like the food there." Mike pulled off her copy of the slip. "Here's your receipt."

Isabel stared at the receipt. "So I don't get it," she said. "You give me this whole speech about how you miss me and how you want another chance. And then I see you at *my* place of work, and you act like you barely know me."

"What did you want me to do?" Mike asked. "You told me at the Ripcurl that you have a boyfriend."

"So?" she snapped.

Mike shook his head. "Maybe you need to get in the water and just take a minute."

"Don't tell me what to do," she said, feeling her anger at Connor and Rory escalate into fury. "And why would I want to give you another chance? You didn't want to meet my parents. You left town as soon as we started sleeping together. Everything I told you about my life, you didn't seem to care. Oh, and let's not forget, you were just trying to get info out of me for your family. So, tell me. Why would I want to give Mike Castelloni another chance?"

Mike didn't say anything.

"Because I'll tell you something," she said. "I do not miss you."

"Yeah, you do," he said softly.

Rage sizzled through her. She snatched the credit-card slip out of his hand. "Gimme my card back. Now."

Mike handed it back to her. "Isabel—"

Before he could finish, she headed for the door. She got into her car, slammed the door, and drove out of the parking lot with so much abandon that she didn't even remember her surfboard until she was halfway home.

CHAPTER SEVENTEEN

Connor's car was still missing. Rory walked around to the front of the house and looked down the long gravel drive. Any moment now, she expected to see a silver Audi round the corner and come zooming down the path, but there was nothing. She turned around and limped her way back across the gravel. The healed blister on her heel had opened up again during her walk home from town that afternoon. Of course, there was always the possibility that Connor might not come home at all. In some ways, she would admire that. Skipping his mom's birthday party seemed like a step in the right direction. But the idea that he would be upset enough to leave her alone for the rest of the night, without so much as a text, made her deeply sad.

She walked back toward the house, past a line of valets wearing black vests and red cummerbunds, fidgeting like teenage guys suited up for the prom. They all looked at her as she went past. She'd settled for wearing the too-short Calypso dress she'd worn to the Georgica the first night. Inside, she could hear the cater waiters in the kitchen, opening and shutting the oven and slamming aluminum baking trays on the island. A cater waiter in a white tux blew through the swinging door, carrying a chafing dish. He turned and smiled at her. Rory mustered a smile in return. She felt completely useless. At least last summer Bianca had given her those dumb candles to light and then float on the surface of the pool. Now she had nothing to do except stalk around the house by herself—a summer guest not on speaking terms with half the people in this house.

"Rory, are you down there?" Mrs. Rule called.

"Yes?" she yelled.

"Can you come up here and help me with something, please? I'm in my room."

Apparently there was one person in the house whom she was still on good terms with. She slipped off her heels and held them in her hand as she limped up the stairs, murmuring "Ow" with every step.

Upstairs she slipped her shoes back on and knocked on Mrs. Rule's door, which stood slightly ajar.

"Come in, said a voice."

Rory pushed open the door and found Mrs. Rule in the center of the room, wearing a floor-length, one-shoulder gown with a high slit up one leg. If Mrs. Rule's objective tonight was to look like she was attending a red carpet soiree, she'd definitely succeeded.

"Does this look okay?" Mrs. Rule said, doing a complete turn so that the dress swished up at the ankles. "Is it too much?"

"It's very pretty," she said.

Mrs. Rule stopped and examined herself in the full-length

mirror. She seemed to like what she saw. "Good," she said. "I wasn't sure. Thought it might be too much."

"Oh no," Rory said.

"Is Mr. Rule here yet?"

"I haven't seen him."

"Could you go down and make sure he's here? And then let him know that I'd like him to come up here in about ten minutes? We should make our entrance together." Mrs. Rule went to her satin-skirted vanity table and pulled out a thick gold-and-pearl-encrusted bracelet from a box.

"Maybe it would be better for you to ask one of your kids to do that," Rory said.

Mrs. Rule looked at her with surprise. "Do you know where Connor is? I asked him to get me some things this afternoon, and he never came back to the house."

Rory bit her lip. "I don't."

"You don't?"

"We decided to take some time to ourselves today," she said, trying to sound breezy.

Mrs. Rule gave Rory a knowing look. "One thing about men is that they always need to know that they're right. You just tell him that you're sorry, and it will all be fine."

That didn't quite work out for you and Mr. Rule, Rory felt like saying.

"And have you been able to say anything to Isabel? About what we talked about?" She leaned over her vanity table mirror and applied some crimson lipstick.

"I don't think that's my place, Mrs. Rule."

192

"It's Lucy," said Mrs. Rule, putting the lipstick down. "And it *is* your place. You're part of this family now. Oh. And I almost forgot." She disappeared into her walk-in closet and came out with a small periwinkle-blue bag. "I got you something." Mrs. Rule handed Rory the shopping bag. The black lettering on the side read TIFFANY & CO. "Go ahead. Take it."

Slowly, almost as if she were fighting her better judgment, Rory reached for the bag. Inside was a small, smooth periwinkle box. She opened it to find a gold necklace with an inky-blue stone pendant resting on the cushioned interior.

"I can't take this," Rory said.

"Of course you can. Put it on. After all, that dress you're wearing needs something."

Rory put the bag and the box on a nearby chair and draped the chain around her neck.

"Here," said Mrs. Rule, helping Rory to fasten the necklace. "Now, look." She pulled Rory over to the full-length mirror. "Isn't that beautiful?"

Rory looked at herself. It was true. The necklace elevated everything—her makeup, her hair, her plain dress. It was the most glamorous thing she'd ever seen on herself.

"It's blue topaz," said Mrs. Rule. "I thought it would look pretty on you."

"You should give this to Isabel. It would look just as good on her. Probably better."

"She wouldn't appreciate it," Mrs. Rule said in a cynical tone. "Now, would you be a dear and go run and tell Mr. Rule to come up here around six thirty? That would really help."

Rory watched Mrs. Rule flit back to the mirror. "Okay," she said. Now that she had this around her throat, there was little else to say.

She left Mrs. Rule's room and couldn't help but notice Isabel's closed door across the hall. A thin sliver of light showed from underneath it.

"Isabel?" she said, gently knocking. "Can I come in?"

Rory listened. There was no sound inside. Apparently Isabel wasn't ready to forgive her yet.

Isabel sat curled up in her tufted chair by the window, nursing her second Jack and Coke and watching cars come up the drive. Her mom had hired the same caterers as she had for her dad's birthday party last year, and luckily their serving policy hadn't changed. Last year a ten-dollar tip had gotten her a nicely mixed drink without ID. Tonight a twenty-dollar tip had gotten a nicely mixed drink brought straight up to her room.

She sipped her drink, savoring the fiery taste of the whiskey. It reminded her of who she used to be out here in the Hamptons—the girl most likely to stay out all night, the girl most likely to break hearts and not care, the girl most likely to instill fear in anyone who wound up on her bad side. Last year, she could have reduced Thayer Quinlan to tears if she'd wanted to. But here she was, being taunted by Thayer in front of Thayer's mom at Citarella, of all places. Waiting tables. Dating a guy who felt like more of a friend than anything else. Unappreciated by a best friend. Ignored by a man who said he was her father. And part of a family whose refusal to be honest was making her sick.

Isabel closed her eyes and took another long sip of her Jack and Coke. Mike had betrayed her, too, most importantly. Of course, she'd sort of asked for it, going to see him like that, throwing herself in his path. And he hadn't disappointed. His smug, self-righteous attitude still rankled her. And at least right now, she knew exactly what to do about him.

She took out her phone and scrolled down to his number. Just a simple text would do. Nothing more.

Don't ever bother me again, she wrote and hit send.

A tiny voice said that she might regret that later. She took another sip. Better keep drinking, just in case.

Mrs. Rule's party looked more like a celebrity wedding than a simple, intimate birthday party. Four-foot-high centerpieces of white lilies, roses, and peonies topped the tables flanking the pool. Crystal chandeliers hung from the ceiling of the clear plastic tent erected between the pool and the beach. A bevy of hurricane candles flickered on every conceivable surface outside. Inside the tent, Rory waded among tables laid with cheese and charcuterie, sushi and tempura, tiny bite-size hamburgers, and mini lobster rolls. *All this to show people that everything's fine,* she thought. What a waste of money.

More white-suited cater waiters were posted here, standing guard behind each area, ready to serve. "Lobster roll?" one of them offered, gesturing to a geometric display of tiny rolls topped with lobster salad.

"No, thanks," she said.

So far most of the guests had yet to leave the flagstone patio in front of the pool and come in here. After a few moments she could see why. Mr. Rule stood in the center of the crowd, sipping his Scotch on the rocks and laughing and chatting. *Maybe a part of him is secretly enjoying this,* Rory thought. After all, nobody was forcing him to show up here and play the happy host. He seemed more than willing to participate. Still, she couldn't approach him and tell him to run upstairs to their bedroom. It made her feel like more of an accomplice in their little charade than she already was.

"Rory," a voice said.

She turned. With a start she watched Evan walk into the tent, and her heart raced.

"Wow," he said, looking around at all the food. "I'm pretty sure we could feed most of Detroit in here." It was the first time she'd seen him since the beach. She almost didn't recognize him. His sport jacket gave him a more polished look, even though he wore it over a T-shirt instead of a button-down. And he seemed to have tried to do battle with his permanent bed head using a comb and a little bit of hair product. Rory wasn't sure if this was Isabel's influence, but it was working. "You look lost," he went on. "Too many choices?"

"It's a little overwhelming," she said.

"Isabel said to wear a jacket. She didn't say anything about a lobster bib, though," he said, pointing to the mini lobster rolls.

"*Annie Hall,*" Rory said, pointing at him.

"Nice," he said.

"It's the scene where he meets her parents. I love that scene."

"I love the one where they're in line to see the movie, and the guy behind them is being so annoying?"

"Oh my god, that's the best," she said. "I love that movie."

"Me, too. I saw it when I was twelve. It took me years to get all the jokes."

In the pause that followed, she ambled over to the sushi.

"Where's Connor?" Evan asked.

"He's coming. I think."

"You think?" He smiled gently. "What does that mean?"

"Well…we had a bit of a fight today."

"Oh. That sucks."

"Yeah, it was just one of those things," she said, feeling him getting closer.

Suddenly Evan put his hand on her arm. "How are you?" he asked, looking into her eyes.

"Evan," she said, moving away.

"I can't stop thinking about you. And Isabel and I…I don't think it's gonna work out. Whatever it is, it's totally separate from you and me."

"Evan, there is no you and me," she said. "What about Isabel?"

"Are you guys talking about me?" Isabel said, walking toward them. The blue silk dress fit her perfectly. It set off her toned, tanned shoulders and made her waist appear even narrower than it was. Looking at her now, Rory knew that she would never have been able to do that dress justice. But she also noticed that Isabel's gait was a little unsteady. "Ah, hair product," she said, tentatively touching Evan's mane. "I like it."

"Yeah, I went crazy with the hair gel," he said. "Didn't want to be afraid of it anymore."

Isabel took another step and stumbled.

"Are you okay?" Evan asked.

"I'm great. Do you want something to drink? Or eat?" She pawed Evan's arm. She had yet to look Rory in the eye. "Or maybe we should get out of here."

"How about we eat something?" Evan said. "What looks good?"

Isabel wrinkled her nose. "Nothing."

"Are you serious?" He chuckled. "Come on, I'm sure something looks appetizing."

Isabel let go of Evan's arm with what looked like a gesture of disgust. "Stop freaking out. I'm getting another drink," she said, and marched out of the tent.

"Is she drunk?" Evan asked.

"We had kind of a fight earlier," Rory said. "I think she's had a rough day."

"She smells like a bottle of Jack Daniel's."

"I'll go to her," Rory said,

She hurried out of the tent and past the pool toward the group of people milling around. The party had doubled in size by now. Waiters passed by with trays topped with all kinds of delicacies: blinis covered with caviar, tiny grilled cheese sandwiches, sushi rolls. Isabel was nowhere to be seen. She spied Mr. and Mrs. Rule standing together in a knot of guests, their arms draped around each other's waists. She'd forgotten all about reminding Mr. Rule to go upstairs.

"Rory!" cried Mrs. Rule. "Rory, come here, I'd like to introduce you to someone." Mrs. Rule didn't seem to even notice that Rory had forgotten her errand.

"Rory, meet Mr. and Mrs. Wilcox," Mrs. Rule said, gesturing to a tall, older couple. "They're dear old friends of ours."

"Hi," Rory said, shaking their hands.

"Rory is Connor's girlfriend," said Mrs. Rule in a doting voice. "Is Connor back yet?" Her voice was sweet, but her gaze was startlingly direct.

"He should be here any minute."

"He's probably finishing up a run," said Mr. Rule.

"That's right, he's quite an athlete," said Mr. Wilcox. "How's the swimming going?"

"Well, he's done with that," said Mr. Rule. "But now running is his passion. Though I like to say that he gets that from me."

"Larry has run five miles a day since the day we met," Mrs. Rule said proudly.

"That's so funny you mention running," said Mrs. Wilcox. "I saw you running the other day. But not around here. It was in Sagaponack. Near Gibson Lane."

Mrs. Rule smiled even wider. "Larry likes to run *all* over town," she said, with a tinkly little laugh.

"But it was late, after dark," Mrs. Wilcox went on. "I wasn't sure it was you, even, because it was so dark, but then I noticed that you had on the Georgica Club Paddle Tennis championship T-shirt. And then I knew it was you. I thought, there's Larry Rule."

Rory saw Mrs. Rule dart a nervous glance her husband's way.

"It probably was me," Mr. Rule said, prompted by his wife's look. "Sometimes I'll start a little too late, and not even realize that it's gotten dark."

"Oh, good," Mrs. Wilcox said, placing a dramatic hand on her chest. "So there's no truth to the rumors."

"What rumors are those?" Mrs. Rule asked.

"Patty," cautioned her husband.

"Oh, Martin, there's no truth to it, obviously," Mrs. Wilcox said, waving him off. She directed her attention to Mrs. Rule. "It's all so silly."

"What is?" Mrs. Rule asked, her gaze becoming even more focused.

"There's some rumor going around town that the two of you are living in different houses this summer," said Mrs. Wilcox.

Mr. and Mrs. Rule's faces stayed blank.

"It's ridiculous, I told you," Mrs. Wilcox said.

Mrs. Rule shook her head. "Wow. That's a new one," she said, glancing once more at her husband.

"I wonder where that came from," Mr. Rule said, though not quite as convincingly.

"I should probably go look for Connor," Rory said. "It was nice to meet you." She stepped back into the crowd as quickly as possible and headed straight for the house. The Rules' discomfort had been too much to witness. As much as she wanted the act to end, it was uncomfortable to watch it start to fall apart.

As she reached the back door, she spotted a group of people making their way toward the party from the driveway. Connor was one of them. Augusta trailed behind him, plus two girls and a guy Rory had never seen before. The mere sight of Augusta with Connor sent her heart beating faster. Of course that's who he'd been with. She should have known. "Connor," she said, stepping in his path.

"Hey," he said. "How's it going?" His eyes roamed past her toward the party as if he was already eager to keep moving.

"Why didn't you text me?" she asked, touching the pendant at her chest.

"Hi, Rory!" Augusta said, marching up to them and grabbing Rory to kiss her on the cheek. "Oh my effing god, that is a gorgeous necklace."

"Oh, thanks," Rory said, letting her hand fall away from the stone.

"Oh, and this is Gisele, Selden, and Rafaella," Augusta said, introducing her friends. "They're visiting from the UK."

The two girls were tall and waifishly thin, dressed in vintage baby-doll dresses and black tights. The guy had intense dark eyes and an impressive five o'clock shadow. He was on a cell phone but held up his fingers in a salute.

"Hi," Rory said. She took Connor's hand. "Can I talk to you? Alone?"

"We'll go find the bar," Augusta said, leading her coterie of jet-setters toward the pool.

"So that's where you've been? Augusta's?" she asked.

"Yeah, I said I needed some time to myself."

"Doesn't sound like that's what you had."

"I'm here now, aren't I?"

"Surrounded by your little posse of admirers."

"Maybe they're the only people I can trust right now," he said, giving her a cold look.

"What is that supposed to mean?"

"Whose side are you on here? Mine or my sister's?"

"There are no sides," she said. "Why do you keep saying that?"

"You're part of this family now. You're my girlfriend. You're living here. To be honest it feels like you're being a little ungrateful when you side with my crazy sister."

Rory felt her insides collapse. "Ungrateful?"

"Yeah, it does. You're in this house, you're here all summer, and you and Isabel are talking shit about my family the whole time. And then telling me that I have no right to defend them. I think I deserve better than that."

His words sawed through her like a dull knife. "I'm not talking shit about your family, Connor. There's something you need to know."

Connor's expression was skeptical. "What?"

"Isabel has a different father," she said quietly.

"Excuse me?" he said.

"His name is Peter Knox. He and his wife were friends with your parents. Your mom...and Mr. Knox...They had an affair. That's why your parents are getting a divorce."

Connor threw up his hand. "Stop it," he said. "Just stop."

"Connor, I'm not saying this to disturb you. It's the truth—"

"Stop it," he said. In the light from the setting sun, his face had gone pale.

"Isabel is someone else's daughter. Not your dad's."

"That's it, Rory," he said, stepping away from her. "I'm done." He stormed off toward the pool.

"Connor, wait!" she yelled, racing after him. Beyond Connor she could see Isabel walking straight toward them, weaving unsteadily on her heels.

"Is it true?" Connor demanded, going up to Isabel.

"Is what true?" Isabel asked. Rory could smell the liquor emanating from her.

"What Rory told me," he said, pointing to Rory. "About Mom. And Mr. Knox. Is it true?"

"Yes." Isabel slapped a hand on Rory's arm. "Thank god she finally told you."

"This is bullshit," he said. "I want proof."

"I am proof," Isabel said. "You want me to call Mr. Knox, put him on the phone for you? I'm happy to."

"Isabel," Rory said.

"No, he has to accept this," she said, her voice a little too loud. "Mom didn't just have an affair. She had a *kid* with another man. Me. And then lied about it. Now do you get it? Now do you get why it makes me so angry to be in this family?"

"You made this up," Connor said. "It's all part of the sick way you justify your craziness to everyone."

"Mom admitted it to me. It's true. Why do you think I've never gotten along with Dad? Why do you think he's always been so hard on me? It makes sense now, doesn't it?"

Connor glanced at Rory.

"I wouldn't make this stuff up, Connor. I just want you to know the truth. You deserve that," Isabel said.

"She's right," Rory admitted.

Connor shook his head, as if it were all too much. "Both of

you are crazy." He looked at Rory, wild-eyed. Then he turned to his sister. "You're completely insane." He brushed past them toward the pool.

Rory and Isabel stood in silence for a moment, until Isabel clapped a hand over her mouth. "I think I'm gonna be sick," she said, and went running toward the house.

Rory stood, wondering whether to run after Isabel. She decided to get Evan instead. She found him standing at the entrance to the tent, staring at the sea.

"Isabel's sick," she said, grabbing his arm. "In the house. You should go to her."

Evan took off without a word. Rory watched him rush toward the house, the gallant boyfriend. She walked back toward the house, still numb. All this time she'd been trying to get up the guts to end things with Connor, and now he'd dumped her. One moment she'd been part of the family. Now he'd cast her out for her betrayal. She knew that she had to let him go, but it still felt like a knife stuck in her heart.

She touched the necklace once more, and it suddenly occurred to her: This wasn't a gift. It was another bribe. Mrs. Rule needed to make sure that she would stay quiet, with the people of East Hampton, and her own son. Rory fumbled with the clasp, until it finally gave way. The necklace slid off her neck and into her hand, so much more easily than she would have guessed.

CHAPTER EIGHTEEN

Isabel opened her eyes. Her head felt like it had been stuffed with rocks. The morning light coming in around the edges of the curtains burned her corneas. The room tilted from one side to the other, like a listing boat. This was, by far, the worst hangover she'd ever had.

She raised herself up on her elbows and tried to blink. The details of last night were hazy—who had put her to bed? When had she gone to bed? How had she gotten so drunk? And then the glimmer of a memory came back to her. Mike. Seeing him at the surf shop. Their fight. Then a lot of Jack and Cokes.

From the direction of her nightstand she could hear a persistent buzzing, like a trapped insect. She felt around the table in the dim light for the source, and then located her phone. She turned it around so that she could see its face. It was almost too bright to look at. And then she saw the text from Mike.

No problem. Take care.

What the hell does that mean? she thought. Then she opened her phone and went to the text screen. There was her message to him, sent last night at 6:16 PM:

Don't ever bother me again.

A stabbing pain shot through her head. She needed to go to the bathroom. She put the phone back down on the bedside table and saw that someone had left her Advil and a glass of water. She jiggled two maroon tablets out of the bottle and swallowed them with the water. Then she forced herself out of bed, splashed some water on her face, and sat on the toilet, trying to ignore the spinning bathroom.

So she and Mike were basically over. He wouldn't show up on her doorstep and beg for her to give him a second chance. And then there was Evan. It was all coming back to her now in humiliating waves—Evan holding her head as she threw up in her bathroom, Evan helping her off with her dress and putting her to bed in, apparently, her underwear. It was all too embarrassing. She staggered back to bed and closed her eyes.

A knock on the door startled her back to full consciousness. "What?" she croaked, keeping her eyes shut tight.

The door opened, and Isabel heard her mother sigh. "Well, good morning, darling daughter. You look fresh as a rosebud."

Isabel opened her eyes an inch to see her mom, still in her nightgown, whip open her curtains. "Please don't do that," she said.

"I want to know what you've said about this family," her mom said. Painful bright light flooded the room.

Isabel roused herself from her pillow and tried to focus on the slim but blurry shape of her mother, standing at the foot of her bed. "What are you talking about?"

"Last night Mrs. Wilcox told me there's a rumor going around about us. That we're living in different homes. And I would like to know how that rumor got started."

Isabel rubbed her eyes. "Are you serious? Did you really think that this wasn't going to get out?"

"You're not answering my question." The harsh morning light made her mother's crow's-feet and frown lines alarmingly visible. "Who did you tell?"

"I've told everybody," Isabel said. "Everyone I can. Everyone I see. Everyone who asks. They all get to hear all about it. Because I'm *so* obsessed with your life."

Mrs. Rule picked up her silk dress, lying in a heap on her duvet, and let it drop back into a wrinkled pile. "Leave it to you to get drunk last night. Your father hasn't seen you in weeks, and that's when you get drunk."

"Can you blame me?"

Her mother took a deep breath. "Don't try to pin this on me. I'm not your excuse, Isabel. Don't use me as a reason to keep doing what you've been doing for years." She shut the door, and Isabel lay back in bed. Her headache was now unbearable.

Rory walked through the swinging door into the breakfast room, which was mercifully empty. In the center of the round rattan table was a leftover floral arrangement from the party last night, and at one end was a stack of newspapers, the same ones that she'd had to run out and buy every morning last summer.

An array of vitamins and supplements lined Mrs. Rule's place setting, as usual. At Rory's place setting stood a jar of lemon curd—Mickey had figured out by now that she'd developed a fondness for it. Looking at it now, she realized how crazily pretentious that was.

She went to the credenza and poured herself a bowl of cereal from one of the twenty or so boxes on display. Her strategy was to eat quickly and hightail it back to her room. There were too many people in this house that she wanted to avoid.

Fee's kind face peeked through the doorway. "Good morning, my dear. You all set out here?"

Rory put down her cereal and felt tears come to her eyes again.

"What is it? What's wrong?"

Rory walked over to her and started crying in her arms.

"Here, here," Fee said.

"Can we go to your room for a minute?" Rory wiped the tears with the back of her hand, but she could barely keep up with them.

"Of course." Holding her by the hand, Fee led her swiftly down the back stairs and along the quiet hall to her room. She closed the door as Rory went to sit on the bed, and then pushed a box of tissues into Rory's hands. "When you're ready, I want to hear all about it," she said gently.

Rory pulled multiple sheets of tissue out of the box and cleaned up her face as much as she could. "Connor and I..." She blew her nose. "Connor and I broke up last night."

Fee didn't look the least bit surprised. "Oh, my dear," she said softly. "How did it happen?"

Haltingly, and with the help of more tissue, Rory managed to string together an edited version of what had gone wrong between them this summer, without mentioning the secret about Isabel's real father. "Last summer was so much easier," she said. "I don't know why."

Fee stroked Rory's arm. "It's always easier to be on the outside. Why do you think this is still my bedroom?" She gestured to the cramped space. "I love working for this family. But I've never forgotten I *work* for them."

"So you're saying it was a mistake to get involved with Connor?"

"No, not at all, dear," said Fee. "He made you happy. There's nothing wrong with wanting to be with someone who makes you happy."

"I guess I thought if I tried hard enough, it would all work out."

"That's what your mother's done to you," Fee said softly. "It's not your job to make things work out. It takes two people. And it doesn't sound to me like he wanted things to work out as much as you did."

Rory nodded. She blew her nose. "But now what? Do I leave here? Do I go back home? I still have my internship. How do I stay here and have it not be massively awkward?"

"It won't be."

"But what if he wants me to leave?"

Fee snorted. "You're talking to the house manager. And you *are* my niece. Nobody is kicking you out of here without getting past me first. Now, let's get you back upstairs for breakfast," she said. "Is there anything special Mickey can get for you?"

Rory thought for a moment. "Blueberry pancakes?"

"Perfect," Fee said, guiding her to the door.

"But only if you let me make them," Rory said. "I haven't so much as measured a cup of water since I've been here."

"I think we can arrange that."

After fortifying herself with pancakes, she decided to go speak to Connor. Better to confront him and let him say whatever else needed to be said. Maybe by now his anger had dissipated, and he'd be able to think and talk a little more clearly.

She walked up the stairs and knocked on his closed door. "Connor?" she said. "It's me. Can I talk to you?"

He opened the door. His hair was wet from the shower. On his shoulder was his zippered gym bag. It looked very full.

"You're leaving?" she asked.

"I'm gonna stay with my dad for a while, yeah."

"Because of me?"

He didn't blink. "You're one of the reasons, yeah."

"I know you're mad," she said. "If you have anything you want to say, I'm here. You can tell me."

"What do you want me to say?" he said, glaring at her. "You're the one with all the information. I'm the idiot who doesn't know anything."

"I didn't tell you those things to hurt you. I hope you know that."

"It doesn't matter." A muscle pulsed in his jaw, and he moved to walk past her. "Is there anything else you want to say?"

"No," she said, feeling a knot form in her throat.

"Tell my mom if she needs me, I'll be at my dad's. And I

guess you'll be here?" he said, throwing her a sardonic look over his shoulder.

Before she could answer, he was heading down the stairs. She stayed on the landing and listened to him leave the house through the back door. A few minutes later she heard the whine of his engine as he started his car, and then the crunch of gravel under his tires. He was gone. But the Connor she'd fallen in love with last summer had left quite a while ago. It had simply taken her until now to see that.

Isabel's bedroom door opened. A girl with a greenish-tinged face, bloodshot eyes, and tangled blond hair who faintly resembled Isabel, peeked out her head.

"Oh my god," Rory said. "You look like hell."

"Thanks for rubbing it in," Isabel said. "I need to get to the kitchen, but I might throw up. Can I hold on to you?"

"Sure."

Rory went to the door, and Isabel stepped out in a threadbare navy bathrobe that looked older than both of them put together. She grabbed Rory's arm and made it as far as the stairs, then plunked herself down on the top one. "Ugh," she said. "I still have the spins."

"Why'd you drink so much?" Rory asked. "Was it because of our fight?"

"I saw Mike," she said, holding her blond head in her hands. "In Montauk. I went there after I left you. We got into a fight. He's such a jerk. I can't believe I wasted one minute thinking about him." She scratched at the tangled mess of her hair and then met Rory's gaze. "Am I making this up, or did you and Connor break up last night?"

"You're not making it up," Rory said. "It's over. He just left to go stay at his dad's."

"Of course he did," she muttered. "I guess he's still in shock. I wouldn't take it personally. He'll come around."

"I'm not sure he will," Rory said. "And I don't think there was anything left to salvage anyway."

"Well, that's his loss," Isabel said.

Rory rubbed her temples. "Maybe I should go home."

"*No,*" Isabel declared. "You are not going home. Don't even think about that."

"Won't it be awkward if I stay?"

"You think I want you to go because you broke up with my brother? No way." She took Rory's wrist again. "Okay, I have to get up again."

Rory helped Isabel down the stairs one step at a time as if she were an elderly woman.

"I'm sorry if I was a bitch yesterday, by the way," Isabel said, when she'd safely reached the bottom. "I didn't mean it."

"Me, neither," Rory said.

"Everything I said about you being a doormat, that was just me talking out of my butt. I think it's been hard for me, you going out with Connor. I've missed hanging out with you."

"I've missed hanging out with you," Rory said.

"Truce?" Isabel said, offering her hand.

Rory gave her a hug instead. "Whoa," she said as she pulled away. "That's a lot of Jack Daniel's I'm smelling."

"Hey, don't judge me," Isabel said.

"Never," Rory said.

CHAPTER NINETEEN

The next day, Rory stared at her computer screen, unable to move, think, or do much of anything. It had been a full thirty-six hours since she and Connor had broken up, and still it didn't seem real. His parting look—a perfect blend of disgust, anger, and injured pride—played on a loop inside her head, blotting out all other thought. Worse, Amelia was humming, loudly, on the other side of the cubicle wall, and it was starting to get on her nerves.

"Hey, Amelia," she said. "You mind keeping it down a little?"

Amelia wheeled herself into view. "Sorry. I'm just really happy. My aunts and uncles are coming in from Massachusetts for the festival. I'm like a celebrity in the family now." She took off her glasses and peered at Rory's face. "What's wrong?"

"I broke up with my boyfriend Saturday night."

"Oh, no," Amelia gasped. "That sucks. Sorry."

"Thanks," she said, suddenly embarrassed to look her in the eye.

"Did he do it? Or did you? Oh. You know what? Don't tell me. That's none of my business."

"He did it," Rory said. "But it's okay. It was sort of…winding down."

"Do you need anything? You want me to run out for ice cream? Beer?"

"I'm fine," she said.

Amelia worked one of her curls around her finger. "You're not gonna leave or anything, right? I mean, I won't know what to do if you're not here every day. Who else am I gonna talk to?"

"No, I'm not gonna leave. Don't worry."

"Because it would seriously suck if you weren't here next month for the screening. I mean, I have you to thank for everything. I'd be so sad if you weren't there."

Rory's work phone rang. She reached for it. "Yes?"

"Hi, Rory, it's Nina," said the voice on the other end. "I just wanted to know, do you know if the Rules prefer salmon or veal?"

Rory took a deep breath. "I really don't know," she said, trying not to sound annoyed.

"I'll do salmon," Nina said, and clicked off.

"What was that?" Amelia asked.

"Another emergency question about what my boyfriend's parents like to eat," she said. "Sorry. My ex-boyfriend's parents."

"My god," Amelia said, rolling her eyes. "They're really stressing about this family, aren't they?"

"They really are."

Her phone rang again. Rory reached for it, already annoyed. "Yes?"

"Hey, Rory, it's Evan."

She shot forward in her chair.

"I'm downstairs, on the sidewalk. I just tried your cell and got voice mail. So I called the main line and they put me through."

"Hi," she said, already smiling.

"Can you take a break for a second? Maybe come down here?"

"Uh…sure," she said. "Hold on. I'll be right there." She slammed down the receiver.

"You being summoned again?" Amelia asked with a wry smile.

"I'll be right back," Rory said, too distracted once again to make eye contact. She picked up her purse and went to the elevator, her heart pounding. In the elevator on the way down, she ran a brush through her hair and put on some lipstick. He'd been in the back of her mind since the breakup, but more as a fantasy than anything real.

He stood waiting outside the door to her building, shading his face from the sun. Earbuds dangled from his hand, and he had on his Captain America T-shirt.

"Hey," she said.

"I had some time before work," he said. "Thought I'd check on you. I heard you and Connor broke up."

Rory slipped on her sunglasses. "Isabel told you?"

"Yeah. I'm sorry. How are you doing?"

"I've been better."

"And he's not trying to get you back?"

"He's the one who did it."

Evan shook his head. "Is he on some weird mind-altering drugs I don't know about?"

She laughed. "That, I can't say."

"I just wanted you to know that if you need anything, I'm here. And the other night at the party, the stuff that I said—"

"It's okay," she cut in. "You don't have to explain."

"No, I sort of do," he said. "All that stuff I said? About Isabel? About not being happy?"

"I didn't say a thing," Rory assured him. "I promise. Not a word."

"That's not it," he said. "I *did* mean all those things. I've given this all a lot of thought. And I think I'm going to end it."

"You can't," Rory blurted. "Please don't."

"But it has nothing to do with you," he said. He smiled. "Okay. Maybe it has a little bit to do with you." His green eyes flashed in that mischievous way. "But we're not right for each other. She's beautiful, and smart, and funny, and cool and everything, but something's off. The other night at the party, when she got so drunk, it was weird. A turnoff. She said some things."

"Like what?" Rory asked, torn between wanting to know and not wanting to know.

"Well, she was really drunk, as you know, and I was helping her into bed, and she called me another name. She called me Mike."

"She was drunk," Rory said quickly.

"I've known there was someone else for a long time."

"There isn't."

"I don't mean she's seeing someone else. I mean she's thinking about someone else. I can just tell. One night when we were out at this bar in Montauk, she got all agitated because someone was there, and she wanted to leave."

216

"Look, she was drunk out of her mind," Rory said. "Don't break up with her, okay? Why are you even telling me this?" She turned back into the lobby of her building.

"I have to do it. Otherwise, it's not fair to her."

"I'm literally going to erase every word of this conversation from my brain."

"It has nothing to do with you," he said.

"I have to go," she said. She gave him a quick wave, then took the steps two at a time up to East End Fest's third-floor offices. Just being in the same physical presence as those words—*I'm going to break up with her*—made her feel like the worst kind of accomplice. Now she had another secret to keep, on top of the secret about Mr. Knox, and on top of Isabel's feelings for Mike. There was no way this was going to end well. Not at all.

AUGUST

CHAPTER TWENTY

Isabel knocked on the door of her father's new house and waited for him to answer. It was one of those homes that had clearly been built to mimic the original cedar-shingled mansions that dotted the Hamptons, but its enormous eaves, elaborately decorated weather vane, and oversize windows gave away its recent origins. She looked out at the oval of front lawn, and beyond it, at Sagaponack Pond, which looked greenish blue under the cloudless sky. Hopefully this wouldn't take long. The only reason she'd come was because of the e-mail. The tone of it was different from the other terse messages that her dad had been sending since June.

Isabel,

I was sorry to miss you the other night. It's now been more than a month since you've been home from school, and I've barely seen you. I understand that you have mixed feelings about spending time at my house, and that, as an eighteen-year-old, you're pretty much free to ignore me if you'd like. But I'd like it if you would consider coming over for a few days, a night, or even just an afternoon. You are my daughter, after all. As much as you probably don't believe that now.

Plus, your mother tells me that you were drunk at her party. I find that very unsettling, yet at the same time, I can't say that I blame you.

Love,
Dad

Her dad sounded almost cool. Maybe there was a reason that all of her siblings were living with him now.

Okay, I'll come over, she'd replied. Friday.

Her dad had only written back one word.

Okeydoke.

Yes, this definitely wasn't the father she knew.

She paced the porch until the door swept open.

"Hi," her dad said. He looked tan and rested and happier than she'd seen him in years. "You made it." He opened his arms for a hug.

"Seriously?" she asked, scrutinizing him.

He lowered his arms. "I thought it was worth a try."

She ducked past him and walked into the house. Loud music played on the sound system. "Since when do you listen to Gwen Stefani?" she asked.

"Come on in," he said. "Make yourself comfortable."

Inside, the house was strikingly modern. One large room with soaring ceilings made up the living room, dining room, and kitchen, which was filled with sleek, futuristic-looking appliances. A tall, double-sided fireplace enclosed with glass doors was the only real partition in the space. Floor-to-ceiling glass doors revealed a pool, a tennis court, acres of green lawn, and the ocean in the distance. The decor was spare and devoid of color—white leather sofas with wooden block frames, seagrass rugs. "It looks like a James Perse store in here," she said.

"Your mother and I never did have the same taste," he said. "Can I get you something to drink?"

"Just some water."

He walked over to the refrigerator, and she stepped closer to the glass doors.

"Has Mom even been over here?"

"Not yet. I think she likes to pretend this place doesn't exist." He approached with her glass of water. "Connor likes it, though."

"I've heard," she said, taking the glass. "He basically moved in, right?"

"Pretty much. And you're welcome to. If you want."

She sipped her water, casting a wary glance over her father and his environment. There was something tempting about decamping here for the rest of the summer, with its laid-back beach-house vibe and cool sound system. But it also seemed empty and forced, like it existed only to prove a point. Isabel sat down on one of the couches. As she'd suspected, it was stiff and uncomfortable.

"So . . . I'm here," she said.

223

"Finally," her dad said. "I didn't think it would happen."

"It's been a busy summer," she said, looking around. "And I didn't know that this was such a big deal for you. I've never thought that you liked me that much."

Her father sat in the chair opposite from her and leaned forward with a deep sigh, steepling his hands. It seemed as if he'd prepared some kind of speech. "Let me try to explain something."

"You don't have to."

"I heard from Connor that he knows about your mother and me. And it's about time you and I talked about it. Father to daughter."

Isabel studied the braided seagrass under her feet.

"When I heard that your mother was pregnant with you," he began, "I told myself that I would always treat you like my own daughter. No matter how I felt about your mother and what she'd done. I wouldn't take that out on you."

Isabel snorted quietly.

"And I think I did that; I think I was true to that. But it was impossible to forget what she'd done. *You* made it impossible to forget. Every time I looked at you, it was a reminder. And then seeing how much your mother loved you...how much she doted on you. How she couldn't do enough for you. It made me wonder if it was because she'd felt something for that man—your real father—that she'd never felt for me."

"So it was my fault?" Isabel asked sarcastically.

"Of course not," her father said. "But I was angry with her. Angrier than I had any ability to express at the time. And I took my anger out on you. Which I can't say that I'm proud of." He glanced in the direction of the glass doors, as if searching for some kind of prop to help him go on. "I'm sorry, Isabel. That's why I wanted to see you. To say I'm sorry. I know I could have been better with you."

"Then make it up to me," she said. "Stop going along with Mom's ridiculous act."

Her father sighed. "You know how much your mother loves the summer. She lives for it every year. I didn't want to ruin it for her."

"But people are going to find out anyway."

"You want me to tell everyone why we're getting a divorce?"

"Of course not. Nobody needs to know why."

He shook his head. "This is what she and I agreed on," he said.

"But she hurt you," Isabel said. "She had an affair with Mr. Knox while she was married to you. Why are you always trying to protect her? Why are we *all* trying to protect her? Lying to your friends is bad enough, but to your own kids? Come on."

Mr. Rule looked down at the concrete-slab floor. "It was a relief when Connor told me he knew."

"Then tell Sloane and Gregory," she said. "Or I will. I can't hold this on my own."

"You always were a strong kid, though," her father said. "I remember teaching you how to Rollerblade. You must have fallen down a hundred times. Each time worse than the time before. Straight down on the concrete in Central Park. But you never cried. You never broke." He chuckled, clearly lost in the memory. "Fearless. I always admired that."

"Just honest," she said, shrugging. "I have to go. I have work."

She walked to the door, hearing her footsteps echo on the concrete floors. All this time she'd thought her dad's needs controlled their house, but it had been her mom's. It had always been about her.

"By the way," she said as she reached the front door. "Do you have a girlfriend?"

Her father cleared his throat. "I am seeing someone, yes."

"I thought so. This place gives off serious girlfriend vibes."

He opened the door for her, and then leaned down and kissed her cheek. "I'd like to start over with you, Isabel. If you'll let me."

"You're not the only person who's been saying that to me." She looked back at him, trying to assess the level of seriousness in his eyes.

"Come over for dinner soon?" he asked. "You used to think I did an okay job on the grill."

"I'll think about it," she said. "Bye."

"Bye."

She walked to her car, which gave off ripples of heat in the late morning sun. Her dad was a flawed man in lots of ways, but at least he seemed ready to admit those flaws. Unlike some other people. Every time she thought about her fight with Mike she got the same roiling sensation in her stomach. She wished she could go back to that day at the surf shop and make everything she'd said to him a little bit harsher. A little bit meaner. Not that it would have changed anything.

She took her phone out of her purse and saw the text from Evan on her screen.

Hey! Coffee before work? Starbucks?

At least there was one part of her life that seemed to be going smoothly. Whatever distance she'd sensed from Evan after her mom's party had thankfully passed.

See you there, she wrote, and got into her car.

CHAPTER TWENTY-ONE

"But how did he do it?" Rory asked. "How exactly?" She crossed her legs underneath her on Isabel's bed and grabbed a pillow to knead with her hands. She needed something to work off the anxiety.

Isabel sat back in the chair, dazed. A strand of hair stuck to her tearstained cheek. "I can't believe this is happening. Two guys in a row? Do I have *leper* tattooed on my back or something?"

"No," Rory said, feeling a lump in her throat. "There is *nothing* wrong with you. He's the one who's obviously screwed up." Rory grabbed the pillow again and squeezed it.

"Are you okay?" Isabel asked. "You seem a little nervous."

"I'm fine," she said, willing herself to be still. "Go on."

"Well, we were talking at one point—about nothing, really—and then all of a sudden he started in on it. How much he liked me, how he thought I was great. But that he wanted to be *fair* to me. Which is such bullshit. I mean, no guy ever cares about being fair to someone. Like that's a reason to break up with someone. But anyway, he said that he had feelings for someone else."

"He *said* that?" Rory asked, willing her face to stay as expressionless as possible.

"Yep," Isabel said, smiling grimly. "Some other girl he's into. But yet, *I'm* so beautiful and smart and funny. Please. And here I thought he was some nice guy. Turns out that he's just a player. I guess we were both wrong about him."

Rory swallowed. "Do you think he's really a player?"

"So then I thought, there's no way I'm going to spend the rest of the summer hanging out with this guy," Isabel went on, "so I quit."

"You quit?" Rory said, even more shocked now.

"That job was lame," Isabel said. "Too much work. The tips were pathetic. And the people were annoying. How many times can you hear that someone wants the chipotle mayo on the side? God, I was about ready to lose it." She rubbed the ball of her foot. "Plus, I was sick and tired of wearing black."

"So what did you say back to Evan?"

Isabel shrugged. "I said okay and left. What was I going to do? Fight him on it? Burst into tears? I have some dignity, after all. I told him whoever this girl was, she could have him."

Rory plucked at a loose string on Isabel's bedspread, trying hard to think. If she didn't say anything, then she'd spare them both an awful, deeply uncomfortable talk. If she did say something, then Isabel might hate her, but at least she'd have a clear conscience. And there *was* the striking possibility that Isabel was right. Maybe Evan was a player. She'd heard about guys who were late bloomers in the romance department, who then went on to give guys like John Mayer a run for their money.

"But you know what?" Isabel went on, picking up a stack

229

of magazines and plopping herself and them down on the bed next to Rory. "I wasn't that into him anyway. All he does is shoot these weird shorts for YouTube. Which I don't even think are that funny. And he doesn't drink, he doesn't surf, he doesn't play sports, he drives this strange beat-up Saab that was discontinued, like, a thousand years ago. And whoever this girl is that he's into, she's probably just as lame and boring as he is."

Rory was quiet.

"I mean, if *I* wasn't right for him, then it's probably someone with no style, no sense of humor, and, let's face it, no looks." She flopped over onto her stomach, almost fully recovered now, and took a copy of *Vogue* off the top of the stack. "So it's all okay. I can do better, and he can't. It's as simple as that." Isabel looked up at Rory. "What's wrong? I hope I'm not depressing you or anything."

"No, no, I think you're probably right," she said, swallowing. "I'm sure you can do better than Evan."

"I *know* I can," Isabel said, opening the magazine.

Rory got up and backed away toward the door. "I think I'm gonna go down and check e-mail for a sec. I'll see you in a little bit."

"Okay," Isabel said, still lost in thought.

Rory left and headed down the stairs, feeling sick to her stomach. This was a disaster, and she felt completely responsible. But at least Isabel seemed like she would survive this.

When she got to her room, there was a text from a familiar 203 number.

Broke up with Isabel today. Can I call you? Can I see you?

She sat down on the bed and thought. If she wrote him back, she would be betraying Isabel. But if she didn't write him back, she would never know if he was more than a crush.

She picked up the phone and stared at the message. All she needed was a little more time. If she gave herself a little more time, she'd know what to do.

Isabel sat in front of the surf shop with the engine running, trying to think of the best opening line. There was always, "Hey, I was just nowhere near your neighborhood," like that line in that movie she saw with Matt Dillon playing a grunge rocker. Or there was something honest, and cute, like, "So...drunk texting: not really my thing." Or there was simply, "Hi." Or, "Hey sorry about that text I sent. I can't stop thinking about it, and it makes me cringe every time, and would you please just forget that I sent it?" But nothing sounded quite right.

She turned off the engine, convinced that she'd figure out the best opener as soon as she was face-to-face with Mike. Between seeing her dad, getting dumped by Evan, and then reliving the entire episode by telling Rory, her brain was a little addled right now. And Mike couldn't be that mad at her, if he was as into her as he said he was. Everyone drunk texted once in a while, for God's sake.

She was reaching for the door handle when Mike stepped out of the shop. He was talking to someone over his shoulder. Instantly, she ducked behind the wheel. She waited, staring at the GPS screen, and then lifted her head.

Mike was talking to a slim brunette. A *pretty*, slim brunette wearing a teeny, tiny tank top and jeans that looked like they were painted on. He was showing her one of the surfboards propped up by the door. With her arms folded across her chest, she seemed to be hanging on his every word, and he seemed to be at least as interested in talking to her, because he was using his hands a lot as he spoke, which she'd never seen Mike do.

So it's a customer. Big deal. She'd laughed and joked with her customers at the restaurant in a way that she would never have done with anyone in real life. It wasn't anything to read into.

Then Mike grabbed a wet suit off a hanger and held it up to the girl. She grabbed it and pressed it to herself, then twirled around on the tips of her toes, pretending to model it for him. Mike laughed. She laughed. Isabel could practically see the cartoon birds and hearts floating in the air between them.

That was it, she thought. She jammed her key in the ignition and turned on the engine. Two seconds later she peeled out of the parking lot, and if Mike happened to see who it was behind the wheel, then she couldn't care less.

CHAPTER TWENTY-TWO

"Lean down to get the ball!" Mrs. Rule called from the other side of the net. "Bend your knees! Deeper!"

God help me, Rory thought as she tried to swat the depressurized tennis ball with her solid paddle.

"Good," Mrs. Rule called, returning Rory's hit. "Make sure you get that racket back earlier!"

Rory rubbed her hairline with the back of her wrist and ran for the ball. The solid metal paddle felt awkward as she swung it back—it had none of the aerodynamics of a regular stringed tennis racket, which now seemed like a breeze to master. She pulled back and swung. The ball bounced right past her, then sputtered at her side, quickly dying on the court.

"Almost!" Mrs. Rule called out. "Almost!"

"Can we stop? Please?" Rory yelled, gasping for breath. She leaned over her knees, trying to get her breath back.

"My goodness," Mrs. Rule said, walking to the other side of the net. She patted Rory's back. "You okay? Was that too much for you?"

"I don't think I'm ready for an actual game yet," she said, still breathing heavily.

"Oh, well." Mrs. Rule sighed. "Let's go get some lunch, then. You've probably worked up an appetite."

The thought of eating right now made Rory want to throw up, but at least it meant a break from this torture. Of course, she had no one to blame but herself. She should have gotten out of this paddle tennis lesson weeks ago.

Once she'd showered and changed into a Georgica Club–worthy tunic dress and her Jack Rogers, Rory realized that she was starving. The patio was full of families out to get some sun and social time on a Saturday afternoon. They found an open table on the covered patio, and Rory dug into her Cobb salad, eating it in gulps.

"The trick to learning any new sport," said Mrs. Rule, "is to throw yourself into it. Practice day and night. Don't be afraid to look foolish. But don't ever have the attitude that you can't do it." She sliced off a small piece of brûléed grapefruit with the side of her fork and put it in her mouth. "My father always said that."

"Were you close with him?" Rory asked, still eating her salad.

"Very. He was quite revered in this town. He was on the board of this club for years and years."

"I didn't know that," Rory said.

"I was his favorite. Which is how I ended up with the house. He said that I was the only one of his daughters who was a true Newcomb."

"And what did that mean?" Rory asked. "Being a true Newcomb?"

"Well, I'm not sure if you know, but the Newcombs go all the way back to the *Mayflower*. I suppose he meant that I had a respect for the family name. For the heritage. The Newcombs weren't people who suffered fools. A Newcomb woman was in the paper only three times in her life: when she was born, when she got married, and when she died. I'm sure you've heard that saying before. It was one of his favorites."

"That must be a little hard to live up to these days," Rory said.

"Not really. I'm sure you've noticed that none of my children like to broadcast their lives on the Internet. Especially Connor."

At the sound of Connor's name, Rory put down her fork and took a long drink of water.

"By the way, I've been wanting to talk to you about Connor," said Mrs. Rule. "I heard about what happened from Fee. I'm sure there's a way that the two of you can patch things up."

"I really don't think so," Rory said.

"Of course there is. Things were going so well, and then all of a sudden, it's over?"

"That's between me and Connor."

"I know it is, but men are so simple when it comes to this sort of thing. If you follow one or two basic things, you'll have him back in no time. And I know how much he cares about you."

"Thank you, but really," Rory said, trying to sound firm, "we're broken up."

"Well, let's enjoy the afternoon, then," Mrs. Rule said in an *I-tried-but-you-just-won't-listen* tone. "Kelly!" Mrs. Rule called out, waving. "Come, sit down for a moment."

Rory looked over and saw Mrs. Quinlan coming toward them. She wore pressed clam diggers and an Hermès print scarf around her neck, and her face glistened slightly from the heat. The hairs on Rory's arms stood on end. Their run-in with the Quinlans in Citarella had happened only a week ago. If she was anything like her daughter, Mrs. Quinlan had probably shared Isabel's news with countless people since then.

"It is so *hot* out," Mrs. Quinlan cried, as she sat down in the empty chair at their table. "The news said it's going to hit ninety-five by the end of the week. Can you believe that?"

"Well, we always get a big heat wave this time of year," Mrs. Rule agreed, picking at her meal. "Do you know Rory McShane? A friend of Connor and Isabel's?"

"Oh, yes, Rory, we met at Citarella," she said.

Rory nodded. *Change the subject*, she thought. *Change the subject*.

"By the way, I'm *so* sorry I couldn't make it to the party," Mrs. Quinlan went on. "Mitchell was *so* sick, and you know what a bear he can turn into when he's got a cold. So I thought it best that we didn't go."

"I got your e-mail," said Mrs. Rule.

"But I heard that it was spectacular," Mrs. Quinlan gushed. "Just spectacular. And I think it's lovely that you and Larry are on such great terms like that. Being there together. Supporting each other in that way. Just lovely."

Mrs. Rule smiled. "I'm sorry?"

"Oh," Mrs. Quinlan said, glancing at Rory. "I thought… well, I heard the news about you and Larry."

"What news?" Mrs. Rule asked sharply.

"That you two separated. Your daughter told me. In Citarella that day."

Mrs. Rule darted a glance in Rory's direction.

"She was quite clear about it. She said that you two were separated and on your way toward getting a divorce. I've been meaning to call—"

Mrs. Rule began to cough. She reached for her water.

"I'm sorry," Mrs. Quinlan said, genuinely abashed. "Was I not supposed to know any of this?" She took Mrs. Rule's hand. "Oh, dear. There's no one else involved, is there?"

Mrs. Rule continued to cough. Rory touched her lightly on the back. The only way this could get worse was if Mrs. Rule started choking, Rory thought. "Are you okay?" Rory asked, still patting.

"I'm fine," said Mrs. Rule, daintily slapping her chest. She smiled as she cleared her throat, but her face was extremely red. "I think I swallowed something the wrong way. Excuse me." She shot up from the table and walked, still coughing, to the ladies' changing room.

Mrs. Quinlan stared at Rory. "I guess I wasn't supposed to know that, was I?" she said.

Rory got to her feet. "I'll be right back." She pushed her way past the tables and went in the direction of the ladies' room. Maybe Mrs. Rule really was choking. She'd studied the Heimlich once, for ninth-grade health class, but that was so long ago she feared she might break one of Mrs. Rule's ribs in the process.

She entered the dim, cool, chlorine-fragrant ladies' room and found Mrs. Rule sitting on the edge of a bench in front of a row of lockers. She was no longer coughing. She seemed to be staring straight ahead. Rory felt something inside her soften.

"Mrs. Rule? Are you okay?" she said, coming to sit down behind her. "Can I help you with something?"

Mrs. Rule didn't turn around. Rory put a hand on her back and could feel a slight heaving. Mrs. Rule was crying.

"It's going to be okay," Rory said. "People aren't going to care."

"Of course they are," she murmured. "It's a prime piece of gossip. I've probably given people enough to talk about for at least five lunches on this patio."

"You can't think about that," Rory said.

"I wish we'd gotten the divorce over with years ago. I was stronger back then." Mrs. Rule sniffed deeply and wiped her face with her hands.

"Here," Rory said, reaching for a box of tissue at a nearby vanity. "Use this."

"I just wanted to get through the summer," Mrs. Rule said, taking a tissue. "I told him we could have it be all over the place come September, but I *just wanted the summer.*"

"It is going to be okay," Rory said, patting Mrs. Rule on the shoulder again. "I promise. You don't have to be perfect."

Mrs. Rule turned to Rory. Her tearstained face was the most vulnerable Rory had ever seen it. "God, you know nothing," she said. Mrs. Rule balled up the tissue and threw it out. "I guess I have to go back there. Not that I have any idea what to say."

Rory stood up and offered her hand to Mrs. Rule. "What about saying that it's true?"

Mrs. Rule looked at herself in the mirror and straightened her ponytail. "If people are really going to be that nosy," she said, taking Rory's hand and standing up, "then I guess they deserve that. Let's go."

They walked back out into the sunshine, where Mrs. Quinlan waited at their table. "Are you okay?" she asked Mrs. Rule. "There is nothing scarier than getting something caught in your windpipe. I remember once, when we were down in Jamaica on vacation—"

"It's true, Kelly," Mrs. Rule said quietly, as she sat back down. "Everything you just mentioned. It's all true. Every last bit of it." She picked up her fork and sliced off a piece of grapefruit. "Did you have any other questions?"

Mrs. Quinlan looked chastened. "No, I don't think I do," she said hesitantly. "But, thank you."

Rory heard her phone buzz from underneath her table. She reached down, rifled through her bag, and finally found her phone at the bottom. It was another text from Evan.

Are you free? Can I see you? I don't want to bother you, but...

Rory read the text over and over. She knew that it was a trap, but at the same time, if she didn't get a break from this crazy family she might lose it once and for all.

I'll meet you later. Where?

My house?

"Rory, can you put that away, please?" Mrs. Rule said. "That's a little rude."

"Uh, sure," Rory said, and dropped the phone back in her bag. For the rest of the lunch, she couldn't touch her salad.

CHAPTER TWENTY-THREE

Rory pulled up in front of a modest brick-and-shingle home on County Road 79, a mile or so outside Sag Harbor Village. Across the street, she spotted a deserted public park with baseball fields and tennis courts. Since lunchtime the sky had turned dark and heavy with impending rain. Despite the ominous weather, she couldn't deny the excitement she felt.

She got out of the car and approached the house, following a narrow path through the grass. Rory looked over her shoulder. Was her car too visible out here? Would Isabel see? She told herself that she was being ridiculous. Isabel wasn't on her way here. It was silly for her to even be thinking about that.

She walked back behind the house, and when she saw Evan and Jeff's guesthouse at the other end of the backyard she could feel butterflies start to flit around her stomach. A pit of gravel lay in front of the house, with weeds growing out of it. A well-used hibachi grill sat right by the front door, a package of white sandwich bread on top of it. The place looked like a cross between a twentysomething crash pad and Grey Gardens, but it didn't matter. It was Evan's place. And he was waiting for her there. He opened the door and stepped out into the overgrown grass.

"Welcome to the shithole," he said with a grand king-of-the-castle sweep of his arms.

Rory laughed. A raindrop plopped onto the tip of her nose, and then another hit the crown of her head. She ran toward him. "I think it's starting to rain."

"Then you better get inside," he said.

She reached him, but he stayed in front of the door, not moving.

"Um, you're not letting me inside," she said, standing in front of him.

Before she knew what was happening, he leaned down and kissed her. She put her arms around his neck and surrendered to the kiss, letting it build until he put an arm around her waist, bringing her closer. Her hands found his hair. His hands traveled up and down her back, holding her closer and tighter to him. The passion that had slowly gone out of her connection with Connor came back now in full force, igniting emotions in her that she'd forgotten she had. She wanted this guy. And even more important, he wanted her.

Slowly, he pulled away. The rain was coming down steadily, and she realized that her clothes were damp. "Do you want to come inside?" he asked.

"Is Jeff home?"

"He's out. And he will be. All day." He took her hand and started to lead her into the house.

242

"Wait," she said, stopping him. "I was sitting in my car for ten minutes trying to decide whether or not to drive away."

He waited for her to continue.

"She's one of my best friends. I can't do this to her. It's not fair."

"But I ended it, Rory. I even told her that I have feelings for someone else."

"But you didn't say that it was me," she said.

He bit his lip and sighed. "No. I didn't think you'd want me to."

"Yeah, you're probably right about that."

"Look, we can take it slow. But there's no reason anymore for us not to be together." He braided his fingers with her own. "Not if we want to be."

"Except that she's my best friend." Rory looked up into his green eyes, searching for a reason not to trust him. "Do you do this a lot?"

"Do what?" he asked, baffled.

"I don't know you. For all I know this is your MO. Going out with one girl, then deciding you like another girl…"

He laughed. "I told you how old I was when I got my first girlfriend."

"Sure," she said.

"So does that answer your question? And do you want to come inside before we both get soaked?" he asked.

They walked into the house, and Evan turned on a lamp. Rory looked around. The guesthouse was indeed small, and the decor made it look like it was trapped in the seventies, though not in a cool, retro way. There was so much shabby, mismatched furniture that she could hardly walk around, and there was a strong smell of mildew. For a moment she missed the Rules' house, with its high ceilings and beautifully decorated rooms, each and every objet d'art and coffee-table book placed just so. But then she caught herself. There was no way that she'd become this much of a snob. Not so soon.

"Do you want something to drink?" Evan asked, opening the orange fridge. "I've got SunnyD and 7UP. Jeff has beer. Or what about to eat? We have ice cream. No, excuse me, we have *gelato*."

"Gelato sounds good," she said, sitting gingerly on the ancient-looking couch.

Evan brought over two mismatched bowls, each containing two huge scoops of lemon gelato. "Okay, get ready for a party in your mouth," he said.

"I can't believe you said that."

Evan laughed.

"Seriously. Sometimes you are just *painfully* unfunny."

"But I'm still cute, right?" he said.

"Yes, you're still cute," she said.

He leaned down and kissed her again, and she felt herself go limp. It was as if they'd been a couple for years. She couldn't believe how easy this was.

"You are so beautiful," he whispered into her ear.

"Okay. Hold on. You just finished dating Isabel Rule. The Grace Kelly of East Hampton. How can you possibly say that *I'm* beautiful?"

Evan looked deep into her eyes, tilting her chin with his hands. "If we're going to work out at all, you're going to have to let me give you a compliment, okay?" he said.

"Okay," she replied.

"Especially when it's true."

When he kissed her the next time, she didn't pull away.

CHAPTER TWENTY-FOUR

Rory lay in bed the next morning, staring at the sunlight streaming through the cracks in the curtains. She still hadn't fallen asleep. Every time she closed her eyes she saw Evan's face, felt his hands on her body, heard his voice. They'd spent the entire afternoon on his couch. It was mostly a blur, but there were plenty of moments that she remembered and could relive, over and over. They didn't do everything—not even close—but that had been just as she'd wanted it. And Evan was a true gentleman. At every point he asked her if she was okay, if it was too much, if she wanted to pull back. Rory felt completely herself around him, even when she took off some of her clothes, which was a relief. She'd never quite lost a feeling of self-consciousness around Connor. She wasn't sure if it was his perfect body or his perfect persona, but she always needed the room to be dark and for blankets to be close by. She'd always thought that her discomfort was a result of being a late bloomer, but after being with Evan she knew now that this wasn't true. She felt safe, and in familiar hands. At one point she even pulled off his shirt, making him say, "Whoa. I feel like a piece of meat. I'm diggin' it."

She started giggling, until he interrupted her with a kiss.

The rain outside sounded a gentle staccato on the roof and windows, making her feel like they were the last two people on earth. *Don't let this end*, she thought over and over. *I don't want this to ever end.*

But it finally did. At some point, while he was getting some soda, she looked at the cable box under the tube TV and saw the time. It was six o'clock.

"I gotta go," she said, throwing her clothes back on.

"What time is it?" he asked, walking back to the couch.

"Six. I should get back for dinner."

"Yeah, Jeff should be home pretty soon. It's probably a good call."

She got dressed, used the miniscule bathroom in the back of the house, and found Evan in the living room, ready to walk her out. "It's still pouring," he said, gesturing to the rain coming down in sheets outside. "Let me give you an umbrella. If we have one. Which we probably don't."

"That's okay. I'll just book it to my car." Drowsy and relaxed from the hours with Evan on the couch, she nestled herself into his arms.

He held her close, then kissed her deeply. "I'll miss you tonight."

"I'll miss you."

"When can I see you again?"

"I don't know," Rory said. She was in no hurry to think about what waited for her at home—guilt, worry, and shame. Having to tell Isabel. For right now she just wanted to bask in this moment. "Text me. We'll figure something out."

"Okay." He kissed her one more time. "It's crazy. I can't even let you go."

"You're gonna have to," she said.

He finally pulled away. "There, I did it," he said. "Now I'm really unhappy."

She laughed. "I'll talk to you tomorrow," she said, and headed out into the rain.

Now she sat up and forced herself to think about the other reason she'd been up most of the night. Isabel. And what on earth she was going to do about that.

As she walked to the shower, she knew that she really had only one choice: to tell Isabel everything, and to tell her as soon as possible.

Just as soon as she figured out *how* to tell her.

Isabel knocked on her mother's bathroom door. "Do you have any Kiehl's left? I'm all out."

Mrs. Rule opened the door in her bathrobe. Her hair was wet and lay in straggly curls over her shoulders. "Take whatever you'd like," she said, as she began to comb her hair in the mirror. "How are you?"

"You'll be happy to know that I quit my job," Isabel said. "I'm no longer shaming the family."

"Was there any reason?" her mother asked, pulling the comb through a knot.

"Not really. I guess one of my coworkers and I had a difference of opinion." Isabel grabbed the bottle of butter-colored moisturizer and was about to head out the door when she stopped. "I went over to Dad's the other day. He wanted to see me."

Mrs. Rule put down the comb. "Is that so?"

"Yeah. His house is totally modern. You'd hate it."

"I'm sure," her mother said.

"Anyway, he apologized to me. For being so weird all those years. Said that he didn't mean to take it out on me."

Mrs. Rule sat down on her cushioned vanity stool and put her hands in her lap. "That's nice to hear," she said stiffly.

"And he said that he'd like to stop pretending, too. It sounds like it's just as painful to him to live this lie as it is to all of us."

"Before you give me a lecture on ethics, Isabel," her mother said, "I'll have you know that the secret is out. Thanks to you and Kelly Quinlan. I saw her at the club. When she asked me if it was true—if we were getting separated—I said yes. So it's done. It's out. I hope you're happy." Her mother shook her wet hair back behind her shoulders and fixed her daughter with a warlike glare. "So, you see, it's all done. I've given in. Everyone's going to hear about it. If they haven't already."

"She already knew. She'd heard a rumor that Dad was living there, and I confirmed it."

"The point is, you can stop feeling victimized now, Isabel," her mother said. "Everything's out in the open. Everyone's going to know that we're getting a divorce. I'll have to cancel at least ten engagements that we had planned. And in about three days I'm going to be the subject of more Schadenfreude than you've ever seen in your life." She reached for a bottle of eye cream on the counter.

"Well, not everything's out," Isabel said. "You still have to tell the family about Mr. Knox."

"I've been through enough for one week, don't you think?"

Isabel was quiet for a moment. "Right," she said. "Because this is all about you."

"I'm still your mother. I still deserve some respect. Even though I know you don't think so." She stood up and brushed past Isabel out of the bathroom, then barricaded herself behind the doors of her walk-in closet.

Isabel looked at herself in the mirror. She was only eighteen, but she felt a decade older. She walked up to the closet doors. "Mom?"

There was no response.

"You're not in there taking a bunch of Celexa, are you?"

There was still no response.

"I know I've been hard on you. I don't mean to be. I think what you did at the club sounds really brave."

There was still no response. She palmed the door and then stepped away. "I know we'll get through this," she said.

Whatever her mother was doing in there, she seemed to want Isabel to go away. For the first time in a long, long while, Isabel left wishing she'd said she was sorry.

On Monday morning, Rory arrived a few minutes late to find a Post-it stuck on her computer monitor.

RORY, PLEASE SEE ME IN MY OFFICE. NINA

Rory dropped her bag on the chair. Something about this didn't seem good. "Amelia?" she called out.

There was no answer.

Rory peeked over the partition. Amelia's chair was empty.

"Well, better get this over with," she muttered, and turned to head toward Nina's office.

Nina gestured her inside through the glass.

"Good morning," Rory said. "You wanted to see me?"

"Good morning," she said flatly, sipping from a takeout cup of coffee. "I hope you had a good weekend."

"I did. Did you?"

"It was fine." She crossed her legs and flicked a piece of dust off the desk. "I received a voice mail from Lucy Rule. Saying how sorry she was, but she and her husband won't be able to attend the gala after all. That other plans came up." She folded her arms and gave Rory a dark look.

"Oh," Rory said. "I really don't know anything about it."

"You don't?" Nina said. "I thought you were living there."

"I am, but they don't let me in on their social calendar."

"The fund-raising committee is very disappointed, to say the least. And I am, too. We were all very happy about this. And you gave us the impression that this was something they were interested in."

"I don't know what to tell you," she said, trying not to sound nervous. "I guess they can't make it."

"Well, in light of this, we've had to shuffle some things around a bit," Nina said. "Amelia's short will no longer be in the festival. I just let her know."

"But why?" Rory asked. "What did she do?"

"Nothing," Nina said blithely. "That's how things go sometimes. People change their minds."

"I understand," Rory said, smiling as tightly as possible.

"So that's all," Nina said. "I just wanted you to be aware. And when you have a moment, could you get me a fresh one of these?" she said, holding up her coffee cup.

"Sure," Rory said, biting her lip.

"Great. You can close the door on the way out."

Rory walked back to her desk, feeling sick. Hopefully Amelia wouldn't be crushed, though she probably would be.

Amelia was back at her desk, writing an e-mail, when Rory returned. "Hey," she said.

"Yeah?" Amelia said without turning around.

"I just spoke to Nina," Rory said. "She told me the news. I'm so sorry."

Amelia swiveled around. "Yeah. If I'd known everything hinged on your boyfriend's parents, I wouldn't have done it."

"I didn't think it hinged on them," Rory said, feeling her face start to get red.

"Right. Of course you didn't," Amelia shot back. "I didn't need you to do me any favors, you know. I was fine on my own." She turned back around to her computer. "Now I have to write my family and tell them I've been kicked out of the festival. For logistical reasons, or some such BS."

"This has nothing to do with either of us," Rory said. "They're the ones who are being totally shallow and petty."

"They've been kissing your ass this whole summer," Amelia said. "You should have seen this coming."

"That's not fair," Rory said. "This isn't my fault, okay?" She threw herself into her chair and turned on her computer.

A few minutes later, Amelia wheeled herself in sight. "Sorry," she said, her face contrite. "It's my third pointless internship. I was hoping this one might be different. I didn't mean to take it out on you." She pushed her glasses up her nose. "You want to get lunch later? Plot everyone's undoing?"

"I need to run out and get coffee for Nina."

"Screw that," Amelia said. "She can get it herself."

"I really am sorry about your family."

"That's okay. I suppose I should have seen what was going on. I guess I wanted to believe that they really thought I was talented."

"You *are* talented, okay? This has nothing to do with you."

Amelia held up her hand for a high five. "You need anything, you call me, okay? High five."

"High five," Rory said, trying to smile as she slapped her hand.

When Rory drove home that afternoon, she spotted Connor's Audi parked in the drive. Her heart lifted unexpectedly—she didn't realize how much she'd missed him. Or how anxious she'd been that he not still be mad at her.

She found Connor in the kitchen, eating some leftover salad and watching the tennis channel. "Hi," she said. "How are you?" It had been just over a week since the last time she'd seen him, and now she couldn't help but feel happy to talk to him again.

"Oh, hey," he said vaguely. "Good to see you."

"How's it going?" she asked, pouring herself a glass of water. "Is everything good at your dad's house?"

"Yup," he said, his eyes on the TV screen. It was obvious

that he was still mad at her. "I stopped by to grab some more clothes."

She sat down across from him. "Are you okay?" she said.

"I'm fine," he said blankly. His gaze stayed riveted on the flat screen.

"Connor, don't ignore me."

"I'm not," he said. "I'm just watching this."

Rory pulled her purse off her shoulder and dropped it on a chair. "I hope we can still be friends."

"Sure," he said in a noncommittal voice.

"Connor, I'm sorry. I thought it was something you should know."

"That's fine," he said. "And now that I know, I'm sure you feel better, right?"

She stood up and grabbed her purse. "Forget it. I'll talk to you later." She pushed through the swinging door. Connor didn't chase or call after her. She needed to see Isabel. Isabel would help her deal with this.

She ran up the stairs to Isabel's room and banged on the door.

"Come in!" Isabel yelled.

Rory opened the door. "Connor's here," she said. "And he won't talk to me."

Isabel sat on her bed wearing her bikini and a loose cotton tunic. "So?" she said. "He's a guy holding a grudge. He'll get over it."

"I have had the worst day," Rory said, collapsing into a chair. "Your parents aren't coming to the opening night of the festival, and my boss freaked. And to punish me for it, they screwed the other intern out of showing her film at the festival. Because I recommended it."

"That doesn't sound like your fault at *all*," Isabel said.

"Maybe not, but I still have a guilt hangover. Not fun."

"They never are."

"Can I use your bathroom? I literally just walked in from work."

"Sure."

Rory flung her bag on the floor, not noticing that the contents spilled out of it onto the carpet.

Isabel opened her laptop. Once again, she began reading the e-mail from Mr. Knox. The one that she'd been waiting for all summer.

Dear Isabel,

I'm sorry that it's taken me this long to get back to you. Production on this film has taken me to three different cities and two different continents since I saw you last. I hope things are going better by now. Just hang in there. And remember to have fun! Only one more month of summer.

Peter

So there it was, she thought. Not exactly the big bonding e-mail she'd been hoping for. Maybe she should take her dad up on his offer of dinner. It couldn't hurt....

Suddenly there was the tinny sound of a few bars of the Beatles. "Nowhere Man." It was Rory's ringtone. Then the chime of a text came through. Isabel stood up and found Rory's phone on the floor, near her bag. The name on the screen made her freeze in her tracks.

EVAN

Slowly, her eyes drifted down to the message below.

Hey, when can I see you again? I miss you. E.

Isabel's eyes glazed over as she read the words. They stopped having meaning, they stopped being words, but still she read them, over and over. Evan. Rory. They'd seen each other. Rory was the person he had feelings for.

Rory was the reason he'd broken up with her.

Rory.

Rory.

A wave of nausea overtook her and began to creep up her throat.

Behind her, the bathroom door opened, but Isabel barely heard it.

"Isabel?" Rory asked. "What's wrong?"

The sight of Rory standing there with an innocent look on her face made Isabel's head spin. "Are you hooking up with Evan?" she asked.

Rory seemed about object, until she looked down and saw the cell phone in Isabel's hand.

"Are you?" Isabel pressed.

"Y-yes," Rory stammered. "But I can explain—"

Isabel tossed the phone on the bed. "When were you going to tell me this? Or were you not going to tell me at all?"

Rory didn't move, except for her lips, which made small, ineffectual attempts at an answer. "I was going to tell you," she finally said. "I promise I was."

"When? Are you the reason he dumped me?"

"No...and we didn't hook up while you guys were together," Rory said.

"What?"

"Yes, there were sparks between us, but I told him not to break up with you. I swear to God, I did."

"Oh my god," Isabel said, turning away from her.

"And from what you said, the other day, it didn't even sound like you were that upset—"

"So that makes it okay for you to go hook up with him behind my back the minute we're not together?" Isabel asked. "I can't believe I trusted you. I can't *believe* I invited you into my home again. All you do is keep things from me. Like last year, hooking up with my brother and hiding it from me. I thought *that* was bad. Now you go after my boyfriend the second we're not together. What is this? Are you obsessed with me or something?"

"Isabel," Rory said, trying to stay calm. "It all just happened. I'm so sorry. We've only hung out once. That's it. Nothing has even begun—"

"Honestly? You're worse than Thayer and Darwin," Isabel said. "At least I always knew where I stood with them. You?

257

You're worse. You *pretend* to be my friend. Only to then sabotage my first relationship in a year."

"I didn't sabotage it, I swear to God," Rory said. "You have to believe me. I didn't. I told him not to break up with you. I did."

"Don't take pity on me," Isabel said. "I want you out of this house. I've had it. I want you to go."

Rory looked stricken, as if she might burst into tears. "Now?" Rory asked.

"Yeah, now."

"It just happened. And you told me yourself, you weren't in love with the guy. That you still have feelings for Mike—"

"Don't even go there. It's not going to help your case. Not at all." Isabel walked to the door. "I feel really sorry for you. I'm not the only one who pushes people away."

She ran out of her room and down the stairs. She needed to get out of this house. She couldn't think, she couldn't breathe, she couldn't even see straight anymore because of the angry tears filling her eyes.

Fool me once, shame on you, she thought. *Fool me twice, shame on me.*

CHAPTER TWENTY-FIVE

The sun was setting when Isabel reached the unpaved back road that led to Mike's house. Her stomach growled. Hopefully Mike had some food. And hopefully, he still lived there. She hadn't asked the guy at the surf shop if Mike had moved, since she didn't want to look like too much of a stalker. But she had a strange feeling that he hadn't. She slowed down as she came upon his driveway, then turned in, shading her eyes from the fading sun.

When she saw the house, she wondered if she'd guessed wrong. Mike couldn't still live here, she thought. It looked too good. Someone had given it a fresh coat of white paint and fixed the screen door. The sloppy pile of mail and circulars had been replaced by a bright, colorful mat. The Christmas lights were gone. Even the lawn looked greener and less overgrown with weeds. But one look at the Xterra in the driveway let her know that she'd been right. Mike still lived here, and he was home.

She stuck her feet in her flip-flops, then bravely got out of the car. The anger she'd felt earlier had faded, but the adrenaline was still there, pushing her forward. She had no planned speech. No opening line. Just simple, bare need.

She walked up the steps, pulled open the screen door, and knocked on the wooden door. Nothing. No sound. She knocked again, louder this time. Finally she heard someone turn the knob from inside the house. The door creaked open, and Mike stood on the steps, looking sleepy and relaxed, as if she'd just woken him up.

"Hey," he said.

"Hi," she said.

He rubbed his eyes. "What are you doing here?"

"I came to say sorry about that text," she said. "And storming out of the shop. I know that was rude. And lame. I was just angry."

"It's okay," he said. "Is that why you came all this way? Just to say that?"

She shook her head and took a step toward him. He pulled her into his arms. The kiss was explosive, unleashing something long pent-up in both of them. He pulled her inside the house, pushing the door shut behind her with his free hand. She yanked his T-shirt up and over his head, feeling his warm skin, his six-pack, the hard, smooth surface of his chest that she'd thought about so many times. He held her tightly, his back against the wall, and kissed her all over her face and her neck, then pulled the tunic up over her head to continue kissing her all the way down her chest. His hand cradled the back of her head as he returned to her lips, kissing her hungrily, so hard that she felt his teeth bite into her lips, and then it traveled down her back, to the knot of her bikini top that he slowly untied.

Together they moved, still kissing, down the hall, just as they had so many times last summer, back to the same room that she remembered so well.

"I missed you," he whispered in her ear, and all she could do was smile, close her eyes, and know that she was exactly where she belonged.

Hours, or maybe days, later—she didn't know—she opened her eyes. The only light in the room was from a lone votive candle on the bedside. It flickered in the breeze coming through the open window. Mike lay beside her, sleeping deeply, turned toward her on his side so that his face rested on her shoulder and his arm hooked around hers. There wasn't a sound, except for the pulse of crickets in the dark outside.

There was no clock in the room, and she'd taken off her watch back at home. For a moment she wondered if Rory had left the house already and where she'd gone, but this wasn't the time to think about that. She could think about it later. For now, she wanted to enjoy this moment.

Mike stirred next to her, moaning softly, and she turned to him, pressing her lips into his hair. *God, he's beautiful*, she thought, looking at his tan arms and chest. How much she'd missed him. How overdue this had all been. How good it felt to be back in his arms, in his bed, in this house.

She turned even more onto her side, and Mike opened his eyes. Delicately, she stroked his arm with her fingers. He smiled, looking into her eyes. "What time is it?" he asked.

"No clue. And I don't really care." She kissed his forehead and then the tip of his nose.

"You've gotten even more beautiful," he said, touching her cheek. "I didn't think that was possible."

"Enough with the flattery," she said. "I might start to believe it."

Mike propped his head up and looked around the room. Then he grabbed his watch from the windowsill. "It's almost nine," he said. "I'm supposed to meet some people right now."

"Right now?"

"Yeah," he said, putting the watch down. He buried his face in her neck and sighed. "I'd love to blow it off, but it's Gordy's birthday party."

She remembered Gordy from that night at the Ripcurl last summer. She hadn't liked him much then, and she was pretty sure she wouldn't like him much now. "Then I guess you should go," she said.

"Want to come with me?" he asked, looking up at her.

"Now?"

"Yeah." His smile was almost goofy. "They'll all remember you. You should come."

"Is that girl with the Farrah Fawcett hair going to be there?"

"Which girl?"

"Forget it," she said. She sat up, holding the covers against her. "Actually, you should go. That's cool. I can go home."

"But why not come?" he asked, propping himself up on his elbow. "I mean, you have to eat, right?"

"Because look at me," she said. "I need to take a shower. I need to change."

"It's at his house. No need to dress up," he said. He pulled her down. "And I don't want to let go of you yet. How does that sound?"

They kissed, but instead of feeling blissed-out and excited, she felt pinned down and trapped. Suddenly she needed to get out of his bed.

"I really should get going," she said, pulling herself up. "Where's my suit?" She got out of bed and knelt down on the floor to get dressed. Out of his eye line, she pulled on her bikini bottoms and tied her top. "Okay, where's my cover-up?"

"So you're leaving," Mike said, with a bereft look on his face.

"Just temporarily. You have a party to go to."

"A party I just invited you to."

"I know. I just don't feel like it yet," Isabel said.

"What's wrong?" Mike asked. "What are you running away from?"

"Nothing," she said, starting to get annoyed. "Why do we have to go out as a couple right this second? Can't we take some time to see where this goes?"

"See where what goes?" he said, sitting up. "What do we have to wait and see about?"

"Maybe I have to wait and see how I feel," she said. "Maybe it's not all about what you want."

"You're the one who came over here and jumped my bones," he said. "Sorry if I'm a little confused right now."

"Ugh. I didn't jump your bones."

"Sorry. I didn't mean that. I feel like you're bolting."

"I'm not bolting. I don't want to go to Gordy's party."

"Right," Mike said.

She looked at him and shook her head. "Okay. You're being annoying right now." She walked out of the room and stomped down the hall. Her tunic lay in a ball in front of the door, and she grabbed it.

He followed her down the hall in his boxers. "Hey, I'm sorry. I guess I'm just feeling a little insecure, okay? I mean, you show up here, we have this amazing time, and now you're out the door."

She knew that she was supposed to tell him that he had no reason to be insecure, but for some reason it felt like too much to ask of her right now. Was she his girlfriend? Did she even want to be? In any event, this wasn't the Mike she knew. He'd never been ready before. She tugged her tunic over her head and slipped her feet back into her shoes. "I'll talk to you tomorrow, okay?"

"Okay," he said. He mustered a small smile. "Thanks for coming over."

"Bye. Have fun at the party." She couldn't get outside into the warm, buzzing night fast enough. *Who would have thought that Mike Castelloni would be clingy*, she thought. *And that I wouldn't want him to be.*

She got to her car and opened the door. She was embarrassed at her hasty departure but also determined to leave. It was only after she'd gotten back on the highway that something occurred to her: Maybe this was the new and improved Mike, the Mike who'd changed, the Mike who could actually be someone's boyfriend. And she wasn't sure if she wanted him.

CHAPTER TWENTY-SIX

"So, okay. I guess I see that this was all my fault."

Rory sat next to Amelia on the Danielses' deck, looking out at the calm, glassy surface of Peconic Bay as it lapped against the piles under their feet. She'd had no one else to call when Isabel had ordered her to leave. Not only had Amelia invited her to stay with her family right off the bat, she'd even listened quietly as Rory burst into tears and started telling her, in gulps and sobs, about what had just happened. All in all, not her most flattering moment, but she'd survived it. Rory had packed her things in under an hour, left without saying good-bye to anyone—not even Fee—and driven herself straight to the Danielses' homey, cheerful yellow house right on the bay. For the past three days Amelia had been a solid friend and a surprisingly gracious host, making sure Rory had plenty of snacks and herbal tea and Mrs. Daniels's delicious fried flounder with tartar sauce.

Rory watched a sailboat glide past them and tried not to think of all the messages that were probably on her phone. The only people she'd texted were Fee—to tell her where she'd gone and why—and Evan—to say she couldn't see him again. After that she'd locked her phone in her trunk and left it there, half to torture herself and half to give herself time to think. But there'd been less thinking than she'd hoped, and instead more feeling—feeling angry, feeling sad, feeling regretful. After three days she was more confused than ever. When she looked back on the events of the past few weeks, she couldn't even figure out the through-line of it all. She should have said no to Evan—but was she really at fault for liking someone? These were the times when she wished there were a wise-talking television judge who assessed your relationships, someone you could lay your case in front of and who would pronounce you in the clear or guilty.

"It's not *all* your fault," Amelia said, kicking her feet in the water. "Maybe just half."

"That's still pretty bad," Rory said.

"It's not going to be like this forever. Isabel will forgive you."

"No, she won't. She hates me. I'm sure the whole family hates me by now, too. And Connor already hated me."

"Connor doesn't hate you. You didn't do anything to Connor. He broke up with you." Amelia put her hand on Rory's arm to stop her from biting her nails. "Stop that. You're making me nervous."

Rory put her hands in her lap. "I should never have gone over to Evan's house. What the hell was I thinking? There are girl rules about this kind of stuff. And I broke them."

"I'm not gonna sugarcoat it for you," Amelia said with a slight edge of impatience. "You kind of did. But you also got pulled into the Guy Spiral."

"What's the Guy Spiral?" Rory asked.

"It's when you go straight from one relationship to the next. You know, you get out of one thing, you feel bad, it didn't work for whatever reason, and it's a bummer. So then, consciously or not, you find the next guy and rush right into that. That's the Guy Spiral. And then *that* doesn't work out, and then you're onto the next thing."

"Right," Rory said, staring at the gold charm bracelet on her wrist. "But things with Connor had been so confusing for so long."

"Clarity isn't always an option," Amelia said, sounding wiser than her years. "Unfortunately."

They watched the sailboats drift by on the surface of the water, and Rory thought of Connor, living at his dad's house. By now there was no way that he didn't know about Evan. "So how do you know so much about relationships?" Rory asked. "What's your story?"

"My boyfriend and I kept breaking up and getting back together all through high school. It was like a bad soap or something. My friends weren't talking to me by graduation, 'cause I'd annoyed them so much."

Rory laughed.

"I think I was so in love with the idea of this guy, but it never became a reality. Every time I went back into it thinking, 'Okay, *this* time, I'm going to get the version of this guy I want.' And I never did. And then when he broke up with me for the last time, on graduation night, I hooked up with some guy I didn't even care about but who I knew had a crush on me, to make myself feel good. And I felt even worse." She looked at Rory. "If it's meant to happen with Evan, then it'll work out," she said. "Take some time."

"I think I should go home," Rory said.

"Don't go home. Not yet."

"I think I probably should," Rory said. "It's time."

"Well, don't decide anything tonight. Sit there."

"Okay," Rory said. "I'm sitting here. Not moving."

She stayed frozen in that position for a good long while, until Amelia stood up and yanked Rory to her feet.

"All right, you've proved your point," she said. "Now let's go eat dinner."

"But isn't that doing something?"

"Oh, shut up," Amelia joked.

Isabel did a perfect swan dive into the pool, swam the entire length, and got out, water streaming off her limbs. Her phone lay on the chaise in the bright sun, and when she picked it up it was red-hot. It had to be almost ninety degrees already, and it was only eleven in the morning. She pressed the button, clicking it on, and saw that she had another text from Mike.

Buford's tonight? Where r u? Call me.

She flung the phone back down and grabbed one of the thick beach towels from the basket by the chaise. His fourth text. With each one that came in, she felt both excited and filled with dread. Pretty soon he was going to start calling, and then she would really be at a loss. As she toweled off she felt another pang of shame at the way she'd bolted from his house. He'd started being needy, but that hadn't been it. And it hadn't only been about going to a party she didn't want to go to. It was something even harder for her to name, and to admit. Maybe what she really wanted, she thought now, was a guarantee that Mike wasn't ever going to hurt her again. And there was no way that she was ever going to get that.

But for the past week since Rory had left, she'd been too down and too lost to sort out her feelings about him. The day after her fight with Rory, her mom had come home from the club pale faced and grim. Isabel gathered from Fee that there'd been an army of well-wishers on the Georgica patio, lining up to dispense sympathy mingled with left-handed compliments, such as "You really had all of us fooled—good going!" and "It must be so hard to know that he's got that bachelor pad in Sag—how humiliating!" Since then her mom had holed up in her room most days, watching daytime chat shows and staying in bed. Not the most uplifting atmosphere when you'd kicked out your best friend and suddenly found yourself completely alone. Well, not completely alone. Not anymore. It had been a no-brainer to call Connor.

"Can you come home? I think Mom needs you," she told him. "And I do, too."

That was all she'd needed to say. He'd come back right away. He was upstairs right now, presumably helping their mom decide between *The View* and *The Chew*.

She lay down on the chaise, slid on her sunglasses, and turned her face to the sun. A few minutes later, she heard the sliding glass doors open and then the sound of footsteps.

"How's the water feel?" Connor asked, dropping a book and his sunglasses on the chaise beside her.

"Pretty good," she answered.

"Man, it's hot out here," he said, pulling off his shirt.

"How's Mom?"

"Not so great," he said. "She's talking about going back to the city early."

"Really?" Isabel asked.

"I don't think she will," he said. "Sweltering humidity and the smell of stinking garbage isn't going to help her feel any better." He sat down on the edge of the chaise and kicked off his flip-flops. "I feel pretty bad for her. It sounds like those women at the Georgica really sank their teeth into her."

Isabel looked at the beads of pool water still drying on her legs.

"And I know you don't want me feeling sorry for Mom, but I do."

A thin breeze came in from the ocean, twisting the American flag around itself.

"Connor, it's not that," she said. "I didn't want you feeling this false loyalty to them."

"Well, I don't anymore, okay?" he asked.

Isabel folded her arms in front of her chest. "I'm sorry about you and Rory. I really am."

"You're the one who kicked her out of here."

"I had my own reasons for that. And it's not like I don't regret it, either."

"Good," he said.

"Excuse me?" she asked. "What did you say?"

"I know Rory," he said, lying back against the chaise. "She's not the type to cheat on anyone. Just because some guy went after her doesn't mean that she deserves to get thrown out of here."

"So you're defending her?" Isabel said.

"She saw all my stuff. I wasn't the perfect guy anymore. She could see all my flaws, and she was calling me out on some of them, and I couldn't handle it. I bailed on *her.* She didn't have a choice." He stood up. "And if she had more in common with this guy than she did with me, then I don't blame her for being into him."

His words rang true. Maybe Rory and Evan were genuinely drawn to each other. She hadn't thought of it that way.

"Anyway, about Mom and Dad, fine," he said. "I believe you. So you can stop hitting me over the head with it. But it's still taking me a while to absorb. I hope you can appreciate that."

"I can."

He slipped his shoes back on. "Do Sloane and Gregory know?"

"Not yet."

"Are you going to tell them?"

"I really don't want to."

"And are you friends with the Knoxes now? Are you in touch with him?"

"I was," she said. "But I'm not sure what kind of future that has, if you want to know the truth."

"Now that you've unloaded on me, I have something to ask of you. Invite Rory back here. Tell her you're sorry. I think that's the least you can do. Don't you think?" He picked up his sunglasses and his book and headed for the sliding glass doors.

"Connor, wait," Isabel said.

He turned around.

"What if she's gone back to New Jersey?"

"I don't think she went home. Ask Fee. She'll probably know."

"Okay. Thanks for coming over."

He shrugged. "You're my little sister. It's impossible for me not to help you. Even when you drive me up the wall and tell me stuff I wish I didn't know. I'll be sending you my therapy bill. I hope you know that."

"Okay," she said with a laugh.

He disappeared into the living room. Isabel watched him go, feeling closer to him than she had in weeks. He'd called her his sister. She hadn't realized how much she'd needed to hear that until now.

CHAPTER TWENTY-SEVEN

Isabel lingered outside the Baybreeze Café, wondering exactly how to swing this. She wanted to pick up her last check—she didn't trust Bill to actually mail it to her. She hadn't spoken to Evan, or seen him, since the dumping, and she had a feeling that he might know about her fight with Rory. There was something unbelievably embarrassing about that.

After pacing back and forth in front of the boutique next door, she took a deep breath and headed straight for the door. Lunch would be long over by now, and hopefully Evan would already be on his break. But before she could get to the door, Evan stepped outside, and almost walked into her arms.

"Isabel," he said, sounding surprised.

"Hi," she said.

"What are you doing here?"

"Picking up my last check," she said, pawing the sidewalk with her toe. At least he was alone, she thought.

"I had Bill mail it to you," he said. "I hope that's okay."

"Oh. Okay. Thanks. Not like it was that much or anything," she said. "But thanks."

"Look, can I talk to you for a minute?" he asked. "If you're not going anywhere."

Isabel checked her watch. The traffic on the way to the North Fork, where Fee had told her Rory was staying, would be intense pretty soon, but she was curious to hear what Evan had to say. "Sure."

They crossed the street toward the pizza place and the Lilly Pulitzer store. The sidewalks were strangely empty. The heat had only gotten worse as the day wore on.

"I feel bad about how I ended things with you," he began.

Isabel cringed. "Don't. It's okay. Seriously."

"Let me finish, all right?" He stopped walking and turned to face her. "I'm not the smoothest when it comes to breakups. It's kind of my weak spot."

"Well, it would be a little screwed up if you were good at them," she conceded.

"Yeah, you're probably right about that." He ran a hand through his hair. "Anyway, there are some things that I wish I said to you that day. And maybe I can say them to you now."

"Okay," she said, kicking the bottom of a lamppost. "I'm all ears."

He looked right into her eyes. "I think you're beautiful, Isabel. Stunning, actually. And smart. And funny. And a hard worker. You're incredible. But we weren't incredible together. There wasn't any spark. You know what I mean? And that had nothing to do with Rory."

Isabel reddened and looked down at the ground.

"Sometimes you can't force it if it's not there. And yeah, okay,

I had feelings for Rory. But I never got the sense that you were crazily into me, either. I felt like we could be amazing friends. Or maybe it's just me who thought that, I don't know."

Still looking down at the ground, Isabel said, "No, it wasn't just you. I thought we'd probably be better off as friends, too."

"But it's kind of a moot point anyway, because Rory's totally blown me off."

"What are you talking about?" she asked, looking up.

He shrugged. "I can't reach her. She won't text me back; she won't call me back. It's driving me crazy. I got this weird message from her that she was going to stay with a friend on the North Fork for a while. And that's it. Nothing else. I've called her, like, six times." He stuck his hands in the back pockets of his 501s and sighed. "And now I figure she's trying to let me down easy. I guess it serves me right."

"Evan, it's not you she's mad at. It's me."

"What?" he asked.

"When I found out that you and Rory were seeing each other, I freaked. I told her to leave. I kicked her out. I'm sure she's avoiding you because of that. Nothing else."

Evan's olive-green eyes went wide. "You kicked her out? Damn."

"I was upset. One of you could have said something to me, by the way."

"Yeah, I know," he said.

"But I don't want to sit at home and stew about it all. So you guys really hit it off. I'm glad. I am."

Evan exhaled. "Could you…could you…I mean, I don't want to put you in a weird place or anything—"

"If I find her, could I put in a good word for you?" Isabel asked.

"Yes." He bit his lip. "If it's not too weird or anything."

"You know I could be totally smug right now and say that you *do* deserve this," she said, smiling. "But I won't. I'll put in a good word for you."

"Thanks. Thank you. Seriously." Evan grabbed her and hugged her. "Thank you."

"Be good to her, okay?" Isabel said. "She really only deserves the best. I'm serious."

"I will," he said, smiling. "I promise, I will."

"Okay. I gotta go."

"Thanks, Isabel. You're a cool girl, you know that?" Evan said.

She smiled at him one last time and then hurried to her car.

Isabel was no expert when it came to navigating the North Fork, but she'd been to it enough times to have a vague sense of where she was going when she made the turn at Riverhead. According to Fee, Rory was staying with someone named Amelia Daniels, and according to Google, the Danielses lived in Southold. It was almost dusk by the time she turned on the correct street. She pulled up in front of the listed address and saw Rory's beige Honda across the street. She'd found the place. She parked the car and got out, smoothing her hair and the front of her dress. Looking as nice as possible would hopefully only support her case.

A short woman wearing a KISS THE COOK apron over a polo

shirt and khaki shorts answered the door. "Yes?" she asked, her face coming right up against the screen.

"Hi, I'm here to see Rory? Rory McShane?" Isabel asked.

"Just a moment," the woman said and left.

Isabel waited on the porch. It had an old-fashioned upholstered swing decorated with what looked like hand-knitted pillows. *Sweet,* Isabel thought. *Maybe Rory likes this place better than my house.*

"Isabel?" Rory stood behind the screen in bare feet. She looked a little scared. "Hey."

"Hey," Isabel said. "Can I talk to you for a minute?"

"Okay." Rory pushed open the screen door and joined Isabel on the porch.

"You have to come back home," Isabel said.

"What do you mean, home?" Rory asked skeptically.

"I mean, my house," Isabel said. "You have to come back. We miss you. *I* miss you. And I overreacted. I'm sorry. I had no right to kick you out. I don't know what came over me; I must have been temporarily insane or something."

"You said that I sabotaged your relationship," Rory said, speaking the words very carefully.

"*God,* no, of course you didn't," Isabel said, practically bouncing up and down. "How could you take that seriously? You can't take anything I say seriously."

Rory arched a brow. "But you said it, Isabel. You still said it."

"I know," Isabel said, contrite. "And I'm sorry for that. I'm really, truly deeply sorry. It was wrong and stupid and childish." She paused. "And I regret it."

Rory looked like she might actually burst out laughing. "O-kay, Ms. Mea Culpa. You don't have to beat yourself up about it or anything. And I'm sorry I didn't tell you about Evan. I should have. I know that now. But I also didn't want you to hate me, and I felt responsible..." Rory sighed with her entire body. "What a mess. And I haven't spoken to him; I'm totally fine with that being over—"

"*No*," Isabel cut in. "It can't be over. Evan needs you. He thinks you're blowing him off. You need to call him. Before he does something drastic. I'm serious."

"How do you know this?"

"He told me. I saw him today. At the restaurant. He looked terrible. He made me promise to tell you how much he cares about you."

Rory still looked pained.

Isabel grabbed Rory's hand. "Ror, it's okay. I think it was my ego that was hurt. Nothing else. I give you my blessing. As weird and pope-like as that sounds."

Rory was quiet. "What about you? You don't have feelings for him anymore?"

Isabel blushed. "Well, I kind of moved on. To Mike." Isabel closed her eyes and held up her hands. "Don't judge."

Rory sat on the porch swing to absorb the shock. "Did you guys hook up?"

Isabel nodded, biting her lip as if waiting for a painful diagnosis.

"And are you dating him?"

Isabel shook her head.

"So how have you moved on?"

"Let me explain. It was awesome. I mean, amazing. And then, I think I got scared. All of a sudden he was acting like a boyfriend."

"But that's good, isn't it?" Rory asked.

Isabel sat next to Rory on the porch swing. "I don't know. For some reason it made me want to run."

"Maybe you're scared," Rory said. "I mean, you did just break up with someone. It's perfectly normal."

"I don't know if I can go through that again," Isabel said. "I don't know Mike as a nice guy. And look at what happened with Evan. I still got hurt."

The screen door opened. "Hey, are you hungry or what?" Amelia asked. She stopped in her tracks at the sight of Isabel.

"Hey, Milly, this is Isabel," said Rory. "Isabel, this is Amelia. We're interns together at the East End Fest."

"Hi," Amelia said. "I've heard a lot about you."

Isabel turned to Rory. "Does she think I'm a bitch?" she asked.

"No, she doesn't at all," Rory said. "I swear."

"What are you guys doing out here?" Amelia asked.

"I was telling Rory how sorry I am for kicking her out," Isabel said.

"And then Isabel was telling me about this guy she may or may not be dating."

"Oh?" Amelia said, slightly interested.

"Yeah, it's nothing," Isabel said, waving it off. "You wouldn't know him."

"Actually, she might," Rory pointed out. "He is from the North Fork."

"What's his name?" Amelia asked.

"Mike Castelloni," Isabel said.

"Mike Castelloni?" Amelia replied. "Yeah, sure I know him. Wait a minute. You're the girl he dated last summer."

"What do you mean?" Isabel asked, suddenly intrigued.

"I heard about you. That he was dating some girl from East Hampton last summer who broke his heart. Some blond girl from Lily Pond Lane."

"Broke his *heart*?" Isabel asked, almost falling off the swing.

"That's what I heard," Amelia said, squinting, as if she needed to concentrate to remember. "That it didn't work out and the girl left, and he was really torn up about it. And Mike was a guy who was never torn up about anyone in high school. Believe me."

Isabel slowly stood up. "I didn't know," she said.

"That's what I heard," Amelia said.

"Amelia!" a voice called from inside the house. "Dinner!"

"Why don't you guys both stay and eat?" Amelia asked. "My mom's making cioppino tonight. Fish stew. It's amazing."

Isabel looked at Rory.

"Stay," Rory said. "It'll be fun. Mrs. Daniels is an incredible cook."

Isabel looked out at the darkening street and could see the lights on in other people's homes. Big Wheels and skateboards and other kids' toys were scattered across front lawns. She could hear the sounds of children and smell the charcoal briquettes of barbecues. There was something cozy and warm about Amelia's neighborhood. For one thing, it was an actual neighborhood, not a silent, deserted street lined with museum-worthy pieces of real estate hidden behind tall hedges. No wonder Rory was in no hurry to leave, she thought. She wasn't, either.

"Okay," she said. "I'd love to."

CHAPTER TWENTY-EIGHT

Driving back into the Rules' estate, Rory thought back to that day two months ago when she'd arrived. She'd had no expectations then, but she had gone into this summer thinking it would just be the same. Why did people always expect to have the same experience over and over again, if it was a good one the first time? No wonder things had been so hard for her, she thought, as she parked. She'd set herself up for disappointment.

She got out of the car and heard the same roll of the waves, felt the same breeze cool her forehead and neck. A week away at Amelia's had given her perspective. Yes, this place was beautiful. But it wasn't her home, and it never would be. It was barely home to the Rules' kids.

The back door opened, and Connor walked out. *He's still gorgeous*, she thought, taking in his firm jaw and his arresting blue eyes. But as he walked toward her, she knew that from now on he would be her friend. And that made her just as happy.

"Hi," she said. "How are you?"

"Good. How are you?" He tilted his head as if ready to hear all sorts of truths tumble out of her mouth.

"I'm fine. Isabel and I made up. No hard feelings."

"She can be kind of a hothead," he said. "But you already knew that by now."

"I did," she said, smiling. "But this time I kind of deserved it." She unlocked her trunk and reached in for one of her bags.

"Rory, I'm sorry," Connor said. "I thought I was ready to have someone really see me. The good and the bad. But I guess I really wasn't."

"That's okay. I get it."

"And I think it's great that you've met someone else. I mean, part of me does want to kick his ass," he said, smiling, "but you deserve to be happy. I want that for you."

"Well, I'm looking forward to school. I hope you and I can hang out in California sometime. I'm only going to be eight hours away."

"Sure, I'll come up there every weekend," he joked. "But seriously, yeah. We'll hang out."

He reached in to get her bags.

"You know what? Leave them," she said.

"You sure?"

"Yeah, I'll get them another time." She closed the trunk.

"All right. My mom's excited to see you. She practically tore Isabel's head off for kicking you out. She's got lunch ready inside."

The thought of an intimate lunch with Mrs. Rule and Connor was slightly intimidating, but she knew that this would be the last one for a while.

Mike's house was quiet in the heat of the afternoon, and as Isabel got out of the car, the only sound was the slow throbbing of frogs coming from the lake a mile or so away. The porch was still neat and brushed clean of dust and dirt, and the only clutter was a tidy stack of mail that sat on the welcome mat. Isabel knocked on the door.

"Coming!" yelled a voice. A girl's voice. Isabel froze. Mike was inside with a girl. *I knew it*, she thought, closing her eyes. She craned her head back toward her car. Was it too late to run away?

The door opened. The slim, pretty brunette Isabel had seen talking to Mike at the store stood in front of her. She had one hand thrust in the back pocket of her very tight jeans. Her tank top was hardly more than a few inches of fabric. "Yeah?" she asked.

Isabel swallowed. "Um, is Mike here?"

"No, he's at work. Is there something I can help you with?" The girl was chewing gum, and suddenly an enormous bubble began to emerge from her lips.

"Could you give him a message for me?" Isabel went on. "That Isabel stopped by?"

The bubble burst against the girl's lips, and her face lit up. "No way," she said, holding out her hand. "I'm Gina. Mike's cousin. Well, second cousin. I've heard so much about you. Hi!"

"Hi!" Isabel shook Gina's hand.

"He's letting me crash here for a few nights," Gina said. "You know. Parental issues." She gave Isabel a knowing smile and cracked her gum. "Anyway, I'll tell Mikey you were here. I'm sure he'll be sorry he missed you."

"Thanks," Isabel said. She had the weird urge to hug this girl, who she realized now couldn't be more than sixteen years old. "Tell him I'd come by his work, but that I don't want to disturb him. But I should be around all day if he wants to call."

Gina reached out and punched Isabel on the shoulder. "You two make such a cute couple," she said. "For real."

Isabel laughed. "Yeah. For real."

Rory knocked on Mrs. Rule's bedroom door. "Mrs. Rule? Are you in here? It's Rory."

"Come in."

Tentatively, delicately, Rory pushed open the bedroom door. Mrs. Rule's bed was covered with matching suitcases, half-filled with clothes. Mrs. Rule emerged from her walk-in closet, carrying a stack of thin cashmere sweaters. "Well, look who finally is back," she said, with genuine warmth. She walked over to Rory and, still holding the sweaters, pressed her into a hug. "It's good to see you."

"What's going on?" Rory asked.

"Oh, I've decided to take a little trip," Mrs. Rule said. "London, Paris, maybe Rome. We'll see." She plopped the sweaters into an open suitcase. "I think it'd be good for me to get a change of scene. East Hampton isn't the only vacation spot in the world."

"No, it definitely isn't," Rory said, wanting to smile. "Are you leaving because people know about the divorce? The people at the Georgica?"

"Well, it hasn't been a picnic, but I was prepared for that," she said, going to her closet and bringing back a stack of skinny jeans in every color of the rainbow. "Well, *almost* prepared. I think Isabel might have been right about that place. It's not the kindest bunch of women in the world. I don't know why I put up with it as long as I did."

"I think what you did was really brave," Rory said. "A lot of other people wouldn't have had the guts to be honest. You did."

"Yes," Mrs. Rule said. "And it's cost me the whole paddle tennis season." She gave Rory a smile that indicated she was half joking and dropped the jeans into the case. "Are you going to be all right here without me? I've asked Fee to look after you girls. And I trust that you'll keep an eye on Isabel for me. Keep her out of trouble."

"I don't think Isabel needs that as much as you think," Rory said. "She's grown up a lot since last year. She deserves a little more credit."

"You're probably right," Mrs. Rule muttered, half to herself. "If it's all right with you, I got the same necklace for Isabel that I got you. I figure you guys can have matching necklaces. Something to remind you of this summer."

"I love that idea," Rory said.

"I leaned on you a lot this summer," Mrs. Rule went on. "I hope you didn't mind."

"Not at all," Rory said. "When do you leave?"

"Mickey's driving me to JFK in two hours."

"All right, then." Before she knew what she was doing, Rory walked up to Mrs. Rule and threw her arms around her. "Have a good trip. And thank you for a wonderful summer."

"You're welcome," Mrs. Rule said, hugging Rory back. "But the summer's not over."

"I think this might be it for me," Rory said. "We'll see." She stepped to the door. "I have to go meet someone. Take care, Mrs. Rule."

"Good luck, Rory. And please, go get yourself some new shoes at Stubbs and Wootton on me," she said, glancing down at Rory's slides. "Those are a disgrace."

When she walked onto Main Beach a few hours later, Evan was waiting for her on the shady verandah, sipping a soda. At the sight of Rory he tossed the soda in a garbage can and strode toward her, ready to envelop her in his arms.

"Hey," he said. "You're back, thank god. It's like I've been living in a Nicholas Sparks movie since you've been gone."

She laughed and hugged him. "It's good to see you."

"It's great to see you," he said. He leaned down and kissed her gently on the lips. "Did you get all my messages?" he asked. "Even the desperate ones? You can delete those, by the way. Not my finest moment."

"Yes, I got them all." She took him by the arm. "Let's walk for a minute."

They left the shade of the snack bar and headed toward the water, weaving their way past blankets and umbrellas and beach chairs. A plane over the ocean tugged a sign advertising a car dealership in Riverhead. "So. I have this whole speech," she said, chuckling.

"Uh-oh," Evan said. "For some reason that doesn't give me a good feeling."

"I'm leaving today," she said. "I think it's time. I want to go home and be with my friends before we all go our separate ways.

287

My boss said it was fine if I left early. I won't get any great recommendation from her, but I wasn't going to anyway."

"Okaaaay," he said. "Not exactly what I was hoping to hear."

"Meeting you was, by far, the best part of my summer. The best, best part." She looked up at him. Evan seemed intent on listening to her. "But I don't want a boyfriend right now. Maybe down the road...but not now. Most of my life I was the girl without the boyfriend. And now I don't remember what it's like to *not* have one. Some girls can do that, go from guy to guy. I can't. It's just not me. Even though I thought it was."

The water hit their feet, but this time Rory didn't react to the icy sensation.

"Okay," Evan finally said. "That makes sense. I get it." The wave went back out, and they watched as a band of tiny birds scattered across the wet sand, searching for food. "Can I still e-mail you every once in a while?" He looked down at her and smiled. "You never know, right?"

Rory chuckled. "Yeah, I guess that's true. You never know."

As they stood and looked out at the water, Rory felt Evan's arm travel across her shoulders, and she leaned in close to him, putting her head against him.

"You're a pretty cool guy, Evan Shanahan," she said.

"I'm glad you finally noticed, Rory McShane," he replied, making her laugh as he squeezed her close.

CHAPTER TWENTY-NINE

"So do you want some snacks for the trip?" Isabel asked, following Rory out the back door. "Or some energy drinks? Coconut water? Greek yogurt?"

"I'll be fine," Rory said. The light from the midday sun was starting to turn golden. "I should probably get on the road. You know how bad the traffic can get." They walked to Rory's Honda. Mrs. Rule's Land Rover was gone. Mickey had taken her to the airport. Connor was back at his dad's house. It already felt as if the summer was over. "You sure you're going to be all right here by yourself?" Rory asked, shading her eyes from the sun. "I feel kind of bad leaving you like this."

"I'll be fine," Isabel said. "I have to get ready for NYU anyway."

"You know, your mom may have a lot of flaws, but she really does love you," Rory said.

"I know," Isabel said. "I guess I have to accept the fact that she's never quite going to be the mom I want her to be."

"Maybe not," Rory agreed. She zipped up her suitcase and shut the trunk.

"I went to Mike's today. He wasn't home, but I left a message. I'll let you know how it goes. And I hope you let Evan down easy."

"I did. I have a feeling we might run into each other again." She threw her arms around Isabel and hugged her. "I'll miss you. Come to New Jersey before I leave for Cali. The Farm and Horse Show is starting next week."

"Wow, so tempting," Isabel said, pretending to roll her eyes. She hugged Rory back. "I'll text you tonight."

"'Kay," Rory said. "See ya. And Isabel?"

"Yeah?"

"Thanks for inviting me this summer. I'm really glad I came."

"Even with all the drama between you and me?"

"Absolutely," Rory said. "I wouldn't have wanted it any other way."

"I would have," Isabel said. "Just kidding."

"Hey, you better visit me at school," Rory said, walking to her car.

"I will. And by the way, don't ever stop making films. Your stuff is a hundred times better than anything I saw at the East End Fest."

"You're only saying that because I'm your friend," Rory said.

"Get in the car, already," Isabel said.

She got into her car and shut the door. Isabel watched as she backed up, waved through the window, and drove down the path, eventually disappearing from sight as she made the turn toward the street.

Isabel stood on the gravel with her hands on her hips. It was hard to believe that she had this house to herself. A host of possibilities flashed through her head: throwing an enormous, raging party; going back to the city and catching up with some of her friends there doing internships; packing a bag and going to stay with her dad for a while. Her dad, she thought. Maybe that was where she belonged, at least for a few days. Then she could figure out a plan.

She turned back to the house, but the sound of crunching gravel made her stop. It was a car. Rory had probably forgotten something.

She turned back around and saw a dark red Xterra making its way up the drive. With her feet rooted to the ground and her heart beating wildly, she watched as the car came to a stop a few feet away, and the car door swung open. Mike hopped down onto the gravel. In his hand he held a bunch of wildflowers. The setting sun gave him a golden sheen as he came toward her.

"Hi," he said.

"Hi." She still couldn't move.

"So these reminded me of you," he said, offering her the flowers. "Wild and beautiful." He touched her cheek.

She laughed and kissed him. "You wanna go surfing?" she asked.

"I'd be honored."

"Let's go," she said, and reached for his hand.

ACKNOWLEDGMENTS

I am indebted to the wonderful team at Poppy and Little, Brown Books for Young Readers, but especially Elizabeth Bewley and Farrin Jacobs for their perceptive notes, gentle guidance, and unwavering belief in these characters. To Joseph Veltre, my new agent: I am so grateful to be in your stable of writers. Tracy Shaw and Sammy Yuen designed another gorgeous cover image, and Christine Ma went over this manuscript with her usual unerring eye. JJ Philbin gave me the best first reading anyone could ask for.

And to Ben van der Veen and Annabelle, the new center of my world…a thousand hugs and a thousand kisses. I love you.

WELCOME to THE HAMPTONS,
where beautiful people come to play.

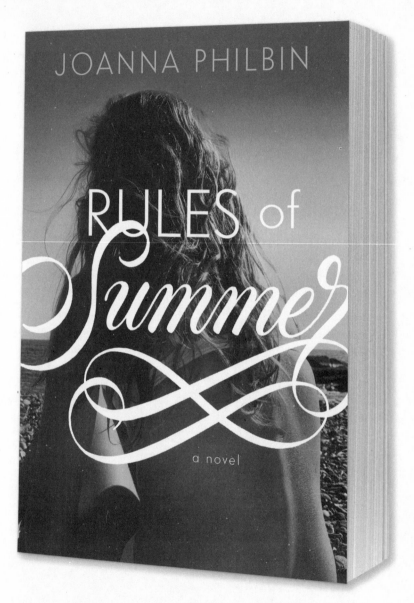

Read Rory and Isabel's story from the beginning.

Available in paperback now.